Where Hearts Heal

Laurel Ridge Series, Book #14

Tara Baisden

Sterling Ridge Press LLC

Copyright

Cover designed by Sterling Ridge Press LLC

Published by: Sterling Ridge Press, LLC www.sterlingridgepress. com

ISBN: 978-1-966093-31-2 Printed in the United States of America

First Edition: September 2025

For permissions, contact: tara@tarabaisden.com or visit www.tar abaisden.com

Also by Tara Baisden

<u>Riverbend Valley Series</u>

#1 A Cowboy's Second Chance

#2 Wanderlust & Wild Horses

#3 Heartstrings on the Horizon

#4 Runaway in Riverbend Valley

#5 Mended Hearts

#6 Healing Hearts

<u>Laurel Ridge Series</u>

#1. Season of Hope

#2. Finding Grace

#3. His Perfect Plan

#4. Love Redeemed

#5 Snowbound Blessings

#6 Sheltered Hearts

#7 Restoring Faith

#8 Love Rekindled

#9 Where She Belongs

Dedication

For my own small-town heroes,
the ones who fix what's broken,
share what they have,
and remind us that the very best love stories begin with friendship,
seasoned with laughter,
and sealed with morning coffee on the porch swing.

Love, Tara

Contents

Chapter 1

The wrench slipped in Megan Miller's grip for the third time; her knuckles scraped against the cold copper pipe beneath her kitchen sink. She repositioned herself on the worn linoleum floor, ignoring the way the cabinet door pressed into her shoulder blade, and squinted at the stubborn shutoff valve that had been dripping steadily for two days.

"Just needs to be snug," she murmured, echoing her father's patient voice from years ago when he'd first shown her the basics of home repair. "Not tight enough to strip the threads, but firm enough to stop the leak."

From her spot at the kitchen table, seven-year-old Lauren looked up from her artwork—a vibrant crayon drawing of what appeared to be a purple elephant wearing a tiara. "Mommy, why are you talking to the sink?"

"I'm not talking to the sink, sweetheart." Megan twisted the wrench counterclockwise, feeling the fitting give slightly. "I'm just thinking out loud."

"Daddy used to do that too, didn't he? When he fixed things?"

Megan's hand stilled for a moment. Lauren had no memories of David—she'd been only two months old when the military training accident took him—but somehow she'd absorbed the stories Megan had shared over the years, weaving them into her understanding of the father she'd never known.

"Yes, he did." Megan's voice softened. "He said that talking through a problem helped him think."

She applied pressure to the wrench again, this time feeling the compression fitting shift. Good. The drip should stop once she—

The fitting crumbled.

Not loosened. Not tightened. Crumbled.

What had been a steady drip became an insistent stream, cold water splashing against the cabinet bottom and soaking into her jeans. Megan scrambled backward, bumping her head on the sink's edge, and watched in dismay as water began pooling on the linoleum.

"Uh oh." Lauren's matter-of-fact observation carried the weight of experience. At seven, she'd witnessed enough of her mother's ambitious repair projects to recognize when things went sideways.

"Uh oh is right." Megan wiped her wet hands on her damp t-shirt and stared at the steady flow of water. The shutoff valve she'd been trying to repair had given up entirely, its ancient threads finally surrendering to time and pressure. She needed to stop the water flow completely, which meant crawling back under the sink to find the main shutoff.

The space beneath the sink was cramped and dark, filled with cleaning supplies and the detritus of daily life—empty spray bottles she kept meaning to recycle, a lone dishwasher tablet that had escaped its box, and now, a growing puddle of surprisingly cold water. Megan felt along the back wall, her fingers searching for the familiar shape of the main water valve.

"Are you okay down there?" Lauren had abandoned her elephant masterpiece and was now peering over the edge of the table, her blue eyes—so much like Megan's own—bright with curiosity rather than concern. Crises were simply puzzles to be solved in Lauren's world, thanks to seven years of watching her mother tackle everything from squeaky hinges to mysterious electrical outlets.

"I'm fine, baby. Just looking for..." Megan's fingers found the valve, and she twisted it clockwise, grateful when the water flow slowed to a trickle, then stopped altogether. "There we go."

She extracted herself from beneath the sink, water dripping from her hair and her shirt clinging uncomfortably to her back.

"Well," she said, more to herself than to Lauren, "this is definitely beyond my skill level."

Lauren tilted her head, studying her mother's bedraggled appearance. "You look like you got caught in the rain."

"I feel like I got caught in something worse than rain." Megan reached for the dishtowel hanging from the oven handle and began dabbing at her wet hair. The cotton fabric smelled of the lavender fabric softener she'd used since moving back to Laurel Ridge, a small comfort that reminded her of her grandmother's linen closet and Sunday afternoons spent learning to fold fitted sheets properly.

The cottage bore traces of three generations of Houser women—her grandmother's china cabinet in the dining room, her mother's collection of vintage mixing bowls, and now Megan's own attempts to create a warm home for Lauren. The kitchen, with its white cabinets and cheerful yellow walls, had always been the heart of the house. But right now, with water pooling on the floor and the sink completely out of commission, it felt more like a disaster zone.

"So what do we do now?" Lauren asked, abandoning her chair to inspect the small lake that had formed near the sink. She walked carefully around the edge, as if the water might suddenly become deeper.

Megan surveyed the damage. The failed shutoff valve lay in pieces—corroded metal and deteriorated rubber seals that spoke of decades of faithful service finally ended. She could try to find a temporary fix, maybe wrap the connection with electrical tape or pipe compound, but the truth was unavoidable: this repair required replacement parts and probably skills beyond her YouTube-educated abilities.

She'd learned a lot in the seven years since David's death. How to change furnace filters and reset circuit breakers. How to unclog drains and tighten loose cabinet hinges. How to be both mother and father, provider and protector, strong enough for two people when Lauren needed her to be. But some problems couldn't be solved with determination and online tutorials.

"We're going to Earl's Hardware," she announced, wrapping the damp dish towel around her shoulders like a cape. "They'll have the parts I need, and maybe someone there can tell me exactly what I'm dealing with."

Lauren's face lit up. "Can I pick out a new paintbrush? The one I have is getting fuzzy."

"We'll see." Megan looked down at her water-stained clothes and sighed. She'd need to change before venturing into public, but first, she should clean up the puddle spreading across her kitchen floor. "Let me get this water mopped up and put on some dry clothes. Then we'll head into town."

As she gathered towels and began sopping up the mess, Megan mentally calculated the cost of repair supplies against her carefully managed budget. The cottage had been a blessing—inherited free and clear from her grandmother—but maintaining an eighty-year-old house required constant vigilance and an ever-growing list of small repairs that seemed to multiply faster than she could address them.

The wooden floors creaked familiarly as she moved between the kitchen and the laundry room, collecting every absorbent fabric she could find. Lauren had returned to her drawing, adding a rainbow over the purple elephant's head, her small tongue poking out in concentration.

"Mommy, why don't we just call someone to fix it?" Lauren asked without looking up from her artwork. "Like when the washing machine made that funny noise?"

Megan paused in her mopping. The appliance repair had cost nearly three hundred dollars—money that had come from the fund she'd earmarked for Lauren's winter clothes. She could afford basic supplies and manage simple repairs herself, but paying someone else's labor rates was a luxury her librarian's salary couldn't support very often.

"Because we're smart and capable, and we can figure this out ourselves," she said, injecting confidence she didn't entirely feel into her voice. "Besides, it's just a matter of finding the right parts. Your Grandpa always said hardware stores were like libraries for people who fix things—everything you need is there, you just have to know how to ask for it."

The comparison felt apt. At the Laurel Ridge Public Library, Megan could locate any piece of information, solve research puzzles that stumped others, and connect people with exactly the resources they needed. Surely a hardware store couldn't be that different. Pipes and fittings instead of books and databases, but the principle remained the same: identify the problem, find the right solution, apply knowledge systematically.

She finished cleaning up the water and surveyed her handiwork. The kitchen looked normal again, except for the shut-off water and the collection of pipe remnants she'd placed on the counter like evidence from a crime scene.

"Alright, Lauren-bug, let me go change clothes and then we'll make our hardware store expedition." She kissed the top of Lauren's head, breathing in the scent of her daughter's strawberry shampoo mixed with crayon wax. "Maybe we can stop by the library afterward and pick up those books you requested. I got a notification that they had arrived."

"The ones about the girl who talks to horses?"

"Those are the ones."

Megan headed upstairs to her bedroom, peeling off her damp t-shirt as she climbed the narrow staircase. The floorboards creaked in a rhythm she knew by heart, and the afternoon sunlight filtering through the landing window created familiar patterns on the wallpaper—tiny rosebuds on a cream background that her grandmother had chosen decades ago and that Megan had never found the heart to change.

In her bedroom, she selected a clean pair of jeans and a white t-shirt and a sage-green cardigan. As she changed clothes, she caught a glimpse of herself in the antique mirror above her dresser—wet hair curling at the ends, cheeks flushed from exertion, and a small smudge of pipe corrosion on her chin. She looked capable and determined, if a bit frazzled.

Which was exactly how she felt most days.

Downstairs, Lauren had added a castle to her elephant drawing, complete with triangular flags and a drawbridge. "Is this for me to keep or for the library bulletin board?" She asked as Megan reappeared in the kitchen.

"It's yours to keep. We have plenty of decorations for the library." Megan gathered her purse and keys from the kitchen counter, then collected the pipe fragments and placed them carefully in a plastic bag. Evidence for the hardware store consultation. "Ready for our adventure?"

Lauren scrambled down from her chair, leaving her crayons scattered across the table in the casual disorder of childhood creativity. "Are we walking or driving?"

"Driving. Earl's Hardware is on Main Street, and I don't want to carry pipe fittings six blocks in this heat." Megan held the door open for Lauren, then turned back to survey her kitchen one final time. The cottage would be without running water in the kitchen until she could complete the repair, which meant no dishwashing, no handwashing, and definitely no more attempts at amateur plumbing until she had the proper parts and, hopefully, some expert guidance.

The August air hit them like a warm embrace as they stepped outside, carrying the scents of late summer—cut grass, blooming roses from Mrs. Patterson's garden next door, and the faint smokiness that lingered from someone's backyard barbecue. Lauren skipped ahead toward their car, a reliable four-year-old Ford SUV that had served them faithfully through countless library commutes and weekend adventures.

As Megan unlocked the car doors, she felt the familiar weight of single motherhood settle around her shoulders—not unpleasant, exactly, but substantial. Every decision was hers to make, every problem hers to solve, every crisis hers to navigate with grace and competence for Lauren's sake. She'd grown accustomed to being both the question-asker and the answer-finder, the one who broke things and the one who fixed them.

But standing in her driveway with a bag of broken pipe fittings and the task of locating replacement parts ahead of her, Megan felt the subtle stirring of something she rarely allowed herself to acknowledge: the wish that someone else might share the load, just occasionally. Someone who could look at the disaster under her sink and know immediately what needed to be done. Someone who could handle the hardware store consultation while she managed other weekend tasks.

She shook off the thought as quickly as it had arrived. Wishful thinking was a luxury she couldn't afford, and besides, she'd managed perfectly well for seven years. One stubborn shutoff valve wasn't going to defeat her.

"Buckled in?" She called to Lauren, who was already securing her seat belt and arranging her small purse—a miniature version of Megan's own—in her lap.

"Ready for the hardware store!" Lauren announced with the enthusiasm of someone who found errands genuinely exciting.

Megan started the car and backed out of the driveway, pointing them toward downtown Laurel Ridge and Earl's Hardware, completely unaware that this simple Saturday morning errand was about to change everything.

The summer afternoon stretched ahead of them, golden and full of possibilities neither of them could have imagined.

Chapter 2

Matt Smith had been organizing hardware inventory for the better part of an hour when the familiar chime of the bell above the door of the hardware store announced another customer. He glanced up from the box of pipe fittings he'd been sorting, automatically preparing his customer service smile and professional greeting—then froze completely.

Recognition hit him like a lightning bolt straight to his chest.

Megan Miller stood just inside the doorway, clutching a plastic bag in one hand and looking around the store with the slightly overwhelmed expression of someone facing an unfamiliar challenge. Except she wasn't the Megan Miller he remembered anymore, was she? The years had clearly changed her, and there was something in her eyes—a depth that spoke of experiences both joyful and difficult—that reminded him how much time had passed since high school. Still, she was unmistakably the girl he'd known in high school—though "girl" was entirely the wrong word for the woman before him now.

The years had transformed her from the pretty, bookish teenager he remembered into something that made his throat go dry. Her chestnut hair fell in soft waves just past her shoulders, and those blue eyes that had always made him stumble over his words in chemistry class were just as stunning as ever. She'd grown into herself, carried herself with quiet confidence, and there was a strength in her posture that spoke of someone who'd learned to handle whatever life threw at her.

"Can I help you with—" Matt's professional greeting died mid-sentence as those familiar blue eyes found his and widened with surprise.

"Matt? Matt Smith?" Megan's voice carried the same warm tone he remembered, though there was a slight tremor of shock threaded through it. "I didn't know you were back in town."

"Megan." Her name felt strange and familiar all at once on his tongue. He set down the box of fittings and stepped around the counter, suddenly hyperaware of his appearance—work shirt rumpled from inventory duty, hair probably standing at odd angles from running his hands through it, and was that a smudge of metal polish on his forearm? "Yeah, I got back about a week ago. Taking over for Dad here at the store so he can retire. Well, semi-retire anyway."

The silence stretched between them for a moment, filled with the weight of twelve years and shared memories of a simpler time. Matt found himself cataloging the changes—the way she held herself with more purpose, the laugh lines around her eyes that spoke of joy despite whatever challenges she'd faced, and the missing wedding ring from her ring finger.

"You look good," he said, then immediately felt heat creep up his neck. *Smooth, Smith. Real professional.*

But Megan smiled, a genuine expression that created a small dimple in her left cheek—a detail he'd forgotten until this moment. "Thank you. You look…" she paused, her gaze taking in his six-foot frame, the way military bearing had straightened his shoulders and broadened his chest, "different. Good different. More grown-up, I suppose."

Matt chuckled, some of his nervous tension easing. "Twelve years in the Marines will do that to a person. What brings you to my humble hardware establishment? Please tell me it's not a major disaster."

Megan's laugh was rueful as she lifted the plastic bag. "Well, that depends on your definition of major. I attempted to fix a leaky shutoff valve under my kitchen sink this morning. The key word being 'attempted.'"

"Ah." Matt nodded knowingly. "Let me guess—the old compression fitting decided to give up the ghost entirely?"

"How did you—never mind, of course you'd know?" She shook her head, and Matt caught the subtle scent of lavender fabric softener and something else—strawberries, maybe from shampoo. "I should have left well enough alone, but the drip was driving me crazy. Now I have no water in my kitchen."

As she spoke, Matt found himself studying her face, noting the way her hands moved expressively when she explained the disaster, the slight self-deprecating tilt to her smile that suggested she was embarrassed but not defeated by the situation. She was still Megan—still kind, still genuine, still possessed of the intelligence that had made her the best student in their graduating class. But there was something else now, a resilience that hadn't been there in high school.

"Well, the good news is that's a fairly straightforward repair," Matt said, forcing himself to focus on her plumbing crisis instead of the way her eyes crinkled when she smiled. "The bad news is that those old compression fittings can be tricky if you're not used to working with them. What kind of valve are we dealing with?"

Megan opened her plastic bag and carefully extracted the corroded remains of her morning's disaster. Matt accepted the pieces, noting the way their fingers brushed briefly during the transfer—a contact that sent an unexpected jolt of awareness up his arm.

"Hmm." He examined the failed fitting, turning it over in his palm. "This has definitely seen better days. Probably original to the house, judging by the corrosion pattern. What year was your place built?"

"Nineteen-forties, I think. It was my grandmother's house." Megan's voice softened slightly. "She left it to me when she passed away a few years ago."

"I remember that cottage," Matt said, the memory surfacing unexpectedly. "White clapboard with green shutters, right? On Maple Street? I always thought it looked like something from a storybook."

"That's the one." Megan seemed pleased that he remembered. "It still looks like a storybook cottage, but the plumbing definitely reads like a horror novel some days."

Matt laughed, genuinely delighted by her humor in the face of domestic disaster. "Well, let's see what we can do to give your story a happier ending. You'll need a new quarter-turn valve—the modern ones are much more reliable than these old compression types. Plus some pipe compound and probably new supply lines while we're at it."

He moved through the store with practiced efficiency, gathering the necessary supplies while Megan followed. The familiar sounds of Earl's Hardware surrounded them—the creak of wooden floorboards worn smooth by decades of customers, the subtle tick of the old regulator clock on the wall, the distant hum of the air conditioning unit that had been threatening to give up.

"I have to admit," Megan said as Matt selected a valve from the display rack, "I'm impressed by how easily you navigate all this. In high school, you were more interested in history than hardware."

"Military training," Matt explained, though that wasn't the complete truth. He'd spent the past week immersing himself in the family business, determined to be worthy of his father's trust and the community's expectations. "Plus, Dad's been preparing me for this transition for months. I may not have grown up loving hardware stores, but I've developed a healthy respect for the problem-solving aspect."

"That makes sense. David always said you were good at figuring things out under pressure." Megan's voice carried a note of something—sadness, maybe, or nostalgia—that made Matt glance at her sharply.

David. Of course. David Miller, his best friend from high school, the guy who'd dated Megan their senior year before they'd both shipped off to basic training. Matt felt a familiar twist in his chest, the complicated mix of grief and guilt that always accompanied thoughts of his fallen friend.

"Yeah, well," he said, focusing intently on selecting the right size supply lines, "some problems are easier to solve than others."

They'd reached the counter, and Matt began tallying her purchases. The silence between them had shifted, becoming heavier with the weight of shared memories and unspoken history. He found himself sneaking glances at her while he rang up her supplies, noting the way afternoon sunlight from the front windows caught golden highlights in her hair, the careful way she watched his hands as he worked.

"This should get you back in business," he said, placing her supplies in a brown paper bag with the Earl's Hardware logo stamped on the side. "Though I have to ask—are you comfortable doing the installation yourself? Those quarter-turn valves can be finicky if you're not familiar with them."

Megan hesitated, and Matt could practically see her internal debate. Pride warring with practicality, independence struggling against the acknowledgment that some jobs required experience she didn't possess.

"I..." she began, then stopped, clearly wrestling with herself.

Matt surprised himself by jumping into the silence. "Look, I could swing by after we close and take a look, if you want. Make sure everything goes together properly. I mean, if you're comfortable with that."

The offer hung in the air between them, unexpected even to Matt himself. Where had that come from? He barely knew this version of Megan, had no idea what her life looked like now, whether she was happily seeing someone that could take care of her plumbing issues, or whether she'd welcome help from her high school friend who'd just returned to town.

But something in her expression—a flicker of relief quickly masked by uncertainty—told him she was tempted.

"I don't want to impose," she said carefully. "I'm sure you have better things to do on a Saturday evening than rescue someone from their plumbing disasters."

"Actually, I don't," Matt admitted with a rueful smile. "I'm still getting reacquainted with Laurel Ridge social life. Plus, it would give me a chance to practice my rusty civilian repair skills. Consider it a favor to both of us."

Megan studied his face, and Matt had the distinct impression she was weighing more than just his plumbing abilities. Whatever she saw there seemed to reassure her, because her shoulders relaxed slightly.

"Okay," she said. "But only if you let me watch what you're doing. I want to learn how to handle this kind of thing myself next time."

"Deal. We close at five. I can be there around five-thirty. Would that work for you?"

"Five-thirty is perfect. You remember where Maple Street is?"

"I remember." The truth was, he'd driven past that white cottage with green shutters more often than he cared to admit during his teenage years just to see if she was there, back when he'd harbored an impossible crush on the smart girl who tutored him in chemistry and never seemed to notice when he stumbled over his words in her presence.

Megan accepted the paper bag of supplies, and Matt noticed she was careful not to let their fingers brush again during the transfer. Interesting.

"Thank you, Matt. I really appreciate this." She paused at the counter, seeming to gather herself. "It's good to see you again. I'm glad you made it home safely."

The simple words carried a weight that made his chest tight. "Thanks, Megan. That means more than you know."

She headed toward the door, and Matt found himself watching her go—the graceful way she moved, the set of her shoulders that spoke of quiet strength, the way she paused to examine a display of garden tools with interest. Just before she reached the door, she turned back.

"Matt? What should I do about the water situation until this evening? I shut off the main valve, so..."

"Leave it off for now," he advised. "No point in risking another flood. You'll be fine without water for a few hours."

"Right. Of course." She smiled again, with the same genuine expression that had always made his teenage heart race. "See you at five-thirty."

The door chime marked her departure, leaving Matt alone with the familiar scents of motor oil and metal polish, the subtle tick of the regulator clock, and the completely unfamiliar sensation of anticipation thrumming through his veins.

He returned to his inventory sorting, but found his mind wandering to memories of high school chemistry class, autumn football games where he'd stolen glances at Megan in the stands, the way she'd looked in her graduation cap and gown standing next to David, radiant with the promise of their shared future.

Twelve years was a long time. People changed, circumstances shifted, and the girl he'd known had clearly grown into a remarkable woman. A widow, he reminded himself, glancing at the spot where she'd stood.

But widow or not, she'd accepted his help. In a few hours, he'd be in her kitchen, fixing her plumbing, probably making small talk about their respective lives and trying not to think about how her presence had just turned his carefully ordered new civilian life completely upside down

Chapter 3

The knock at the front door came at exactly five-thirty, punctual in a way that made Megan smile despite her nervous energy. She'd spent the last hour alternately checking her appearance in the hallway mirror and reminding herself this was simply a practical arrangement—an old friend helping with a repair, nothing more complicated than that.

"He's here!" Lauren announced from her perch on the living room sofa, where she'd been watching Matt while working on a new crayon masterpiece. This one featured a castle surrounded by flowers, though the purple elephant from this morning had somehow found its way into the courtyard.

Megan smoothed her hands over her jeans and opened the door to find Matt, a well-worn leather tool bag in one hand and a slight smile playing at the corners of his mouth. He'd changed from his work clothes into a clean flannel shirt and newer jeans.

"Evening," he said. "Ready to tackle that rebellious plumbing?"

"More than ready," Megan replied, stepping aside to let him enter.

"Matt!" Lauren bounded off the sofa with the boundless energy of childhood, her drawing forgotten. "Are you really going to fix our sink? Mommy says you know all about pipes and stuff."

"I know some about pipes and stuff," Matt said, crouching down to Lauren's eye level with an ease that surprised Megan. "But the most important thing about fixing anything is understanding how it works first. Would you like to help me figure out what's going on under there?"

Lauren's eyes went wide with delight. "Can I really help? Mommy usually says I'm too little for tools."

"Tools can be dangerous if you don't know how to use them safely," Matt explained patiently. "But there are lots of ways to help that don't involve the pointy or electrical parts. You could be my official flashlight holder, if your mom says that's okay."

Megan felt something warm and unexpected unfurl in her chest as she watched Matt's interaction with her daughter. Most adults either ignored Lauren entirely or spoke to her with that patronizing tone that made Megan's teeth clench. But Matt addressed her with genuine respect, as if her questions and curiosity were not just tolerable but actually valuable.

"I think official flashlight holder sounds like a very important job," she said, earning a brilliant smile from Lauren and an approving nod from Matt.

"Excellent. Now, let me take a look at what we're dealing with."

Matt set his toolbox on the kitchen counter and surveyed the space with the systematic approach of someone trained to assess situations quickly and thoroughly. Megan found herself watching him move through her kitchen, noting how his presence seemed to fill the room. He was taller than she remembered from high school, broader through the shoulders, and there was a confidence in his movements that spoke of experience and capability.

"Mind if I take a look underneath first?" he asked, glancing at her for permission.

"Please go ahead. I'll grab the flashlight for Lauren."

While Megan rummaged through the utility drawer, Matt knelt beside the sink and peered into the cabinet space. She could hear him moving things around, his voice taking on a thoughtful quality as he examined the problem.

"Okay, I can see what happened here," he said, emerging from beneath the sink. "That compression fitting was definitely past its expiration date. But the good news is that everything else looks solid. This should be a straightforward replacement."

Lauren had positioned herself beside him, clutching the flashlight with both hands like a sacred trust. "What made it break?"

"Time, mostly," Matt explained, settling cross-legged on the linoleum floor and patting the space beside him. "Metal gets old just like everything else. After forty or fifty years of doing the same job, sometimes it just gets tired and decides to retire."

"Like Grandpa Henry when he stopped working at the coal mines?"

"Exactly like that."

Megan pulled out one of the kitchen chairs and sat down where she could watch the repair process. "What should I be looking for if this happens again?"

"Good question. The main thing is recognizing when you're out of your depth. You did exactly the right thing by stopping when the situation got worse instead of better."

As he talked, Megan studied his hands—strong and scarred from work, with calluses that spoke of someone who used tools regularly.

His movements were economical and sure, with no wasted motion or uncertainty. When he reached for his wrench, Lauren immediately angled the flashlight to illuminate the work area without being asked.

"See how the old fitting crumbled when your mom tried to tighten it?" Matt pointed to the damaged pieces. "That's because the metal had corroded—eaten away by water over time. The new fitting is made from better materials that should last much longer."

"How much longer?" Lauren asked, peering intently at the brass valve in his hand.

"Probably longer than you and I will be around to worry about it."

The repair proceeded with a rhythm that felt almost meditative. Matt explained each step as he worked, his voice never hurried or impatient despite Lauren's steady stream of questions. Why did the pipe thread one way but not the other? What was the white paste he was applying? How did he know how tight was tight enough without breaking something?

Megan discovered that she was genuinely learning, not just watching. Matt included her in his explanations, asking if she could see what he was doing and whether his reasoning made sense. There was no condescension in his tone, no suggestion that plumbing was too complicated for her to understand. Instead, he treated her like an ordinary person capable of mastering new skills.

"The key is feeling the resistance," he said, his hand guiding hers on the wrench handle. "Too loose and it leaks. Too tight, and you damage the threads. There's a sweet spot where everything settles into place."

The casual contact sent an unexpected jolt of awareness through her—the warmth of his palm covering her knuckles, the clean scent of his skin, the solid reassurance of his presence. She found herself hyperaware of how close he was sitting, the way the kitchen light caught the darker flecks in his blue-gray eyes, the unconscious grace with which he moved around the cramped space beneath her sink.

This was dangerous territory, she realized. She was supposed to be learning about plumbing repair, not cataloging the attractive qualities of her high school friend.

"I think I've got it," she said a little too quickly, and carefully extricated her hand from his guidance.

If Matt noticed her sudden need for distance, he didn't comment on it. Instead, he turned his attention back to Lauren, who had been following the entire exchange with the focused intensity of someone determined not to miss a single detail.

"What do you think, flashlight holder? Should we test our work?"

"Yes!" Lauren scrambled to her feet and positioned herself by the main shutoff valve under the sink. "I know where the water switch is!"

"Careful and slow," Matt instructed. "Turn it just a little at first."

The pipes gave a gentle shudder as water began flowing through them again, and Megan held her breath as she watched the new connection. No drips, no streams, just the quiet efficiency of properly functioning plumbing.

"Success," Matt announced, and Lauren let out a cheer that made them both laugh.

"This calls for a celebration," Megan said, relief and gratitude washing over her in equal measure. "Can I get you some coffee? Sweet tea? I think there's still some of Lauren's lemonade in the refrigerator."

"Coffee sounds perfect."

As Megan busied herself with the Keurig coffee maker, she listened to Matt and Lauren's continued conversation about tools and repairs. Lauren had apparently decided that Matt was the most interesting adult she'd encountered, and was peppering him with questions about everything from screwdrivers to the hardware store to whether he'd ever fixed anything really, really big.

"What's the biggest thing you ever fixed?" Lauren asked, settling into her chair at the kitchen table while Matt gathered his tools.

Matt considered this seriously. "Probably a helicopter."

"A real helicopter? That flies in the sky?"

"A real helicopter. Though it wasn't flying when I worked on it, which was definitely for the best."

"Were you in the army?"

"Marines. For twelve years."

"Wow!" Lauren's eyes went wide with the mathematical implications. "Did you know my daddy? He was a Marine too."

Megan tensed involuntarily. Lauren asked about David sometimes, usually with the matter-of-fact curiosity of childhood, but this felt different—more loaded with possibilities she wasn't sure she was ready to explore.

"I did know your daddy," Matt said gently. "We were good friends in high school, and we served together for a while. He was a very good man."

"Mommy says he would have liked to meet me."

"I'm sure he would have loved you very much."

The simple honesty in Matt's voice made Megan's chest tight with emotion she hadn't expected. She concentrated on making coffee with unnecessary precision, grateful for the task that let her process the moment without having to respond immediately.

When she turned back to the table with two steaming mugs, Matt and Lauren were bent over her drawing, discussing the merits of crayon castle construction. The domestic scene struck her with sudden force—this was what her kitchen was supposed to feel like. Warm and welcoming and full of easy conversation. Complete in a way it had never been.

"So my mom told me you're the head librarian now," Matt said, accepting his coffee with a nod of thanks. "That's wonderful. I remember how much you loved books in school."

"Still do. Though these days I spend more time with budget spreadsheets and program planning than actual reading." She settled into the chair across from him, cradling her mug in both hands. "What made you decide to come back to Laurel Ridge? I would have thought after all those years in the Marines, you might want to see more of the world."

"I saw plenty of the world," Matt said quietly. "Sometimes you realize that home is exactly where you want to be."

There was something in his tone that suggested deeper waters beneath the simple statement, but Megan didn't press. Everyone had their reasons for the choices they made, and she understood better than most that some stories needed time before they could be shared.

"The hardware store suits you," she said instead.

"I've always known that Dad would retire one day and that I'd step up and run the store. I've always been good with my hands. And honestly, it was time. When my reenlistment came up for the Marines, I knew I was ready to move on."

The faint flush creeping up his neck was endearing in a way that made Megan's stomach flutter unexpectedly. This was Matt—quiet, competent Matt—who had just spent an hour patiently teaching her daughter about plumbing while treating them both with more genuine respect than some people managed in years of acquaintance.

"Well, I can't thank you enough for this," she said, gesturing toward the sink. "You've probably saved me a couple hundred dollars in repair bills."

"Happy to help." Matt finished his coffee and began gathering his tools with the same methodical precision he'd shown throughout the repair. "We should get together soon. It would be nice to catch up."

The invitation hung between them, friendly but loaded with possibility. Megan felt the familiar flutter of anxiety that accompanied any step beyond the careful boundaries of her established life. But underneath the nervousness was something warmer—anticipation, maybe, or simple pleasure at the prospect of spending time with someone who seemed genuinely interested in her company.

"I'd like that. Maybe we could have lunch sometime?"

"It's a date." The words slipped out easily, then Matt seemed to realize what he'd said. "I mean, it's a plan. Lunch... sometime soon."

"I knew what you meant." Megan smiled, touched by his sudden awkwardness.

She walked him to the front door, Lauren trailing behind with questions about when Matt might come back to fix other things. As they reached the porch, Megan noticed him glance at the railing she'd been meaning to tighten for months.

"I noticed your porch railing seemed a little loose," he observed casually.

"I know. It's on my list."

"I could take a look at sometime, if you want. Probably just needs some new screws."

The offer was practical, neighborly, and completely reasonable. It was also dangerous in ways that had nothing to do with home repair and everything to do with the warmth spreading through her chest at the thought of seeing him again.

"We'll see," she said, which wasn't exactly a yes but wasn't a no either.

Matt nodded, hefting his tool bag over his shoulder. "Well, you know where to find me if you need anything."

From the porch, Megan watched him walk to his truck—a solid, dependable vehicle that suited him perfectly. He raised one hand in a brief wave before driving away, leaving her standing in the doorway with Lauren pressed against her side.

"I like him," Lauren announced with seven-year-old certainty. "He's nice, and he knows about helicopters, and he didn't get mad when I asked a million questions."

"He is nice," Megan agreed softly.

They went back inside, Lauren chattering about flashlight holding and the important job of being a repair assistant. But Megan was only half-listening as she moved through the familiar evening routine of fixing dinner.

The cottage felt different somehow. Not just because the plumbing worked again, though that was certainly a relief. There was something else—a lingering warmth that had nothing to do with the August heat and everything to do with the way Matt had filled her kitchen with easy conversation and patient kindness.

She wondered what it would be like to have that kind of presence in her life regularly. Someone to share the small disasters and daily victories. Someone who treated Lauren with respect and made her laugh. Someone who looked at her like she was worth knowing, worth spending time with, worth more than just polite consideration.

The thought should have terrified her. For seven years, she'd built her life around self-sufficiency and careful emotional boundaries. She was content with her work, devoted to Lauren, active in her church and community. She didn't need anyone else to make her life complete.

But as she started mixing the ingredients for a chicken casserole, Megan couldn't shake the realization that contentment and completion were not necessarily the same thing. And Matt Smith's presence in her kitchen had reminded her of the difference in ways she wasn't sure she was ready to examine.

Chapter 4

"Will Matt come back tomorrow?" Lauren asked as she slipped her arms into her favorite pajamas—the ones covered with dancing horses that Megan's mother had found on clearance at the end of last summer.

Megan looked up, struck by the hopeful note in her daughter's voice. They'd barely finished their evening routine of bath time and toothbrushing, and already Lauren's thoughts had circled back to their evening visitor.

"I don't think so, sweetheart. Tomorrow's Sunday—we have church, remember?" Megan smoothed the quilt over Lauren's narrow bed, breathing in the familiar scents of strawberry shampoo and freshly washed sheets. "And Matt probably has his own Sunday plans."

"But he could come to church with us, couldn't he?" Lauren climbed into bed and settled against her pillows, surrounded by the collection of stuffed animals that had somehow multiplied over the years. Her favorite, a worn teddy bear named Mr. Buttons, found its usual spot tucked against her chin. "I bet he'd like Pastor Andrew."

Her daughter had inherited David's generous spirit and thoughtful heart along with his stubborn cowlick, always assuming the best of people and eager to include anyone who showed her kindness.

"Well, we don't really know what Matt's plans are," Megan said carefully, settling on the edge of the bed. "But it was nice of him to help us with the sink, wasn't it?"

"He's really good at fixing things. And he wasn't mean about me asking so many questions." Lauren's blue eyes—so much like Megan's own—were bright with excitement despite the late hour.

"Questions are important," Megan agreed, stroking Lauren's hair back from her forehead. "That's how we learn new things."

"Matt said my daddy was a good man." Lauren's voice grew softer, more thoughtful. "Do you think my daddy would have taught me about fixing things too?"

The question hit Megan's chest like a physical blow. Lauren rarely asked about David. Lauren had never known a life with a father present. But tonight, Lauren had glimpsed something she'd never experienced: what it might be like to have a man who took her questions seriously, who included her in grown-up tasks, and who made her feel valued and heard.

"I think your daddy would have taught you anything you wanted to learn," Megan managed, her voice steady despite the emotion threatening to overwhelm her. "He would have been so proud of how smart and curious you are."

Lauren was quiet for a moment, processing this with the serious consideration she gave to all matters of importance. Then, in the way children had of asking the questions that cut straight to the heart of things, she said, "Why do some kids have daddies and I don't?"

The bedroom suddenly felt too small, the air too thin. This was the conversation Megan had been preparing for since Lauren was old enough to notice family structures, but it never got easier. How do you explain death to a child who has never known anything but life? How do you talk about loss when you're still learning to live with it yourself?

"Well," Megan began carefully, choosing her words with the precision of someone defusing a bomb, "families come in all different shapes and sizes. Some families have mommies and daddies, some have just mommies or just daddies, some have grandparents or aunts and uncles raising kids. God makes families in lots of different ways."

"But why don't I have a daddy when God made other kids have them?"

Lauren's question was purely logical, without self-pity or complaint—just a seven-year-old trying to understand the mathematics of family composition. But it struck Megan with renewed force how much her daughter had missed, how many father-daughter moments had been stolen by that training accident seven years ago.

"Your daddy wanted to be with us more than anything," Megan said softly, taking Lauren's small hand in hers. "But sometimes God calls people home to heaven before we're ready to let them go. It doesn't mean He loves some families more than others. It just means that some people have different jobs to do, and sometimes those jobs are in heaven instead of here on earth."

"What kind of job does Daddy have in heaven?"

"I don't know exactly. But I think it must be something very important, because God needed someone very special to do it."

Lauren considered this with the same intense focus she applied to her drawings, her small brow furrowed in concentration. "Do you think he watches us sometimes? Like when I'm learning new stuff?"

"I think he does, and I think he loves you very much. And I think he'd want you to keep learning new things and asking good questions."

"Like about fixing sinks?"

"Like about fixing sinks."

Lauren smiled then, the shadow of sadness lifting from her features as quickly as it had appeared. "Matt's really good at teaching, isn't he? He made it seem easy, even though it was probably hard."

"He is good at teaching," Megan agreed, remembering the patient way Matt had guided her hands on the wrench, the careful explanations that never made her feel foolish for not knowing. "Some people have that gift."

"I hope he comes back soon. Not just for fixing things, but for talking too. He listens like grown-ups are supposed to listen, but most of them don't."

From the mouths of babes. Lauren had managed to articulate something Megan had felt but hadn't quite named—the rare quality of being truly heard, truly seen, that Matt possessed. How many adults rushed past children's questions or answered with half their attention elsewhere? But Matt had given Lauren his complete focus, treating her curiosity as legitimate and worthy of his time.

"We should probably say our prayers now," Megan said, deflecting before Lauren could ask more questions about when they might see Matt again.

They recited their nightly prayer together, Lauren's sweet voice joining Megan's in the familiar words of gratitude and protection. But tonight, as Lauren asked God to bless Mommy and Grandma and Grandpa Houser and Grandma and Grandpa Miller and Mr. Buttons and the new goldfish at school, Megan found herself listening with fresh attention.

"And please bless Matt too," Lauren added spontaneously. "Thank you for sending him to fix our sink and help him to have good dreams about helicopters."

Megan's throat tightened at her daughter's innocent addition to their prayer list. In the space of one evening, Matt had somehow earned a place in Lauren's nightly conversation with God—an honor typically reserved for family and beloved pets.

"Amen," she whispered, pressing a kiss to Lauren's forehead.

"Amen," Lauren echoed, already settling deeper into her pillows. "Mommy? Will you leave the hall light on tonight?"

"Of course, baby girl. Sweet dreams."

Megan turned on the small nightlight and left Lauren's door cracked open—their established routine for perfect sleeping conditions. The hallway stretched before her, filled with the comfortable shadows of home and the ticking of her grandmother's mantle clock downstairs.

Instead of heading to her own room, Megan was drawn back to the kitchen downstairs. She moved quietly through the familiar space, straightening things that didn't need straightening and trying to process the emotions Lauren's questions had stirred up.

The kitchen faucet gleamed in the soft light from the range hood. Megan turned on the tap and watched clear water flow into the basin, marveling at the simple miracle of indoor plumbing that she'd taken for granted until this morning. But it wasn't really about the plumbing, was it? It was about the man who had fixed it, and the way his presence had filled more than just the physical space beneath her sink.

She'd spent seven years carefully constructing a life that was complete, manageable, and safe. She was a good mother, a competent professional in her job, and an active member of her community. She'd learned to change light fixtures and unclog drains, to navigate parent-teacher conferences and pediatric appointments, to be both mother and father to a little girl who deserved the world.

But tonight, watching Matt interact with Lauren, seeing the way her daughter had blossomed under his attention, Megan had caught a glimpse of what they'd both been missing.

Not that they were incomplete without a man in their lives. That wasn't the issue. But there was something about masculine energy, about the particular way men approached problems and conversations and relationships, that brought out different aspects of Lauren's personality. And if Megan was being honest, different aspects of her own personality as well.

She'd forgotten how it felt to have someone competent and caring step into her domestic space and simply... handle things. Not because she couldn't handle them herself—she'd proven that for seven years. But because sharing the load, having someone who wanted to help not out of obligation but out of genuine concern, created a different kind of harmony in a home.

Megan turned off the water and leaned against the sink, letting herself acknowledge what she'd been trying to avoid all evening. She was attracted to Matt Smith. Not just grateful for his help or pleased to see an old friend, but genuinely, physically, romantically interested in the man who had accidentally slipped back into her life.

The realization should have terrified her. For seven years, she'd kept her heart carefully protected, dating occasionally but never letting anyone get close enough to matter. She'd told herself it was for Lauren's sake—no point in bringing confusion or instability into her daughter's life. But if she was honest, it had been for her own protection too. Loving someone meant risking loss, and she'd already lost enough for one lifetime.

But tonight, seeing Lauren's face light up when Matt treated her questions as important, watching him move through her kitchen with quiet competence and genuine kindness—tonight, the wall around her heart had developed some serious cracks.

And Lauren's bedtime questions had revealed another truth she'd been avoiding: her daughter was hungry for male attention, for the particular kind of relationship only a father figure could provide. Megan had tried to fill every role, but there were some things a mother simply couldn't give her daughter, no matter how much love and dedication she poured into the effort.

Did that mean she should pursue something with Matt? The logical part of her mind immediately began cataloging all the reasons why it would be complicated. They had a history, but it was a history complicated by David's memory. Matt was still settling into civilian life, and she had no idea what he really wanted or whether his interest extended beyond friendly helpfulness. And then there was Lauren to consider—what if things didn't work out? What if Matt decided he wasn't ready for an instant family? What if he broke her daughter's heart along with her own?

But another part of her mind, the part that had been dormant for so long she'd almost forgotten it existed, whispered different possibilities. What if it worked? What if Matt's return to Laurel Ridge was about more than just taking over his father's hardware store? What if, after seven years of careful independence, God was offering her a second chance at love and partnership and the kind of family Lauren had never known?

The thought made her breath catch in her throat. It had been so long since she'd allowed herself to dream about shared futures and daily companionship and someone to talk to at the end of long days. So long since she'd imagined what it might be like to trust someone with her heart again.

Megan pushed away from the sink and moved through the darkened living room to the front window, where she could see the empty street beyond her small yard. Matt's truck was long gone of course, but she wondered what he was doing now. Was he in his apartment above the hardware store, reflecting on the evening the way she was? Did he feel the same spark of possibility that had been dancing through her thoughts all evening?

Or was she reading too much into simple neighborly kindness? Maybe Matt was just being helpful to an old friend who'd needed plumbing help. Maybe his easy way with Lauren was nothing more than the natural courtesy of someone who'd been raised to be polite to children. Maybe the moments when their eyes had met over the sink repair, when she'd caught him watching her with something warmer than casual interest, had been her imagination.

But even as she tried to talk herself out of the hope spreading through her chest, Megan couldn't quite manage it. There had been something in the way Matt looked at her tonight, something in the way he'd lingered over coffee and seemed reluctant to leave. Something in the way he'd suggested lunch at Martha's Diner with the kind of careful casualness that suggested he'd been thinking about it for longer than the moment it took to speak the words.

She moved back through the house, turning off lights and checking door locks, but her mind remained focused on the question Lauren had asked earlier: Why do some kids have daddies and I don't?

Maybe the answer wasn't about what Lauren didn't have. Maybe it was about what God might be preparing to give them both.

As Megan climbed the stairs to her bedroom, she found herself offering up a tentative prayer of her own. Not for Matt specifically—that felt too presumptuous, too much like trying to dictate God's plan. But for wisdom. For discernment. For the courage to remain open to whatever possibilities He might have in mind, and the wisdom to recognize them when and if they appeared.

Because if tonight had taught her anything, it was that her carefully constructed life of independence and self-sufficiency might not be as complete as she'd convinced herself it was. And maybe, just maybe, that was okay.

Maybe it was time to stop protecting her heart so fiercely and start trusting it again.

Chapter 5

The morning sun streamed through the tall stained-glass windows of Laurel Ridge Community Church, casting jeweled patterns of blue and gold and burgundy across the polished wooden pews. Matt settled into his family's customary spot—third row from the front, right side—between his mother, Sylvia, and his younger brother, Graham, with his father, Earl, completing their familiar foursome.

It felt strange and comforting all at once to be back in this sanctuary where he'd spent countless Sunday mornings as a child and teenager. The scent of aged wood and fresh flowers filled the air, mingling with the quiet murmur of congregation members greeting each other and settling into their seats. Some things, Matt reflected, never changed in the best possible way.

"Have I told you how good it is to have you home, son?" Earl murmured, adjusting his reading glasses as he opened his bulletin. His father's voice carried the satisfaction of a man who'd waited years to have his family complete in the pew again.

"Good to be here, Dad," Matt replied.

Pastor Andrew Whitman took his place at the simple wooden pulpit, his warm smile encompassing the gathered congregation. He was younger than Matt had anticipated—probably mid-thirties—with an easy, approachable manner that immediately put people at ease. The kind of pastor who could discuss theology over coffee or help you move furniture on a Saturday afternoon with equal enthusiasm.

As the service began with familiar hymns and responsive readings, Matt found his attention wandering despite his best intentions. Not from boredom—he'd genuinely missed small-town worship during his years of deployment—but because of the woman sitting across the aisle and three rows back.

Megan sat with Lauren and her parents. They had aged just like everyone else he had once known, but he recognized them instantly. Even from this distance, Matt could see Lauren's small hands folded neatly in her lap, her head tilted attentively toward Pastor Andrew as if determined not to miss a single word. Megan herself looked serene and lovely in a simple blue dress, her attention focused on the service with the kind of genuine engagement that spoke of deep faith rather than mere tradition.

"Beloved friends," Pastor Andrew began, his voice carrying easily through the sanctuary, "this morning we're going to talk about God's amazing capacity for forgiveness—not just forgiving us, but giving us the strength to forgive ourselves and step into the new life He has planned."

Matt shifted slightly in his seat, feeling the words settle somewhere deeper than his ears. After years of carrying guilt and regret, the theme struck closer to home than he was entirely comfortable with.

"Sometimes we get stuck believing that our past mistakes disqualify us from future blessings," the pastor continued, his gaze sweeping the congregation with gentle authority. "But God's love isn't limited by our limited understanding of what we deserve. His grace creates possibilities where we see only obstacles."

The message continued, weaving scripture and practical wisdom together with the skill of someone who understood that faith needed to make sense in daily life. Matt was genuinely engaged, taking mental notes about forgiveness and second chances and the courage required to accept God's gifts even when they came in unexpected packages.

When Pastor Andrew invited the congregation to pray, Matt bowed his head and found his thoughts turning not just to abstract theological concepts, but to very specific recent developments. Like the way Megan's hand had felt under his when he'd guided her use of the wrench. Like Lauren's trusting smile when she'd held the flashlight for him. Like the growing awareness that coming home to Laurel Ridge might involve more than just taking over the hardware store.

The service concluded with a hymn Matt knew well—Great Is Thy Faithfulness. Around him, voices lifted in harmony, creating the kind of communal small-town worship experience he'd missed more than he'd realized.

As the final notes faded and Pastor Andrew offered the benediction, the congregation began the leisurely process of gathering belongings and transitioning to fellowship time. This was clearly still a community that didn't rush their Sundays, Matt observed with approval.

"Matt Smith, as I live and breathe!"

He turned to find Mrs. Henson, his third-grade Sunday school teacher, approaching with the same warm smile he remembered from twenty years ago. She was smaller than he remembered, her hair now silver instead of brown, but her eyes held the same kindness that had made her classroom a favorite refuge during his childhood.

"Mrs. Henson," Matt said, genuinely pleased. "You haven't changed a bit."

"Flatterer," she said with a laugh, patting his arm with affectionate familiarity. "Though I have to say, the Marines certainly did good things for you. Your parents are so proud to have you home."

"We certainly are," Sylvia agreed, slipping her arm through Matt's with maternal pride. "Though I'm still getting used to having him tower over me like this again."

The conversation continued as they moved toward the recreation hall behind the church, where the weekly fellowship time was already in full swing. Long tables covered with checked tablecloths held platters of homemade cookies, coffee urns, and pitchers of sweet tea. The atmosphere was warm and welcoming, filled with the comfortable buzz of people who genuinely enjoyed each other's company.

Matt accepted a cup of coffee and scanned the room, supposedly looking for old friends but actually searching for a particular head of chestnut hair and a seven-year-old with an infectious smile.

"Looking for someone?" Graham asked, appearing at his elbow with a knowing grin and a plate of chocolate chip cookies.

"Just getting reacquainted," Matt replied mildly, though his younger brother's raised eyebrow suggested the deflection wasn't entirely successful.

"Uh-huh." Graham took a bite of cookie and surveyed the room with exaggerated casualness. "And I suppose your reacquaintance has nothing to do with Megan Miller and her daughter over by the coffee station?"

Matt followed his brother's gaze and felt something warm unfold in his chest. Megan was indeed by the coffee station, laughing at something her mother was saying while Lauren tugged gently on her skirt, clearly eager to move on to more interesting activities than adult conversation.

"We're old friends," Matt said, which was true as far as it went.

"Old friends," Graham repeated with the kind of fraternal skepticism that came from sharing childhood bedrooms and adolescent secrets. "Right. And I suppose that's why you kept glancing back at her during church like she hung the moon."

Before Matt could formulate a suitably dismissive response, the conversation became moot. Lauren had spotted him across the room and was making a beeline in his direction with the single-minded determination of a child on a mission.

"Matt!" she called out, her face lighting up with genuine delight. "You came to church! Did you like Pastor Andrew? He's really nice, and he tells good stories about Jesus."

"I did like him," Matt agreed, crouching down to Lauren's eye level. "And you're right about the good stories. Were you listening the whole time?"

"Mostly," Lauren admitted with the honesty that made adults simultaneously charmed and nervous. "Sometimes I color on my bulletin, but Mommy says that's okay as long as I'm quiet."

"That sounds very reasonable."

By now, Megan had approached with her parents in tow, her cheeks slightly flushed with what Matt hoped was pleasure rather than embarrassment at her daughter's enthusiastic greeting.

"Matt, I'm sure you remember my parents," she said, her voice warm despite the faint tension around her eyes. "Mom, Dad, this is Matt Smith—Earl and Sylvia's son. He's the one who helped us with our plumbing crisis yesterday. You might remember him from when I was in school."

"Ah, the hero of the kitchen sink," Bill Houser said, extending a firm handshake. He was a tall man with kind eyes and a steady presence that spoke of years in education. "Megan told us how you saved the day. Much appreciated. And I'm sorry to say... my memory isn't the best anymore. I can't remember you from back in the days when Megan was in school."

"No worries, Mr. Houser... high school was years ago. I'm just glad I could help your daughter yesterday," Matt replied, noting the way Helen Houser was studying him with the subtle intensity of a mother evaluating potential suitors. Not uncomfortable exactly, but certainly thorough.

"It was very neighborly of you," Helen added, her smile warm but speculative. "I remember you from when you were in school with Megan and David. You boys were always getting into some sort of mischief together."

The mention of David created a brief moment of silence, not awkward exactly but weighted with shared memory. Matt felt the familiar twist in his chest, but it was gentler somehow, softened by time and the peaceful atmosphere of the fellowship hall.

"Good mischief, mostly," he managed, earning a laugh from Bill and an approving nod from Helen.

"Matt," Lauren interjected, apparently deciding the adult conversation had gone on long enough, "would you like to come to dinner at our house tonight? Mommy's making chicken potpie."

The invitation hung in the air for a moment, innocent and devastating in equal measure. Matt could practically feel the attention of nearby congregation members shifting in their direction, the kind of gentle surveillance that small communities specialized in. Nearby, he caught sight of his own parents watching with expressions of interest.

Megan's face went through several shades of pink, and Matt could see her wrestling between maternal pride at Lauren's hospitality and mortification at her daughter's public invitation.

"Lauren, sweetheart," she began carefully, "you can't just invite people to dinner without asking—"

"But there's always room at our table," Lauren insisted with seven-year-old logic. "You said so yourself before. And Matt's nice, and he fixes things, and he knows about helicopters."

"She's got a point about the helicopters," Graham murmured from somewhere behind Matt, earning a warning look from Sylvia.

Matt was charmed by the entire situation—Lauren's earnest invitation, Megan's flustered embarrassment, the obvious affection of their families, and the gentle curiosity of their church community. This was what he'd missed during his years of service: the messy, wonderful complications of being known and cared about by people who remembered his childhood mistakes and celebrated his adult victories. Small-town life at its finest.

"I'd be honored to come to dinner," he said, addressing Lauren directly but keeping his eyes on Megan's face. "If your mom doesn't mind the short notice."

"She doesn't mind," Lauren announced with confidence. "Do you, Mommy?"

Megan met his gaze for a moment, and Matt saw something flicker in her blue eyes—surprise, pleasure, maybe a touch of nervousness.

"No," she said softly, "I don't mind at all. Dinner's usually around six, if that works for you."

"Six is perfect."

"Wonderful," Helen Houser said with the satisfied tone of a grandmother whose granddaughter had just accomplished something particularly clever. "Megan's chicken potpie is legendary in our family. You're in for a treat."

"I'm looking forward to it," Matt said, and found that he genuinely was.

As the fellowship time began to wind down and families started gathering their belongings, Matt felt a pleasant sense of anticipation settling over him. Yesterday evening's repair visit had been about helping a neighbor and reconnecting with an old friend. Tonight's dinner invitation felt like something different—a step forward into possibilities he hadn't quite allowed himself to consider fully.

"See you at six," Megan said as they prepared to part ways, her smile more relaxed now that the initial awkwardness had passed.

"I'll be there," Matt replied, already looking forward to another evening in the warm circle of her kitchen table, with Lauren's chatter and Megan's quiet grace creating the kind of domestic harmony he was beginning to crave more than he cared to admit.

As he walked back to his parents' car, Graham fell into step beside him with a knowing grin.

"Just old friends, huh?" his younger brother said.

Matt smiled. "Yeah," he said. "Something like that."

Chapter 6

At exactly six o'clock, Matt's knock echoed through the cottage, and Lauren raced to answer the door before Megan could finish drying her hands on the kitchen towel. The scent of her grandmother's chicken potpie recipe filled the house—tender chicken, mixed vegetables, and fluffy biscuit topping that had been baking to golden perfection for the past hour.

"Matt's here!" Lauren announced loudly, as if the entire neighborhood needed to know.

"I can see that," Megan said, smoothing her hands over the simple green dress she'd changed into after church. She'd debated the outfit choice longer than warranted, finally settling on something that looked welcoming without trying too hard.

Matt stood in the doorway looking comfortable and handsome in khakis and a button-down shirt, holding a small bouquet of wildflowers. "For the hostess," he said, offering them to Megan with a slight smile.

"They're beautiful. Thank you." She accepted the flowers, their fresh, earthy scent mixing pleasantly with the dinner aromas. "Lauren, can you help me find a vase while Matt gets settled?"

The next few minutes passed in the comfortable bustle of final dinner preparations—Lauren carefully arranging the wildflowers in her grandmother's crystal vase, Matt complimenting the delicious smells wafting from the kitchen, and Megan feeling pleasantly flustered by having a guest who seemed genuinely at ease in her home.

"I hope you're hungry," she said, pulling the potpie from the oven and setting it on the trivet in the center of her small dining table.

"Smells incredible," Matt said, and Megan caught him taking in the details of her dining room—the antique china cabinet, the framed photos of Lauren through the years, and the small touches that made this house unmistakably home.

They settled around the table, Lauren chattering about the morning's Sunday school lesson while Megan served generous portions of potpie alongside fresh green beans from the local farmer's market and warm dinner rolls. The domesticity of it all struck her with unexpected force.

"This is outstanding," Matt said after his first bite. "Is this a family recipe?"

"My grandmother's. She taught me to cook it when I was Lauren's age, insisting that every proper lady should know how to make at least one dish that could feed unexpected company."

"Smart woman. Though I'm hardly unexpected company at this point."

"No," Megan agreed, meeting his eyes across the table. "You're not."

Lauren seemed oblivious to the undercurrents in the room, busy arranging her green beans by size and explaining to Matt why the smallest ones tasted the best.

As the meal progressed, conversation flowed more easily than Megan had dared hope. Matt asked thoughtful questions about her work at the library, expressing genuine interest in her programs for children and seniors. She described the challenges of running a small-town public library with limited funding, the joy of connecting readers with the perfect book, and the satisfaction of watching literacy programs help struggling students gain confidence.

"I remember you tutoring kids in high school," Matt said. "Always patient, never making anyone feel silly for not understanding something right away. Sounds like you found the perfect career."

"Most days I think so. Though there are times when dealing with budget committees makes me wonder if I should have gone into something more lucrative." She laughed softly. "But then a child discovers a love for reading, or an elderly patron thanks me for helping them research their family history, and I remember why I do this."

"That's the mark of a true calling," Matt observed. "When the purpose matters more than the paycheck."

"Speaking of callings, what made you choose the military right out of high school? I remember you being more interested in books and history than adventure stories."

Matt was quiet for a moment, considering his answer while Lauren continued her methodical consumption of dinner. "Honestly? I wanted to see the world, and David convinced me we should do it together. The Corps seemed like the best way to get an education and travel while serving something bigger than ourselves."

"Did you see the world?"

"More of it than I ever expected. Some places I'd love to visit again as a tourist. Others..." He shrugged. "Well, some experiences are better left as memories."

Megan heard the weight behind his casual tone and recognized the careful way he'd phrased his response—honest but guarded, aware that Lauren was listening to every word. "And David? Did he love it as much as he thought he would, in your opinion? I always thought he was born for military life."

"He did. David was definitely meant for military life—the camaraderie, the mission, the sense of purpose. He thrived on the challenges, always pushing himself to be better, to do more." Matt's voice grew softer, more reflective. "He used to say the Marines gave him a way to protect people who couldn't protect themselves. That was David—always thinking about taking care of others."

Lauren looked up from her green beans with sudden interest. "Like how he would have taken care of me and Mommy?"

"Exactly like that," Matt said gently. "Your daddy had a big heart and strong hands, and he would have used both to make sure you and your mom had everything you needed."

Megan felt her chest tighten at Matt's words, recognizing the truth in them while simultaneously aching for what Lauren had never known. She'd tried so hard to give her daughter a complete picture of David without dwelling on the loss, but hearing Matt describe her late husband's character felt like receiving an unexpected gift.

"What happened to him?" Lauren asked with seven-year-old directness. "I know he went to heaven, but how come he had to go so soon?"

Matt glanced at Megan, clearly seeking guidance about how much detail was appropriate. She gave him a slight nod, trusting his judgment.

"Sometimes accidents happen during training," Matt explained carefully. "Your daddy was learning to do something very important and very dangerous, because that was his job. But something went wrong, and God called him home before he could come back to you and your mommy."

"Were you there when it happened?"

"No, sweetheart. I was in a different place, doing a different job. But I heard about it right away, and I was very sad. All of his friends were sad, because your daddy was a very special person."

Lauren processed this information with the serious concentration she applied to all important matters. "Do you still miss him?"

"Every day," Matt said without hesitation. "But I'm also grateful I got to know him and be his friend. And I think he would be very proud of how smart and kind you are, and how well your mommy has taken care of you."

The conversation had become heavy enough that Megan felt the need to lighten the mood. "Who wants dessert? I made Lauren's favorite chocolate chip cookies yesterday."

"Yes!" Lauren bounced slightly in her chair, her brief, somber mood lifting immediately. "Matt, you have to try them. Mommy makes the best cookies in the whole world."

"I'd love to try them," Matt agreed, though Megan noticed he was watching her carefully, as if gauging whether the previous conversation had been too difficult.

She served cookies and milk, grateful for Lauren's chatter about cookie preferences and the important distinction between crispy edges and chewy centers. But as the evening continued, she kept stealing glances at Matt, recognizing something in his expression that she hadn't seen before—a weariness, perhaps, or a sadness that went deeper than simple grief for his lost friend.

After Lauren finished her dessert and was dispatched to brush her teeth, double-check her homework for school, and get ready for bed, Megan and Matt sat alone at the dining table.

"Thank you," Megan said quietly. "For the way you talked to Lauren about David. She asks sometimes, but I never know how much detail is appropriate or helpful."

"She's a remarkable kid. David would have been crazy about her."

"I like to think so." Megan traced the rim of her coffee mug with one finger. "Can I ask you something personal?"

"Of course."

"When David died, how did you handle it? The grief, the questions, the way everything changed?"

Matt was quiet for a long moment, and when he spoke, his voice carried a rawness that made Megan realize how carefully he'd been moderating his words all evening.

"Honestly? Not well at first. I kept waiting for him to show up somewhere, convinced there had been a mistake. Then I got angry—at the Corps, at God, at David for taking a risk that got him killed. Then I threw myself into work, into deployments, into anything that would keep me too busy to think about how wrong everything felt without him. I avoided coming home for a long time, and anytime a leave came up, I chose to visit anywhere else but here."

He paused, running his hand through his hair. "It wasn't until I started thinking about coming home for Christmas about 4 years after he passed, that I realized I'd been stuck somewhere between angry and numb for years. David wouldn't have wanted that for me, but I didn't know how to move forward without feeling like I was leaving him behind. I was stuck and grieving for a long time."

"And now?"

"Now I'm trying to figure out what moving forward looks like in civilian life. Coming back to Laurel Ridge, taking over the store, reconnecting with people who knew him—it feels like honoring his memory instead of running from it."

Megan nodded slowly, recognizing the struggle he was describing. "I went through something similar after I moved back here with Lauren. Everyone wanted to help, but I felt like I had to prove I could handle everything on my own. If I needed help, it meant I was failing as a mother, failing to be strong enough for both of us."

"When did that change?"

"Gradually. My parents helped, David's parents were wonderful, and the church community just quietly showed up when I needed them. I learned that accepting help wasn't admitting weakness—it was allowing other people to love us the way David would have wanted us to be loved."

"That's harder than it sounds."

"Much harder. But Lauren needed to see that we were part of something bigger than just the two of us. And honestly, I needed it too."

Matt leaned back in his chair, his expression thoughtful. "Speaking of community, I've been wondering—are there volunteer opportunities around town? Ways I can get involved beyond just running the store? I want to be useful, to contribute something meaningful."

"Actually, yes. Our church has a ministry called Hands of Grace that might be exactly what you're looking for."

"Hands of Grace?"

"We do home repairs and practical help for people who need it—elderly folks, single parents, families going through difficult times. Basic maintenance, accessibility modifications, whatever needs doing."

Megan felt her enthusiasm for the ministry warming her voice. "It's about serving our neighbors with willing hands and faithful hearts."

Matt's eyes lit up with interest. "That sounds perfect. When do you meet?"

"Well, we have planning meetings on Wednesday evenings, usually once or twice a month, but the real work happens on various Saturdays. This coming Saturday we're building a wheelchair ramp for Mrs. Simmons—she's my neighbor, and she's been having trouble getting in and out of her house and up and down stairs since her hip surgery."

"I'd love to help. I've got construction experience from military projects."

"Really? You wouldn't mind spending your Saturday morning hammering nails?"

"Are you kidding?" Matt's smile was genuine and eager. "What time should I be there?"

"We usually start around eight in the morning. I can give you the house number and details—Mrs. Simmons lives just three houses down from me."

"Perfect. Should I bring my own tools?"

"Bring whatever you have, but we usually have a good selection of church tools available. The main thing is just showing up ready to work and serve."

As they talked about the ministry, Megan watched Matt's face transform. The weariness she'd noticed earlier seemed to lift, replaced by anticipation and purpose that made him look years younger.

"This is exactly what I was hoping for," he said. "A way to be useful, to connect with people, to do something that matters. Thank you for telling me about it."

"Thank you for wanting to be part of it. We can always use skilled volunteers, especially ones who know what they're doing with power tools."

Their conversation was interrupted by Lauren's return to the dining room, freshly scrubbed and wearing her horse pajamas. "Matt, are you going to read me a story tonight?"

"Lauren!" Megan said, mortified by her daughter's assumption. "Matt doesn't have to—"

"I'd be happy to read a story," Matt interrupted gently. "If it's okay with your mom."

"Come on, I'll show you my favorite books."

Megan watched her daughter drag Matt upstairs, marveling at how easily he'd slipped into this domestic routine. From her spot at the dining table, she could hear Lauren's voice explaining the merits of various picture books, followed by Matt's patient responses and eventual agreement on their selection.

The sound of his voice drifted down from Lauren's bedroom as he began reading—steady, warm, engaging enough to capture a seven-year-old's attention without being theatrical. Megan smiled as she cleared the dinner dishes, remembering countless nights when she'd performed this same ritual alone.

Having Matt's voice fill the cottage created a completeness she enjoyed. Not that she and Lauren weren't sufficient as a family—they absolutely were. But there was something precious about the sound of masculine laughter mixing with Lauren's giggles, about the deeper voice adding harmony to their household's evening rhythm.

Twenty minutes later, Matt reappeared in the kitchen where Megan was finishing the last of the dishes.

"She's out like a light," he reported. "Apparently, the adventures of a brave princess and her talking horse were exactly what she needed to wind down."

"You have a gift with children," Megan observed, drying her hands on the dish towel. "Lauren rarely settles down that quickly."

"She's easy to talk to. Honest, curious, trusting—all the best qualities of childhood."

They moved to the living room, where the lowering evening sun filtered through the sheer curtains and the comfortable furniture invited lingering conversation. Matt settled at one end of the sofa while Megan chose the armchair across from him.

"I should probably head home soon," Matt said, though he made no move to leave. "Early morning at the store tomorrow."

"Of course. But I'm glad you came tonight. It was good to catch up."

"More than good. I'd forgotten how much I missed having genuine conversations with people who matter."

The simple statement hit Megan hard. People who matter.

"Matt, can I say something?"

"Anything."

"I know tonight we talked about David, about losing him, about how we've both tried to move forward. But I want you to know—you don't have to carry that grief alone anymore. David was part of your story, and now, coming back here, you're part of ours. That doesn't diminish what he meant to any of us. It just means the story continues."

Matt was quiet for a long moment, and when he looked at her, his eyes held a vulnerability that made her heart ache.

"I've been afraid," he admitted quietly. "Afraid that moving forward meant forgetting him. Afraid that finding happiness somehow dishonored his memory. Afraid that I didn't deserve the things he'll never have."

"Oh, Matt." Megan felt tears prick her eyes at his honesty. "David wouldn't want that for you. He'd want you to live fully, love completely, and find every bit of joy and purpose God has planned for you. That's not betraying his memory—that's honoring it."

"You honestly think that's true?"

"I do. David had a big heart. He wanted everyone around him to be happy and successful. He cheered for other people's victories and mourned their losses as if they were his own. The last thing he'd want is for his death to limit your life... or mine for that matter."

Matt leaned forward, his elbows on his knees, his hands clasped tightly together. "When I came back to Laurel Ridge, I thought I was just coming home to run the store and settle down. But being here, talking to you, seeing Lauren, remembering what David and I both loved about this place—I think maybe God had bigger plans than I realized."

"Maybe."

They sat in comfortable silence for a moment, the weight of shared understanding settling around them like a blanket. Outside, the summer evening was giving way to dusk, and the cottage felt like the safest place in the world.

"I really should go," Matt said finally, though his tone suggested reluctance.

"I know. And I should check on Lauren and get ready for tomorrow."

But neither of them moved immediately. Instead, they remained suspended in this moment of connection, both recognizing that something fundamental had shifted during the evening. They'd moved beyond polite rekindling of old friendship into something deeper, more honest, more dangerous.

When Matt finally stood, Megan walked him to the door, hyper-aware of his presence beside her, of the easy way he moved through her home as if he belonged there.

"Thank you for dinner," he said at the door. "For the food, the conversation, the story time—all of it. This is the most at home I've felt since coming back."

"Thank you for being here. Lauren loved having you, and I..." She paused, searching for words that were honest without being too revealing. "I enjoyed having someone to really talk to. Someone who understands."

"Saturday morning, eight o'clock?"

"I'll be there. Should I pick you up, or do you want to meet at Mrs. Simmons's?"

"I'll meet you there. I'm looking forward to it."

He hesitated for a moment, and Megan wondered if he was going to say something else. Instead, he simply smiled and touched her arm briefly.

"Good night, Megan."

"Good night."

She watched him walk to his truck, noting the confident set of his shoulders, the easy stride that spoke of a man comfortable in his own skin. As he drove away, she remained in the doorway, breathing in the cooling evening air and trying to process everything that had happened.

The dinner conversation had revealed more than she'd expected about both of their journeys since high school. Matt's struggle with survivor's guilt and his search for meaning beyond military service.

Her own battle to balance independence with community, strength with vulnerability.

But more than their individual stories, what struck her most was how naturally they'd shared them. The easy way conversation had flowed from surface pleasantries to deeper truths. The comfort they'd found in being understood by someone who shared their most significant loss.

This was dangerous territory, she realized... emotional danger of opening her heart to someone who could truly see inside it.

As she locked the door and turned off the porch light, Megan acknowledged what she'd been trying to avoid all evening. She was falling for Matt.

The question was whether she had the courage to pursue that possibility, knowing it would require trusting her heart—and Lauren's—to someone who might not be ready for the complications of an instant family.

But as she climbed the stairs to her bedroom, Megan smiled despite her fears.

Chapter 7

Megan stabbed her salad with more force than necessary, trying to focus on the monthly acquisition reports spread across her desk rather than the persistent thoughts of Matt that had been circling her mind since yesterday's dinner. The shared office she occupied with her assistant librarian and best friend felt smaller than usual, filled with the comfortable clutter of two people who spent their days surrounded by books and the endless administrative details of running a small-town public library.

"Okay, what's wrong?" Heather Morgan looked up from her own lunch, setting down her sandwich with the decisive motion of someone preparing for serious conversation. "You've been stabbing that poor lettuce like it offended you."

Megan looked up, recognizing the determined expression that meant Heather would not let this go. They'd shared this office for three years, ever since Heather had moved back to Laurel Ridge after her divorce and taken the assistant librarian position. In that time, Heather had become more than just a coworker—she was the sister

Megan had never had, the friend who could read her moods better than anyone except maybe her mother.

"Nothing's wrong, exactly," Megan said, pushing a cherry tomato around her container with unnecessary precision. "I'm just processing some unexpected developments."

"Unexpected developments?" Heather raised one perfectly shaped eyebrow. "That sounds intriguing and deliberately vague."

Megan took a deep breath, recognizing that she'd been wanting to talk about this situation with someone who would understand. "Matt Smith is back in town."

The effect was immediate and dramatic. Heather's sandwich slipped from her fingers, landing on her desk with a soft thud as her mouth fell open in shock.

"Matt Smith? Our Matt Smith? Quarterback, Marines, David's best friend Matt Smith?"

"The very one."

"Oh, my goodness." Heather leaned back in her chair, running both hands through her hair. "When? How? Why didn't I know about this? Wait—is this why you've been acting weird all morning?"

"I haven't been acting weird," Megan protested, though even she could hear the lack of conviction in her voice.

"Megan Grace Miller, you reorganized the children's section twice this morning and color-coordinated the pencil jar. You only clean and organize and fret around when you're processing big emotions." Heather's eyes narrowed with the focus of someone scenting a story. "How long has he been back? Where did you see him? What did he look like? Did you talk to him? Tell me everything immediately."

Despite her emotional turmoil, Megan smiled at her friend's rapid-fire interrogation. This was vintage Heather—curious, enthusiastic, and completely incapable of letting interesting developments pass without thorough examination.

"He's been back a little over a week from what I understand, taking over Earl's Hardware from his father. I ran into him on Saturday when my kitchen plumbing decided to self-destruct." Megan kept her tone carefully casual.

"And?"

"And he helped me get the parts I needed for repairs."

Heather stared at her for a long moment, clearly waiting for additional information. When none was forthcoming, she leaned forward with predatory interest.

"That's it? You run into the man you had a crush on your junior year of high school—yes, don't even try to deny it—and all you're going to tell me is that he sold you pipe fittings?"

"I did not have a crush on Matt Smith," Megan said automatically, though the protest sounded weak even to her own ears.

"Please. You tutored him in chemistry that year and turned approximately fourteen shades of red every time he walked into the classroom. I sat behind you, remember? I watched you doodle 'Mrs. Matthew Smith' in your notebook margins."

"That was years ago!"

"Some things don't change." Heather's expression grew more thoughtful, less teasing. "Though I suppose a lot of other things do. Man... I miss him! It's been forever since I've seen him. What's he like now? Does he seem... different?"

Megan considered the question seriously, trying to separate her emotional response from objective observation. "He's more confident, more settled in himself. The military definitely changed him—he carries himself differently, speaks more thoughtfully. But he's still kind, still patient. He was wonderful with Lauren."

"He met Lauren?" Heather's voice rose with excitement. "Oh, this is getting good. Keep going."

"It's not 'getting good,'" Megan said firmly. "He fixed our plumbing, that's all. He was being neighborly."

"Uh-huh. And this neighborly plumbing repair happened at your house... with Lauren present?"

Sometimes Megan forgot that Heather had majored in psychology before switching to library science. Her friend's ability to read subtext and identify emotional undercurrents could be unnervingly accurate.

"It was a simple repair job," Megan insisted. "Nothing more complicated than that."

"Right. And I suppose the fact that you're blushing just thinking about it is totally unrelated to any feelings you might or might not be developing."

"I'm not blushing!"

"You absolutely are. You're doing that thing where your neck gets pink first, then it spreads to your cheeks. You always do it when you're flustered about something important."

Megan pressed her hands to her cheeks, annoyed to discover that they were indeed warm. "Fine. Maybe I'm a little... aware of him. But that doesn't mean anything significant."

"Aware of him," Heather repeated slowly, as if tasting the words. "That's an interesting way to describe attraction to a man who... if I remember correctly was absolutely gorgeous in high school, and who used to make you tongue-tied just by existing in your general vicinity."

"He didn't make me tongue-tied."

"Megan, you once asked him if he needed help with his 'mathistry' homework. Chemistry and math got so tangled up in your brain that you invented a new subject."

The memory made Megan groan and bury her face in her hands. She'd forgotten about that particular incident, but Heather's recollection brought it back with mortifying clarity. Matt had been so kind about her verbal fumble, gently correcting her and accepting her tutoring offer with the same patient smile he'd shown Lauren Saturday night.

"That was a long time ago. We're different people now."

"Are you?" Heather's voice had grown gentler, more serious. "Because from where I'm sitting, it sounds like Matt Smith still has the power to make you forget basic vocabulary."

Megan was quiet for a moment, considering her friend's observation. It was true that something about Matt's presence seemed to short-circuit her usual composure, but she'd attributed that to surprise at his return rather than lingering attraction.

"It's complicated," she said finally.

"How so?"

"He was David's best friend, Heather. He was our best friend in high school too. He was part of our circle back then. He and David served together, planned their futures together, were supposed to come home and be each other's godfathers to each other's children." The words came out in a rush, carrying the weight of guilt she'd been trying to ignore. "How can I look at Matt and think about... about possibilities... without feeling like I'm somehow betraying David's memory?"

Heather was quiet for a long moment, her expression thoughtful rather than immediately reassuring. When she spoke, her voice carried the careful precision of someone choosing words with deliberate care.

"Can I ask you something, and will you promise to really think about the answer instead of giving me the response you think you're supposed to give?"

"Okay."

"Do you think David would want you to spend the rest of your life alone?"

The question hit Megan like a physical blow, striking directly at the heart of her internal conflict. "That's not fair."

"It's completely fair. And it's the question you need to answer honestly if you're going to have any hope of moving forward." Heather leaned across the small space between their desks, her eyes intense with the focus she brought to helping people find what they truly needed. "David loved you, right? Completely, generously, with his whole heart?"

"Yes."

"And he was a good man? Kind, unselfish, wanting the best for the people he cared about?"

"You know he was."

"Then tell me how that man would react to knowing that his widow had found someone who could love her and Lauren well. Someone who treated them with kindness and respect and genuine care."

Tears pricked Megan's eyes as she considered the question she'd been avoiding. Because the truth was, she did know how David would react. He would be thrilled. He would probably have thrown a party and insisted on giving his blessing personally. David had always wanted everyone around him to be happy and loved and fulfilled.

"He'd want us to be happy," she whispered.

"Exactly. So, the question isn't whether developing feelings for Matt would dishonor David's memory. The question is whether you're brave enough to honor David's memory by allowing yourself to be happy again."

The logic was sound, but it didn't address Megan's deeper fears. "What if it doesn't work out? What if Matt isn't interested in that kind of relationship? What if he's just being kind to his old friend's widow? What if I let myself care about him and he decides he doesn't want the complications of an instant family?"

"What if it does work out?" Heather countered. "What if he's every bit as attracted to you as you obviously are to him? What if he's been waiting his whole life for exactly this kind of family? What if God brought him back to Laurel Ridge specifically because you and Lauren need him as much as he needs you?"

"Now you're just being romantic."

"I'm being realistic. Megan, you're thirty years old. You're beautiful, intelligent, kind, and you have a daughter who lights up every room she enters. Any man would be lucky to be a part of your lives. And Matt Smith isn't just any man—he's someone who already cares about you, obviously. He's someone who knew and loved David, someone who understands your history and your heart."

"I'm scared."

"Of course you are. You'd be crazy not to be scared. Love is terrifying under the best circumstances, and your circumstances are pretty complicated." Heather's voice grew gentler. "But being scared isn't a good enough reason to close yourself off from something that could be wonderful."

"I don't even know if he's interested in anything more than friendship."

"Only one way to find out."

"How?"

"Spend time with him. Talk to him. Be open to possibilities instead of immediately shutting them down because they feel risky." Heather smiled with the satisfaction of someone providing excellent advice. "And in the meantime, tell me more about this plumbing repair. Did he roll up his sleeves? Because I remember Matt having very nice forearms."

Megan laughed. "You're incorrigible."

"I'm invested in your happiness. There's a difference." Heather picked up her sandwich and took a decisive bite. "So what else happened? And don't leave out any details about forearms or tool usage or domestic moments that made you realize how empty your house feels when it's just you and Lauren."

"It doesn't feel empty," Megan protested, though even as she said it, she remembered the completeness Matt's presence had brought to her kitchen Sunday night.

"Uh-huh. Tell me about the dinner."

"What dinner?"

"The one you obviously invited him to after he fixed your sink. The one where Lauren got attached to him and he charmed your parents and you realized that having a man in your house felt natural instead of intrusive."

Sometimes Heather's perceptiveness was genuinely unsettling. "How do you know all that?"

"Because I know you, and I know how your brain works. You felt guilty about accepting his help, so you offered dinner in return. Lauren was curious about him because she's never had consistent male attention, and your parents were delighted because they've been worried about you being alone for years." Heather tilted her head, studying Megan's face with scientific interest. "How close am I?"

"Uncomfortably close. Lauren actually invited him over for dinner after church."

"And how was the dinner?"

"Nice," she said carefully. "Very nice."

"Just nice?"

"Okay, it was wonderful. He was wonderful. He read Lauren a bedtime story, and we talked about real things, important things. He understood about David, about losing him, about trying to build a life after everything changed." The words came out faster as Megan's carefully maintained composure began to crack. "And yes, I noticed his forearms, and yes, having him in my home felt natural instead of intrusive, and yes, I may have found myself wondering what it would be like to have that kind of conversation or a man present in my life every evening instead of just once."

"There we go," Heather said with satisfaction. "Now we're getting to the truth."

"The truth is complicated."

"The truth usually is. But that doesn't make it less true." Heather leaned forward, her expression serious again. "Megan, you deserve to be loved. Completely, passionately, by someone who chooses you and Lauren every single day. You deserve partnership and companionship and someone to share the load with. And if that someone happens to be Matt, who knew and loved David and understands your history and makes Lauren giggle and has nice forearms, then maybe that's not a complication. Maybe that's a gift."

The office fell quiet except for the familiar sounds of library life beyond their door—hushed conversations, the soft thud of books being shelved, the occasional ring of the checkout computer. Megan stared at her half-eaten salad, trying to process everything Heather had said.

"I don't know how to do this," she admitted finally.

"Do what?"

"Be open to love again. Date. Trust someone with my heart and Lauren's. Risk having everything I've built fall apart if it doesn't work out."

"Nobody knows how to do it," Heather said gently. "That's what makes it brave. But Megan, you've already proven you can survive the worst thing that could possibly happen. You lost David, and you rebuilt everything from nothing. You raised a beautiful daughter and created a good life and became the kind of person other people depend on. If you can do all that, you can certainly handle giving your heart to someone who might just treasure it."

Megan felt tears threatening again, touched by her friend's faith in her strength and simultaneously terrified by the implications of actually acting on her feelings.

"What if I'm reading too much into his kindness? What if he was just being helpful and I'm creating romantic possibilities that don't exist?"

"What if you're not?"

The simple question hit a nerve.

"I should probably get back to work," she said, though she made no move to clear her lunch containers or return to the acquisition reports.

"Probably," Heather agreed. "But first, answer me one more question."

"What?"

"When you think about Matt—not about the complications or the fears or what might go wrong, but just about him—how do you feel?"

Megan closed her eyes, allowing herself to focus on the simple truth beneath all her anxieties. When she thought about Matt's patient smile, his gentle way with Lauren, the steady competence of his hands as he worked, the understanding in his eyes when they'd talked about loss and healing—when she thought about just him, without all the surrounding worries—she felt something she hadn't experienced in seven years.

She felt hopeful.

"Interested," she said quietly, opening her eyes to meet Heather's knowing gaze. "I feel interested."

"Good," Heather said with a satisfied smile. "Interest is an excellent place to start."

Chapter 8

Matt stood outside the Laurel Ridge Public Library at 1430 hours—2:30 PM in civilian time, he corrected himself with a slight grimace—studying the stately brick building with its arched windows and ivy-covered walls. The Carnegie-era architecture spoke of permanence and community investment, much like the hardware store he was learning to call his own domain. But where Earl's Hardware felt familiar and practical, the library seemed to inhabit a different world entirely, one built around ideas and imagination rather than nuts and bolts.

He felt oddly uncertain for a man who'd spent twelve years navigating military bureaucracy and foreign terrain. This was just a library. Just books. Just a perfectly reasonable errand for a civilian business owner who needed to expand his practical knowledge and maybe find some decent fiction to fill his evening hours.

The fact that Megan Miller worked here as head librarian was purely coincidental.

Matt pushed through the heavy oak doors and immediately found himself enveloped in the distinctive scent of books. The main circulation area spread before him like foreign territory: rows of wooden shelves stretching in orderly lines, computer terminals humming quietly, and reading areas furnished with chairs that looked designed more for contemplation than efficiency.

A few patrons moved quietly through the space—an elderly gentleman reading newspapers in the periodical section, a mother with two young children selecting picture books, and a teenage girl hunched over homework at one of the study tables. The atmosphere was hushed and scholarly, making Matt hyperaware of the sound his work boots made against the polished floor.

He wasn't entirely sure where to begin.

"Can I help you find something, Matt?"

Matt turned toward the circulation desk and felt his breath catch slightly. Megan stood behind the wooden counter, her chestnut hair pulled back in a neat ponytail that emphasized the elegant line of her neck. She wore a sage-green cardigan over a white blouse, looking every inch the professional librarian, but her blue eyes held the warmth he was beginning to associate with her presence in his life.

"Hi Megan. I... uh... was hoping to find some books," he said, then immediately felt foolish for the obvious statement.

Megan's lips curved into a gentle smile that suggested she'd heard similar declarations before. "Well, you've come to the right place. What kind of books were you thinking about?"

"Home improvement guides, mainly. And maybe some fiction." Matt approached the desk, noting how naturally she seemed to belong in this space. "I'm trying to expand my skill set beyond basic repairs and Marine-issued reading material."

"Marine-issued reading material?" Megan's eyebrow arched with curious amusement. "I'm almost afraid to ask what that includes."

"Technical manuals, mostly. Some history. The occasional thriller when we could get our hands on decent paperbacks." Matt relaxed slightly as their conversation settled into familiar territory. "Let's just say my literary horizons could use some broadening."

"I think I can help with that." Megan stepped around the circulation desk, gesturing for him to follow her deeper into the library. "Home improvement first, or fiction?"

"Practical stuff first. I'm discovering that running a hardware store and tackling some home improvement projects requires more knowledge than I initially realized." Matt followed her toward the back of the building, watching the confident way she navigated between the stacks. "Dad made it look easy, but there are aspects of the business I need to learn."

"What kind of home improvement projects are you tackling?" Megan led him to a section marked with neat labels showing construction, plumbing, and general repair guides.

"Kitchen renovation, mostly. The apartment above the store hasn't been updated since the Carter administration, and I'm starting to feel like I'm living in a time capsule." Matt surveyed the shelves with the same systematic approach he'd once used to assess tactical situations. "Basic plumbing I can handle, electrical work that may be a bit more beyond my knowledge, and maybe some cabinet installation."

Megan pulled a thick volume from the shelf and handed it to him. "This one covers most residential systems. The author assumes you have basic competence but explains things clearly without being condescending." She paused, tilting her head slightly. "Though after watching you work on my kitchen plumbing, I suspect you're more capable than you're letting on."

"That was basic pipe fitting. Installing a new kitchen requires skills I haven't learned yet." Matt accepted the book. "I prefer to know what I'm doing before I start swinging hammers."

"Wise philosophy. My dad always said measure twice, cut once." Megan selected another book, this one focused specifically on kitchen remodeling. "This one has good step-by-step photographs and planning worksheets."

Matt accepted the second book, noting how thoughtfully she'd chosen guides that matched his apparent skill level and specific needs. "You seem to know your way around these subjects pretty well for a librarian."

"I know my way around books about these subjects," Megan corrected with a slight smile. "There's a difference. Though I've learned a few things through necessity over the years."

"Like Saturday's plumbing adventure?"

"Yeah... something like that." Megan's cheeks colored slightly, and Matt found the faint blush utterly charming.

Their laughter seemed unusually loud in the library's hushed atmosphere, and Matt noticed the teenage girl at the study table glancing their way with mild irritation. He lowered his voice instinctively.

"What about fiction?" he asked.

"What kind of stories do you enjoy?" Megan headed toward another section, her professional demeanor shifting into something more enthusiastic. "Mystery, adventure, literary fiction, science fiction?"

"Mystery sounds good. Something with puzzles to solve and characters who know what they're doing." Matt followed her past several rows of fiction, noting how the organization seemed both logical and mysteriously complex. "I have to admit, navigating a library is more complicated than I remember."

"It's all about understanding the system." Megan stopped in front of a section marked 'Mystery/Thriller,' and began scanning the spines. "Once you learn the basic layout, everything makes sense. Though I suppose that's true for most environments."

"Including hardware stores?"

"Especially hardware stores. I still get lost trying to find specific items at your father's place." She pulled a book from the shelf and examined the back cover. "Have you read any John le Carré?"

"No, but the name sounds familiar."

"Spy novels, but literary ones. Complex characters, realistic situations, excellent writing." Megan handed him the book. "This one's considered his masterpiece."

Matt studied the cover, noting the serious tone suggested by the artwork and blurb. "Is this going to require a college degree to understand?"

"It might challenge you, but in a good way." Megan's eyes held a hint of mischief. "I have faith in your intellectual capabilities, Marine."

The teasing note in her voice sent warmth spreading through his chest. "That's a dangerous assumption. My reading interests have been pretty limited to technical manuals and Tom Clancy novels."

"There's nothing wrong with Tom Clancy. But there's a whole world of books out there waiting for you." She moved along the shelf, selecting another volume. "If le Carré seems too dense, try this—Louise Penny writes excellent mysteries set in a small Canadian village. Cozy but not simplistic."

Matt accepted the second book, finding himself drawn more to Megan's enthusiasm than the actual titles she was recommending. The way her face lit up when discussing books, the confident manner in which she navigated her professional domain, the gentle way she guided his choices without making him feel ignorant—all of it created an attractive picture of competence and warmth.

"You really love this work, don't you?" he said, watching her pull a third option from a different section.

"I can't imagine doing anything else." Megan's expression grew thoughtful. "There's something magical about connecting people with exactly the right book at exactly the right moment in their lives. Sometimes they know what they want, sometimes they have no idea, but there's always something here that can help or inspire or comfort them."

"Like you did with Lauren's horse books... I noticed she had quite the collection before I read to her?"

"Exactly. She's going through a phase where she's fascinated by the idea of communicating with animals. Those books feed that curiosity while teaching her about responsibility and empathy." Megan selected another mystery novel, this one with a more contemporary cover. "Reading shapes how we see the world."

Matt studied her profile as she spoke, noting the passion that animated her features when she discussed her work. This was Megan in her element—confident, knowledgeable, and genuinely excited about sharing what she loved with others.

"What about you?" she asked, turning back to face him. "What books shaped how you see the world?"

The question caught him off guard. "I'm not sure I've ever thought about it that way."

"Come on, there must have been something. A favorite book from childhood, something you read during your service that stuck with you."

Matt considered the question seriously, surprised by how difficult it was to answer. "There was a biography of George Washington I read during my second deployment. Written by Ron Chernow. It made me think differently about leadership and sacrifice."

"Excellent choice. Chernow's a brilliant historian." Megan's approval felt more valuable than it probably should have. "What about it changed your perspective?"

"The way Washington understood that sometimes the most important thing a leader can do is step away from power when the job is finished. He could have been king essentially, but he chose to return to private life. That idea of service without ego—it influenced how I thought about my own military career."

Megan's expression grew more serious, her blue eyes reflecting genuine interest rather than polite conversation. "That's a profound way to approach service. Most people don't think that deeply about what they read."

"Maybe I should read more books that make me think." Matt gestured toward the volumes she'd selected for him. "Assuming I can handle the intellectual challenge."

"I think you'll surprise yourself." Megan's smile returned, warmer than before. "And if you get stuck on something, you know where to find me."

"Matt Smith!" a voice called from the next aisle over. "As I live and breathe!"

Both Matt and Megan turned toward the sound as Heather Morgan appeared around the end of the bookshelf, her arms full of returned books and her face bright with delighted recognition.

"Heather." Matt felt his face break into a genuine grin. "It's good to see you."

"Look at you!" Heather set down her stack of books and approached with the kind of enthusiasm that had made her the social coordinator of their high school group. "All grown up and handsome as ever. When did you get back to town?"

"About a week and a half ago. I'm taking over the hardware store for Dad."

"So I've heard," Heather glanced meaningfully between Matt and Megan. "And now you're expanding your literary horizons? How wonderful."

"Megan's been helping me select some books." Matt found himself slightly self-conscious under Heather's gaze.

"Oh, I'm sure she has. Our Megan is excellent at matching people with exactly what they need."

"Heather," Megan said with the tone of someone issuing a gentle warning.

"What? I'm just saying you have excellent instincts about these things." Heather's innocence was transparently false. "Remember in high school when we used to study together? The four of us—you, me, Matt, and David. Those were good times."

"They were," Matt agreed.

"Well," Heather said after a moment, "I should get these books re-shelved. Matt, we should get together soon and catch up. You, me, and Megan."

"I'd like that," Matt said honestly.

"Excellent. I'll coordinate something." Heather gathered her books and gave them both a meaningful look. "You two enjoy your literary discussion."

As Heather disappeared back into the stacks, Matt and Megan found themselves alone again.

"She's not subtle," Megan said with a slight laugh.

"Never was." Matt picked up the books Megan had selected. "I should probably let you get back to work."

"Actually," Megan said, her voice carrying a hint of reluctance, "did you want to see our local history section? We have some great books about the New River Gorge area, and if you're planning to stay in Laurel Ridge, you might be interested in learning more about the region you grew up in."

"That sounds interesting."

The truth was, he would have agreed to a tour of the library's plumbing system if it meant spending more time in Megan's company. Something about being in her professional space, watching her navigate with such competence and enthusiasm, made him want to linger and learn more about this part of her life.

For the next twenty minutes, Megan showed him historical photographs of Laurel Ridge's founding, geological surveys of the surrounding mountains, and collections of local folklore that had been gathered by community volunteers over the decades. Matt was genuinely engaged by the material, but more than that, he was captivated by Megan's knowledge and the way she brought the information to life through her storytelling.

"Your family's business is mentioned in several of these histories," she told him, opening a volume about local commerce. "Earl's Hardware has been serving this community for over thirty years. That's a real legacy."

"Dad always said the store was about more than selling supplies. It was about being a place people could come when they needed help solving problems." Matt studied a photograph of Main Street from the 1990s, noting how little the essential character of the area had changed. "I'm still learning what that means in practice."

"It means being patient with customers who aren't sure what they need. It means sometimes fixing things for people who can't afford to pay for labor. It means being part of the community fabric." Megan's voice held warm understanding. "Just like this library is more than books—it's about connecting people with information and stories and each other."

Matt looked up from the historical photographs to find Megan watching him with an expression that made his pulse quicken. There was something in her blue eyes that went beyond professional courtesy or casual friendship.

"I should probably head back," he said reluctantly, glancing at his watch. "Dad's expecting me to help with the afternoon shipment."

"Of course." Megan walked with him back toward the circulation desk. "Let me check these out for you."

The process of creating his new library card and processing his book selection gave them a few more minutes of conversation, during which Matt asked unnecessary questions about due dates and renewal policies, anything to extend their interaction.

"Two weeks for each book," Megan explained as she stamped the due date cards. "But you can renew them if you need more time."

"What if I finish them quickly and want more recommendations?"

"Then you know where to find me." Megan handed him the books with a smile.

"Thanks, Megan."

"You're welcome, Matt."

Matt headed toward the door, then paused and turned back. "Megan?"

"Yes?"

"Thank you... honestly. For the recommendations, and for taking the time to show me around. I appreciate it."

"It was my pleasure."

As Matt pushed through the oak doors and emerged into the afternoon sunshine, he felt lighter than he had in months. The books in his arms represented more than just evening entertainment—they were a connection to Megan and her world, a reason to return and continue conversations that had become the highlight of his civilian transition.

Chapter 9

Matt stood outside the Laurel Ridge Public Library at 1430 hours—2:30 PM in civilian time, he corrected himself with a slight grimace—studying the stately brick building with its arched windows and ivy-covered walls. The Carnegie-era architecture spoke of permanence and community investment, much like the hardware store he was learning to call his own domain. But where Earl's Hardware felt familiar and practical, the library seemed to inhabit a different world entirely, one built around ideas and imagination rather than nuts and bolts.

He felt oddly uncertain for a man who'd spent twelve years navigating military bureaucracy and foreign terrain. This was just a library. Just books. Just a perfectly reasonable errand for a civilian business owner who needed to expand his practical knowledge and maybe find some decent fiction to fill his evening hours.

The fact that Megan Miller worked here as head librarian was purely coincidental.

Matt pushed through the heavy oak doors and immediately found himself enveloped in the distinctive scent of books. The main circulation area spread before him like foreign territory: rows of wooden shelves stretching in orderly lines, computer terminals humming quietly, and reading areas furnished with chairs that looked designed more for contemplation than efficiency.

A few patrons moved quietly through the space—an elderly gentleman reading newspapers in the periodical section, a mother with two young children selecting picture books, and a teenage girl hunched over homework at one of the study tables. The atmosphere was hushed and scholarly, making Matt hyperaware of the sound his work boots made against the polished floor.

He wasn't entirely sure where to begin.

"Can I help you find something, Matt?"

Matt turned toward the circulation desk and felt his breath catch slightly. Megan stood behind the wooden counter, her chestnut hair pulled back in a neat ponytail that emphasized the elegant line of her neck. She wore a sage-green cardigan over a white blouse, looking every inch the professional librarian, but her blue eyes held the warmth he was beginning to associate with her presence in his life.

"Hi Megan. I... uh... was hoping to find some books," he said, then immediately felt foolish for the obvious statement.

Megan's lips curved into a gentle smile that suggested she'd heard similar declarations before. "Well, you've come to the right place. What kind of books were you thinking about?"

"Home improvement guides, mainly. And maybe some fiction." Matt approached the desk, noting how naturally she seemed to belong in this space. "I'm trying to expand my skill set beyond basic repairs and Marine-issued reading material."

"Marine-issued reading material?" Megan's eyebrow arched with curious amusement. "I'm almost afraid to ask what that includes."

"Technical manuals, mostly. Some history. The occasional thriller when we could get our hands on decent paperbacks." Matt relaxed slightly as their conversation settled into familiar territory. "Let's just say my literary horizons could use some broadening."

"I think I can help with that." Megan stepped around the circulation desk, gesturing for him to follow her deeper into the library. "Home improvement first, or fiction?"

"Practical stuff first. I'm discovering that running a hardware store and tackling some home improvement projects requires more knowledge than I initially realized." Matt followed her toward the back of the building, watching the confident way she navigated between the stacks. "Dad made it look easy, but there are aspects of the business I need to learn."

"What kind of home improvement projects are you tackling?" Megan led him to a section marked with neat labels showing construction, plumbing, and general repair guides.

"Kitchen renovation, mostly. The apartment above the store hasn't been updated since the Carter administration, and I'm starting to feel like I'm living in a time capsule." Matt surveyed the shelves with the same systematic approach he'd once used to assess tactical situations. "Basic plumbing I can handle, electrical work that may be a bit more beyond my knowledge, and maybe some cabinet installation."

Megan pulled a thick volume from the shelf and handed it to him. "This one covers most residential systems. The author assumes you have basic competence but explains things clearly without being condescending." She paused, tilting her head slightly. "Though after watching you work on my kitchen plumbing, I suspect you're more capable than you're letting on."

"That was basic pipe fitting. Installing a new kitchen requires skills I haven't learned yet." Matt accepted the book. "I prefer to know what I'm doing before I start swinging hammers."

"Wise philosophy. My dad always said measure twice, cut once." Megan selected another book, this one focused specifically on kitchen remodeling. "This one has good step-by-step photographs and planning worksheets."

Matt accepted the second book, noting how thoughtfully she'd chosen guides that matched his apparent skill level and specific needs. "You seem to know your way around these subjects pretty well for a librarian."

"I know my way around books about these subjects," Megan corrected with a slight smile. "There's a difference. Though I've learned a few things through necessity over the years."

"Like Saturday's plumbing adventure?"

"Yeah... something like that." Megan's cheeks colored slightly, and Matt found the faint blush utterly charming.

Their laughter seemed unusually loud in the library's hushed atmosphere, and Matt noticed the teenage girl at the study table glancing their way with mild irritation. He lowered his voice instinctively.

"What about fiction?" he asked.

"What kind of stories do you enjoy?" Megan headed toward another section, her professional demeanor shifting into something more enthusiastic. "Mystery, adventure, literary fiction, science fiction?"

"Mystery sounds good. Something with puzzles to solve and characters who know what they're doing." Matt followed her past several rows of fiction, noting how the organization seemed both logical and mysteriously complex. "I have to admit, navigating a library is more complicated than I remember."

"It's all about understanding the system." Megan stopped in front of a section marked 'Mystery/Thriller,' and began scanning the spines. "Once you learn the basic layout, everything makes sense. Though I suppose that's true for most environments."

"Including hardware stores?"

"Especially hardware stores. I still get lost trying to find specific items at your father's place." She pulled a book from the shelf and examined the back cover. "Have you read any John le Carré?"

"No, but the name sounds familiar."

"Spy novels, but literary ones. Complex characters, realistic situations, excellent writing." Megan handed him the book. "This one's considered his masterpiece."

Matt studied the cover, noting the serious tone suggested by the artwork and blurb. "Is this going to require a college degree to understand?"

"It might challenge you, but in a good way." Megan's eyes held a hint of mischief. "I have faith in your intellectual capabilities, Marine."

The teasing note in her voice sent warmth spreading through his chest. "That's a dangerous assumption. My reading interests have been pretty limited to technical manuals and Tom Clancy novels."

"There's nothing wrong with Tom Clancy. But there's a whole world of books out there waiting for you." She moved along the shelf, selecting another volume. "If le Carré seems too dense, try this—Louise Penny writes excellent mysteries set in a small Canadian village. Cozy but not simplistic."

Matt accepted the second book, finding himself drawn more to Megan's enthusiasm than the actual titles she was recommending. The way her face lit up when discussing books, the confident manner in which she navigated her professional domain, the gentle way she guided his choices without making him feel ignorant—all of it created an attractive picture of competence and warmth.

"You really love this work, don't you?" he said, watching her pull a third option from a different section.

"I can't imagine doing anything else." Megan's expression grew thoughtful. "There's something magical about connecting people with exactly the right book at exactly the right moment in their lives. Sometimes they know what they want, sometimes they have no idea, but there's always something here that can help or inspire or comfort them."

"Like you did with Lauren's horse books... I noticed she had quite the collection before I read to her?"

"Exactly. She's going through a phase where she's fascinated by the idea of communicating with animals. Those books feed that curiosity while teaching her about responsibility and empathy." Megan selected another mystery novel, this one with a more contemporary cover. "Reading shapes how we see the world."

Matt studied her profile as she spoke, noting the passion that animated her features when she discussed her work. This was Megan in her element—confident, knowledgeable, and genuinely excited about sharing what she loved with others.

"What about you?" she asked, turning back to face him. "What books shaped how you see the world?"

The question caught him off guard. "I'm not sure I've ever thought about it that way."

"Come on, there must have been something. A favorite book from childhood, something you read during your service that stuck with you."

Matt considered the question seriously, surprised by how difficult it was to answer. "There was a biography of George Washington I read during my second deployment. Written by Ron Chernow. It made me think differently about leadership and sacrifice."

"Excellent choice. Chernow's a brilliant historian." Megan's approval felt more valuable than it probably should have. "What about it changed your perspective?"

"The way Washington understood that sometimes the most important thing a leader can do is step away from power when the job is finished. He could have been king essentially, but he chose to return to private life. That idea of service without ego—it influenced how I thought about my own military career."

Megan's expression grew more serious, her blue eyes reflecting genuine interest rather than polite conversation. "That's a profound way to approach service. Most people don't think that deeply about what they read."

"Maybe I should read more books that make me think." Matt gestured toward the volumes she'd selected for him. "Assuming I can handle the intellectual challenge."

"I think you'll surprise yourself." Megan's smile returned, warmer than before. "And if you get stuck on something, you know where to find me."

"Matt Smith!" a voice called from the next aisle over. "As I live and breathe!"

Both Matt and Megan turned toward the sound as Heather Morgan appeared around the end of the bookshelf, her arms full of returned books and her face bright with delighted recognition.

"Heather." Matt felt his face break into a genuine grin. "It's good to see you."

"Look at you!" Heather set down her stack of books and approached with the kind of enthusiasm that had made her the social coordinator of their high school group. "All grown up and handsome as ever. When did you get back to town?"

"About a week and a half ago. I'm taking over the hardware store for Dad."

"So I've heard," Heather glanced meaningfully between Matt and Megan. "And now you're expanding your literary horizons? How wonderful."

"Megan's been helping me select some books." Matt found himself slightly self-conscious under Heather's gaze.

"Oh, I'm sure she has. Our Megan is excellent at matching people with exactly what they need."

"Heather," Megan said with the tone of someone issuing a gentle warning.

"What? I'm just saying you have excellent instincts about these things." Heather's innocence was transparently false. "Remember in high school when we used to study together? The four of us—you, me, Matt, and David. Those were good times."

"They were," Matt agreed.

"Well," Heather said after a moment, "I should get these books re-shelved. Matt, we should get together soon and catch up. You, me, and Megan."

"I'd like that," Matt said honestly.

"Excellent. I'll coordinate something." Heather gathered her books and gave them both a meaningful look. "You two enjoy your literary discussion."

As Heather disappeared back into the stacks, Matt and Megan found themselves alone again.

"She's not subtle," Megan said with a slight laugh.

"Never was." Matt picked up the books Megan had selected. "I should probably let you get back to work."

"Actually," Megan said, her voice carrying a hint of reluctance, "did you want to see our local history section? We have some great books about the New River Gorge area, and if you're planning to stay in Laurel Ridge, you might be interested in learning more about the region you grew up in."

"That sounds interesting."

The truth was, he would have agreed to a tour of the library's plumbing system if it meant spending more time in Megan's company. Something about being in her professional space, watching her navigate with such competence and enthusiasm, made him want to linger and learn more about this part of her life.

For the next twenty minutes, Megan showed him historical photographs of Laurel Ridge's founding, geological surveys of the surrounding mountains, and collections of local folklore that had been gathered by community volunteers over the decades. Matt was genuinely engaged by the material, but more than that, he was captivated by Megan's knowledge and the way she brought the information to life through her storytelling.

"Your family's business is mentioned in several of these histories," she told him, opening a volume about local commerce. "Earl's Hardware has been serving this community for over thirty years. That's a real legacy."

"Dad always said the store was about more than selling supplies. It was about being a place people could come when they needed help solving problems." Matt studied a photograph of Main Street from the 1990s, noting how little the essential character of the area had changed. "I'm still learning what that means in practice."

"It means being patient with customers who aren't sure what they need. It means sometimes fixing things for people who can't afford to pay for labor. It means being part of the community fabric." Megan's voice held warm understanding. "Just like this library is more than books—it's about connecting people with information and stories and each other."

Matt looked up from the historical photographs to find Megan watching him with an expression that made his pulse quicken. There was something in her blue eyes that went beyond professional courtesy or casual friendship.

"I should probably head back," he said reluctantly, glancing at his watch. "Dad's expecting me to help with the afternoon shipment."

"Of course." Megan walked with him back toward the circulation desk. "Let me check these out for you."

The process of creating his new library card and processing his book selection gave them a few more minutes of conversation, during which Matt asked unnecessary questions about due dates and renewal policies, anything to extend their interaction.

"Two weeks for each book," Megan explained as she stamped the due date cards. "But you can renew them if you need more time."

"What if I finish them quickly and want more recommendations?"

"Then you know where to find me." Megan handed him the books with a smile.

"Thanks, Megan."

"You're welcome, Matt."

Matt headed toward the door, then paused and turned back. "Megan?"

"Yes?"

"Thank you... honestly. For the recommendations, and for taking the time to show me around. I appreciate it."

"It was my pleasure."

As Matt pushed through the oak doors and emerged into the afternoon sunshine, he felt lighter than he had in months. The books in his arms represented more than just evening entertainment—they were a connection to Megan and her world, a reason to return and continue conversations that had become the highlight of his civilian transition.

Chapter 10

Matt pulled his pickup truck to the curb in front of Mrs. Simmons's house at eight o'clock on Saturday morning ready for volunteer work. The September air carried a crisp promise of autumn that made physical labor appealing rather than burdensome. He gathered his tool belt from the passenger seat and surveyed the modest white house with its sagging front porch that had prompted this weekend's Hands of Grace Ministry project.

Mrs. Eleanor Simmons was eighty-three years old and had lived in the same house for over sixty years, raising four children and watching them scatter to cities with better job opportunities. The front porch, where she'd spent countless evenings watching neighborhood children play, had buckled and separated from the house foundation, creating a safety hazard that her fixed income couldn't address.

Matt hadn't expected the substantial crowd of volunteers already gathered in Mrs. Simmons's front yard.

His father stood near a pile of lumber, clipboard in hand, talking with his brother, Graham. His mother, Sylvia, was arranging what appeared to be an entire breakfast buffet on a folding table someone had set up in the shade, while Pastor Andrew Whitman moved through the group of volunteers with the calm authority of someone accustomed to organizing community efforts.

And there, standing near the front steps with Lauren beside her, was Megan.

Even in work clothes—faded jeans, a light blue t-shirt, and sturdy canvas sneakers—she looked both practical and beautiful. Her chestnut hair was pulled back in a ponytail, and she held a clipboard of her own, apparently coordinating volunteer assignments.

Matt felt something warm and complicated settle in his chest at the sight of her, a reaction that went beyond a simple appreciation for an attractive woman.

"Matt!" Lauren's voice carried across the yard as she spotted him. She abandoned whatever task she'd been assigned and ran toward him with the kind of unguarded enthusiasm that made him smile.

"Good morning, Lauren," he said, adjusting his tool belt as she reached him. "Are you here to supervise the construction crew?"

"I'm here to help," Lauren announced with the serious dignity of someone who took her responsibilities seriously. "Mommy says I can hand people tools and clean up scraps, but I have to stay away from the power saws because they're dangerous."

"Your mom is absolutely right about that." Matt looked across the yard to where Megan was now talking with a couple he didn't recognize. "It looks like she's got everything well organized."

"Mommy's really good at stuff like that." Lauren's pride in her mother's abilities was evident in every word.

Before Matt could respond, Pastor Andrew approached with a warm smile.

"Matt, I'm so glad you could join us. Your father tells me you have experience with construction work."

"Some," Matt agreed. "The Marines taught me to be resourceful with repairs, and Dad taught me a few things when I was growing up."

"Perfect. We can always use someone with some basic knowledge." Pastor Andrew gestured toward the gathered volunteers. "Before we start, I'd like us all to come together for a word of prayer and blessing over this work."

The volunteers gathered in a loose circle in Mrs. Simmons's front yard—twenty people ranging in age from Lauren to several church members in their sixties. Matt stood between his father and Megan, close enough to catch the faint scent of her perfume.

"Heavenly Father," Pastor Andrew began, his voice carrying clearly in the morning air, "we thank you for the opportunity to serve our sister Eleanor and to use the gifts you've given us for the benefit of our community. Bless this work and keep us safe as we labor together. Help us to build more than just a porch today—help us to build connections, fellowship, and love. In Jesus's name, Amen."

"Amen," the group responded in unison, and Matt felt the familiar warmth that came from being part of something larger than himself.

As the volunteers dispersed to their assigned tasks, Matt gravitated toward the actual construction work while Megan moved seamlessly between different groups, checking on progress and coordinating the various elements of the project. He watched her direct the older volunteers toward tasks that matched their abilities while ensuring the younger, more energetic participants were channeled toward the heavy lifting and demolition work.

"Megan's got a natural gift for leadership," Earl commented as he and Matt began removing the old porch boards. "Always did, even in high school. Remember how she organized that fundraiser for the family whose house burned down senior year?"

Matt did remember, though the memory was filtered through the lens of seventeen-year-old priorities that had focused more on football and military recruiters than on appreciating Megan's organizational abilities.

"She makes it look effortless," Matt said, pausing to watch Megan explain the day's timeline to Mrs. Simmons, who stood in her doorway with a walker, clearly delighted by all the activity surrounding her home.

The morning progressed with the kind of organized chaos that characterized successful community projects. The old porch came down faster than expected, revealing structural issues that required additional attention but nothing beyond the group's collective capabilities. Matt worked primarily with his brother Graham and two other men he'd known casually in high school, the physical labor and shared purpose creating easy camaraderie.

But throughout the morning, he found his attention repeatedly drawn to Megan.

She moved through the work site with quiet confidence, solving logistical problems before they became actual problems and ensuring that everyone felt useful and included. When one of the older volunteers struggled with a task, she smoothly reassigned him to something more manageable without making him feel inadequate. When the teenage volunteers from the church youth group arrived late and slightly unfocused, she put them to work organizing materials in a way that made them feel important while keeping them productive.

And through it all, Lauren stayed close to Matt whenever her other duties allowed, asking questions about tools and construction techniques with the same curiosity she'd shown about his military service.

"Why do you measure twice before you cut?" she asked as Matt prepared to trim a support beam.

"Because if you cut it wrong, you can't put the wood back together again," Matt explained patiently. "It's better to take extra time getting the measurement right than to waste materials fixing mistakes."

"Like when I color outside the lines in my coloring book?"

"Exactly like that. Except in construction, the lines are really important for making sure everything fits together properly."

Lauren nodded solemnly, as if filing this information away for future reference. "Can I help measure?"

Matt glanced toward Megan, who was close enough to overhear their conversation. At her encouraging nod, he handed Lauren the end of his tape measure.

"Hold this right here, exactly on the mark," he instructed, positioning her small hand carefully. "Don't let it move while I check the other end."

The simple task gave Lauren obvious pleasure.

He'd never seriously considered being a parent before. Military life hadn't been conducive to family planning, and his relationships during his service years had been casual. But helping and working with Lauren through the morning's activities had him thinking about what it would mean to wake up every day and have a child in his life.

The thought startled him.

By noon, the new porch framework was complete, and the support structure was solid. The church women had produced a lunch that seemed far too elaborate for a simple work project—fried chicken, potato salad, green beans, cornbread, and three different desserts arranged on folding tables in Mrs. Simmons's front yard.

"You ladies have outdone yourselves," Pastor Andrew announced as the volunteers gathered around the food. "This looks like a church picnic feast."

"Speaking of which," Sylvia called out, "don't forget tomorrow's picnic after church service. Weather's supposed to be perfect for outdoor games and fellowship."

Matt filled his plate and looked around for a place to sit, noting that most of the volunteers had claimed spots on blankets or quilts spread under the large oak tree that dominated Mrs. Simmons's front yard. He was pleased when Megan appeared beside him with her own plate, Lauren close behind.

"There's room over here," Megan said, gesturing toward a partially occupied quilt in the shade. "If you don't mind eating with the Miller girls."

"I can't think of anything I'd enjoy more," Matt said, and meant it completely.

They settled onto the quilt together, Lauren immediately launching into a detailed critique of the morning's construction progress while Megan and Matt listened with varying degrees of amusement.

"The hammer you taught me to use was just the right size," Lauren told Matt seriously.

"Tools should always fit the person using them," Matt said.

"Will you teach me how to use other tools sometime?" Lauren asked with the directness that seemed to be her default approach to life.

Matt glanced at Megan, who was watching their interaction with an expression he couldn't quite read. "If your mom thinks it's a good idea, I'd be happy to show you how to use some basic tools safely."

"Can he, Mom? Please?"

"We'll see," Megan said diplomatically.

Pastor Andrew joined their small group, settling onto the grass with his own plate of food. "Mrs. Simmons is absolutely thrilled with the progress," he reported. "She says it's the most excitement she's had in months."

"It's a good project," Matt said. "Practical help that makes a real difference in someone's daily life."

"That's the heart of Hands of Grace Ministry," Pastor Andrew agreed. "We're not trying to solve every problem in the world, just the ones right here in our community that are within our power to address."

"Are you planning to attend tomorrow's church picnic?" Megan asked Matt, her tone casual but her eyes holding a question.

Before Matt could respond, Lauren took matters into her own hands with characteristic directness.

"You should sit with us at church tomorrow," she announced. "And then you can stay for the picnic and play games with us."

"I'd like that very much if you're sure I wouldn't be intruding."

"You wouldn't be intruding at all," Megan assured him, her voice carrying genuine welcome. "We'd enjoy the company."

"Then I accept," Matt said, meeting Lauren's delighted grin with one of his own.

The afternoon work progressed smoothly, with the new porch taking shape under the coordinated efforts of the volunteers. Matt worked primarily on the more technical aspects of the construction, but he was constantly aware of Megan's presence as she moved through the work site, ensuring that everyone stayed hydrated and that the project maintained its schedule.

He was also increasingly aware of Lauren, who had apparently decided that he was her designated construction mentor for the day. She stayed close whenever her mother's assignments allowed, observing his work with the focused curiosity of a child.

"Why do you check that everything's straight with that tool?" she asked, pointing to his level.

"Because if the porch isn't level, water will run the wrong direction and cause problems," Matt explained. "Everything in construction needs to be straight and square, or it won't work right."

"Like if I built a bookshelf crooked, the books would fall off?"

"Exactly. Good thinking."

Lauren beamed at the praise, and Matt realized how much he was enjoying her company. She was bright and observant, asking intelligent questions and remembering the answers he gave her. More than that, she seemed to genuinely enjoy being around him, seeking him out throughout the day.

By four o'clock, the new porch was complete—solid, level, and ready to be stained. Mrs. Simmons emerged from her house with the aid of her walker to inspect the work, her face bright with pleasure and gratitude.

"It's beautiful," she declared, running her hand along the smooth railing. "Better than it was when it was first built years ago."

The volunteers gathered around to admire their collective handiwork, and Matt felt the satisfaction that came from completing useful work with his hands. But more than that, he felt the warmth of being part of a community that took care of its members, of being surrounded by people who measured success not in personal achievement but in service to others.

As the volunteers began cleaning up their tools and packing away the remaining food, Lauren appeared at Matt's side one last time.

"Don't forget church tomorrow," she said with the seriousness of someone issuing an important reminder. "We sit in pew number six on the left side."

"Pew number six, left side, got it," Matt replied.

"Good. And wear nice clothes, because it's church."

"I'll wear my best shirt," Matt said with a grin.

Chapter 11

The church grounds stretched behind the white clapboard building in a tapestry of well-maintained grass, mature oak and maple trees, and the covered pavilion that served as the center of outdoor gatherings. Picnic tables were already arranged in conversational groupings, while several church members were setting up games and activities for the afternoon's fellowship.

The church grounds buzzed with activity as families claimed tables and the church women began arranging the potluck dishes with practiced efficiency. The September air carried the mingled scents of various casseroles, fresh breads, and the last roses of summer blooming along the church's foundation, creating an atmosphere that felt both festive and comfortingly familiar.

"Megan! Matt!" Sylvia Smith called from a table near the center of the pavilion. "We saved seats for you."

As they joined the Smith family's table, Megan noticed how naturally Matt settled into conversation with longtime church members who remembered him from his youth. Earl regaled them with stories about Matt's childhood attempts to "help" in the hardware store, while older parishioners shared memories of his high school achievements and expressed their pride in his military service.

"It's good to have you home, son," said Robert Harrison, a man in his seventies who'd taught Sunday school for decades. "The community's stronger when young folks like you are part of it."

After they'd eaten from the abundant spread of casseroles, salads, and desserts, Lauren spotted several of her friends from the children's Sunday school class and asked permission to join them.

"Stay where I can see you," Megan instructed, "and remember your manners."

"I will!" Lauren promised, already bouncing toward her friends with her plate carefully balanced in both hands.

Megan felt suddenly self-conscious, as if the congregation might be observing their interaction and drawing conclusions she wasn't ready to address.

"She fits right in everywhere, doesn't she?" Matt observed, watching Lauren settle happily among the other children.

"She's never met a stranger," Megan agreed. "Sometimes I think she's more socially confident than I am."

"I find that hard to believe. You seemed perfectly comfortable organizing yesterday's work project and managing all the volunteers."

"That's different." Megan took a sip of her sweet tea, trying to articulate the distinction. "When I'm doing something useful, I feel confident. But social situations... sometimes I still feel like that bookish girl from high school who was more comfortable with novels than parties."

"You were never awkward in high school. You were just selective about where you invested your energy."

"Is that a diplomatic way of saying I was antisocial?"

"It's an honest way of saying you knew what mattered to you and didn't waste time on things that didn't." Matt's gaze held hers with an intensity that made her breath catch slightly. "I always admired that about you."

Before Megan could respond to the compliment, Pastor Andrew approached their table with the kind of enthusiastic energy that usually meant he was about to organize group activities.

"Who's ready for some games?" he announced. "We've got horseshoes set up for the competitive folks, beanbag toss for the more relaxed participants, and I'm hoping to get a volleyball game started for anyone who's feeling athletic."

"Volleyball sounds fun," Matt said, glancing at Megan with raised eyebrows. "What do you think? Are you feeling athletic?"

Megan hadn't played volleyball since college, but something in Matt's challenging tone made her want to prove she could still hold her own. "I think I could manage a game or two."

"Excellent!" Pastor Andrew said.

The volleyball net had been set up on a level section of grass behind the pavilion, creating a perfect arena for friendly competition. As they divided into teams, Megan found herself on the same side as Matt, along with Heather—who had arrived late after playing piano for a nursing home service—and three other church members.

"Fair warning," Heather announced as they took their positions, "I haven't played volleyball since college, and I wasn't very good then."

"Just keep the ball in the air," Matt advised. "We'll make it work."

The first serve came their way, a gentle lob that Matt returned with easy competence. The rally developed slowly, with players on both sides making valiant efforts to keep the ball airborne despite varying skill levels. When it finally came to Megan, she managed a respectable bump that sent the ball toward Matt, who spiked it over the net with enough force to score the point without embarrassing the other team.

"Nice setup," he told her.

"Nice finish," she replied.

The game continued with the kind of friendly competition that made everyone feel successful regardless of their athletic ability. Matt's natural leadership kept their team organized without being overbearing, while his patient encouragement helped less confident players contribute meaningfully to the game.

Megan laughed more than she had in months, caught up in the pleasure of physical activity and the easy camaraderie. When she managed an impressive save near the net, diving to keep a difficult ball in play, Matt's cheer of approval sent warmth spreading through her chest.

"I didn't know librarians were so athletic," he teased as they rotated positions.

"There's a lot you don't know about librarians," Megan replied with mock seriousness. "We're full of surprises."

"I'm beginning to realize that."

The way he said it, with casual flirtation, made Megan suddenly aware of how their playful interaction must appear to the other players and the families watching. She glanced around quickly and noticed several congregation members observing their game.

As their team won the second set and began discussing a tie-breaking third game, Lauren appeared at the edge of the court with several of her friends in tow.

"Mom! Matt! Can you teach us how to play?" she called.

"What do you think?" Matt asked the adult players. "Should we let the kids take over the court?"

"Absolutely," Pastor Andrew agreed. "Teaching the next generation is more important than defending our winning streak."

The transition from adult competition to children's instruction created a different but equally enjoyable dynamic. Matt proved to be a natural teacher, demonstrating basic volleyball techniques with patience that made each child feel capable of improvement. Megan worked alongside him to organize the kids into teams and change the rules to accommodate their smaller stature and developing coordination.

"Like this?" Lauren asked, mimicking Matt's serving motion with exaggerated concentration.

"Perfect," Matt assured her. "Now just remember to keep your eye on the ball and follow through with your arm."

Lauren's serve barely sailed over the net and landed within the court boundaries, generating cheers from both teams and a proud grin that seemed to light up her entire face.

"I did it!" she announced.

"You absolutely did," Matt confirmed.

As the afternoon progressed and the games wound down, families began gathering their belongings and preparing to head home. The September sun was angling lower through the trees, casting long shadows across the church grounds and creating the kind of golden light that made ordinary moments feel touched with magic.

"It's been a good day," Matt said after they had helped put away all the games and folding chairs. "I'd forgotten how much I missed this kind of community fellowship."

"Laurel Ridge does church picnics well," Megan agreed.

"Will you be at Martha's for dinner on Wednesday?" Lauren asked Matt as they walked toward the parking area together.

"Lauren," Megan said with gentle reproach, though she was trying not to smile.

"Mommmm... I'm just asking," Lauren defended.

"I could, if your mom would like me to," Matt said, glancing at Megan for her reaction.

"You'd be welcome," she said, meaning it completely.

As they reached their cars in the church parking lot, Lauren once again initiated the goodbye hug that was apparently becoming her standard farewell protocol with Matt. Megan again noticed how naturally he accepted the affection, returning Lauren's embrace with care that spoke of someone comfortable with children.

"Thank you for teaching me volleyball," Lauren told him seriously.

"Thank you for being such an excellent student," Matt replied with equal seriousness.

After Lauren climbed into their car and was busy arranging her Sunday school crafts and bulletin announcements, Matt turned to Megan with an expression that seemed to hold questions he wasn't quite ready to ask.

"I had a really good time today," he said simply.

"So did we. You fit right back into the community like you never left."

"It feels good to be part of something again," Matt admitted. "Military life doesn't always offer this kind of... belonging."

The word hung in the air between them, loaded with meaning that went beyond simple community membership. Megan understood Matt was talking about more than just church picnics and volleyball games—he was talking about finding a place where he could build a life.

"I'm glad you're home," she said.

"So am I."

"I look forward to more days like this with you."

Matt smiled, "I do too. More than you could imagine. Take care, Megan."

Megan drove home with Lauren chattering happily about the day's activities from the backseat. But her own thoughts were occupied with the memory of Matt's easy laughter during the volleyball game, the way he'd celebrated Lauren's small victories as if they were his own, and the comfortable feeling of having him beside her throughout the afternoon's activities.

Megan found herself hoping for more Sundays exactly like this one—filled with community, fellowship, and the growing possibility of sharing it all with someone.

Chapter 12

Megan was shelving returned books in the mystery section when the sound of work boots against the library's polished floor and the familiar scent of fresh coffee reached her. She looked up from the stack of novels in her arms to find Matt approaching with two insulated to-go cups and a smile that made her pulse quicken.

"Morning," he said, offering her one of the cups. "I thought you might need some caffeine reinforcement for your Friday morning."

"That's very thoughtful." Megan accepted the coffee, noting that he'd somehow remembered exactly how she liked it—two sugars, a splash of cream, from Martha's Diner based on the distinctive cup design. "Thank you."

"And I wanted to return these," Matt continued, producing the small stack of books she'd recommended during his previous visit. "Finished the last one last night."

"How did you like the Louise Penny? I wasn't sure if the small-village setting would appeal to someone used to more action-packed environments."

"Actually, I loved it. The way she develops the community relationships, how everyone knows each other's business but still cares about each other—it reminded me of what I've been missing about small-town life." Matt's eyes held genuine enthusiasm as he spoke about the book. "And Inspector Gamache's approach to solving problems... that resonated with me more than I expected."

"I'm so glad. Would you like me to help you find the next one in the series?"

"If you have time. Though I was also hoping you might recommend something different. Maybe another mystery series, or even some non-fiction if you think I can handle it."

They moved deeper into the library, their conversation flowing easily as Megan guided him toward different sections. She genuinely enjoyed their discussion of books and reading preferences, noting how thoughtfully Matt approached her recommendations and how his questions revealed someone who read for both entertainment and personal growth.

"This author writes excellent historical mysteries," Megan said, pulling a volume from the shelf. "Set during World War I, but the protagonist is a nurse turned investigator. Strong, capable woman who doesn't let societal expectations limit her."

"Sounds like someone I know," Matt said, his gaze meeting hers with an intensity that made her breath catch.

Before Megan could respond to the compliment, Heather appeared around the end of the bookshelf with a stack of interlibrary loan materials and a knowing expression.

"Matt! How nice to see you again," she said. "Expanding your literary horizons even further, I see."

"Megan's an excellent guide," Matt replied diplomatically.

"Oh, our Megan has wonderful taste in just about everything." Heather's tone carried layers of meaning that made Megan want to sink into the floor. "Books, people, life choices in general."

"Heather," Megan said with gentle warning.

"What? I'm just saying you have good judgment." Heather's innocent expression fooled absolutely no one. "Well, I'll let you two continue your... literary consultation."

As Heather disappeared back toward the circulation desk, Megan felt heat creep up her neck. "I apologize for—"

"Don't," Matt interrupted with a smile. "She cares about you. That's obvious."

They continued selecting books, but Megan sensed a shift in Matt's demeanor, a building anticipation that made her hyperaware of his presence beside her in the quiet stacks. When they'd gathered several promising titles, he helped carry them back toward the circulation desk, but instead of heading directly to check them out, he paused near the reading area where comfortable chairs invited lingering conversation.

"Megan," Matt began, his voice carrying a note of careful intention. "I was wondering if you might like to have dinner with me tonight."

The question—simple and direct—was loaded with implications that made Megan's heart race. This wasn't a casual encounter at Martha's Diner or an impromptu meal shared with Lauren. This was Matt asking her on an actual date.

"Tonight?" she heard herself say, immediately recognizing the slight note of panic in her voice.

"I know it's short notice," Matt said quickly, misinterpreting her hesitation. "If you're not available, or if you'd prefer a different evening—"

"No, it's not that." Megan's mind immediately began cataloging reasons why dinner tonight might not be practical. "It's just that Lauren will expect our usual Friday night routine, and I don't have anyone to—"

"I volunteer!" Heather's voice carried clearly from the circulation desk, where she'd obviously been listening to every word of their conversation. "I would absolutely love to spend an evening with Lauren. We could make popcorn and have a movie night."

Megan turned toward her friend with a mixture of gratitude and exasperation. "Heather, you don't have to—"

"I want to," Heather insisted, abandoning all pretense of not eavesdropping and approaching them directly. "You two deserve an evening out together."

Matt's smile held gentle encouragement. "The childcare situation is solved. What do you say?"

Megan was caught between Matt's hopeful expression and Heather's barely contained excitement, her carefully constructed reasons for declining evaporating one by one. She felt a flutter of anticipation in her chest.

"I..." she began, then stopped herself, recognizing the absurdity of her hesitation. Why was she being like this? It was just Matt. It was just dinner. "Where were you thinking?"

"Sue's Pizza?" Matt suggested. "My cousin owns the place, and they make excellent thin crust. Nothing fancy, just good food and conversation."

Sue's Pizza had been a Laurel Ridge fixture for the past few years with its checkered tablecloths and casual atmosphere.

"That sounds nice... yes, Matt, I'd like to go out to dinner with you."

"Great." Matt's relief was evident in his smile. "Would six o'clock work for you? I could pick you up."

"Six is fine."

"Perfect. I'll see you then."

As he headed toward the circulation desk to check out his books, Heather immediately appeared at Megan's side with a predatory gleam that suggested intensive questioning was about to begin.

"Finally!" Heather whispered urgently. "An actual date. Just the two of you. Without your cute seven-year-old chaperone."

"It's just dinner," Megan said weakly.

"It's a beginning," Heather corrected with satisfaction. "And I'm going to make sure Lauren has such a good time tonight that she'll be begging for more Aunt Heather babysitting adventures."

Megan watched Matt complete his checkout process.

"I haven't been on an actual date in four years," Megan admitted quietly to Heather.

"Then you're overdue."

"What if I've forgotten how to do this?" she asked Heather. "What if I'm awkward or boring or—"

"What if you're exactly who you've always been—smart, kind, funny, and interesting—and what if Matt already knows that because he's been spending time with you for weeks now?" Heather's tone was gentle but firm. "Megan, stop looking for reasons to be afraid. Start looking for reasons to be excited and be happy."

Matt finished his transaction and approached them with his books tucked under his arm and car keys in hand. "Six o'clock," he reminded Megan. "And don't worry about dressing up or anything."

"I'll be ready," Megan promised.

"Looking forward to it." Matt's parting smile was warm and genuine, carrying none of the nervous energy she was experiencing. He seemed completely comfortable with the idea of their dinner, as if taking her out was the most natural thing in the world.

After he left, Megan stood in the middle of the library feeling as if the familiar space had suddenly become foreign territory. The afternoon sunlight streaming through the tall windows seemed brighter, the usual sounds of library life seemed more distant, and the steady rhythm of her carefully ordered life felt disrupted in ways both thrilling and terrifying.

"What am I going to wear?" she asked Heather, the practical question emerging from her swirling thoughts.

"Something that makes you feel pretty and confident," Heather replied immediately. "That blue casual dress you wore to the church dinner last month would be perfect. Casual enough for pizza but nice enough to show you tried."

"I should make sure we have ingredients for popcorn at home, and maybe rent you and Lauren a movie—" Megan said, her mind shifting into organizational mode.

"Megan." Heather placed gentle hands on her friend's shoulders. "Breathe. I've got the Lauren logistics covered. Your only job is to go home after work, put on something that makes you feel good, and prepare to have a wonderful evening with a man who clearly thinks you're worth pursuing."

The simplicity of the plan was both comforting and terrifying. For seven years, most of Megan's Friday evenings had followed a predictable pattern: library work, dinner with Lauren, quiet activities at home, early bedtime. Tonight, she would sit across a table from Matt, sharing conversation and pizza while trying to remember how to be someone other than just a mother and librarian.

"This is good for you," Heather continued. "You've been so focused on taking care of everyone else that you've forgotten how nice it can be to let someone take care of you for a change."

As the afternoon progressed and closing time approached, Megan alternated between excitement and anxiety. Every few minutes, she would catch herself wondering what she and Matt would talk about for an entire evening, or whether she would remember how to navigate the subtle complexities of adult conversation without the comfortable buffer of Lauren's chatter or community activities.

But underneath the nervousness was something warmer—anticipation, maybe, or simple pleasure at the prospect of spending uninterrupted time with someone whose company she genuinely enjoyed. Matt made her laugh. He listened when she talked. He treated her daughter with respect and kindness. He had steady hands and a gentle heart and a way of making ordinary moments feel touched with possibility.

Maybe Heather was right. Maybe instead of looking for reasons to be afraid, she should start looking for reasons to be excited.

Chapter 13

Megan stood in front of her bedroom mirror, smoothing the fabric of her blue dress and questioning every decision she'd made in the past hour. The dress was perfect—casual enough for Sue's Pizza but flattering enough to show she'd made an effort—but her reflection revealed nervous energy that no amount of outfit adjustments could disguise.

"You look beautiful, Megan," Heather called from downstairs. "Stop overthinking and come down here so I can give you a proper pep talk."

Megan descended the stairs with as much dignity as her nervous stomach would allow, finding Lauren curled against Heather's side with Mr. Buttons tucked under one arm and obvious excitement brightening her features.

"Mommy, you look pretty. Like a princess going to a ball."

"Thank you, sweetheart. It's just dinner at Sue's Pizza," Megan said, though she couldn't help smiling.

"With Matt," Lauren said.

"Yes, with Matt." Megan settled into the armchair across from them, trying to project calm confidence while her pulse thrummed with anticipation. "And you're going to have a fun evening with Heather watching movies and eating entirely too much popcorn."

"We're going to have a blast," Heather confirmed, then fixed Megan with a look of mock seriousness. "But first, let me remind you that this is supposed to be fun. You like Matt. He obviously likes you. You've been spending time together for weeks now, and it's felt natural and comfortable. Tonight is just more of the same, except with better food and no seven-year-old commentary."

"What if I run out of things to talk about? What if it's awkward without Lauren there to fill the silences?"

"Then you're both in trouble, because you've been talking easily for weeks," Heather said with gentle teasing. "Megan, you're overthinking this. Just be yourself—the smart, funny, caring, strong woman you've always been. That's who Matt asked to dinner, not some perfect version of yourself that doesn't exist."

The sound of a truck engine in the driveway interrupted her anxiety spiral, and Lauren immediately bounced off the couch to peer through the front window.

"He's here!" she announced.

Megan felt a flutter in her stomach as she gathered her purse and lightweight cardigan. Through the window, she could see Matt walking up the front path wearing khakis and a navy button-down that emphasized his broad shoulders and the confident way he carried himself.

"Have fun," Heather said, giving her a quick hug. "And don't come home before nine-thirty. Lauren and I have serious movie watching to accomplish."

Matt's knock was prompt and gentle, and when Megan opened the door, his smile did something warm and complicated to her breathing.

"Ready for the best pizza in Laurel Ridge?" he asked, offering her his arm with old-fashioned courtesy.

"You're overselling it," Megan replied with a grin.

"Trust me," Matt said as he guided her toward his truck. "Sue's been perfecting her recipes for years. She takes pizza very seriously."

Matt opened the passenger door for her, a gesture that felt both natural and special, and Megan settled into the comfortable seat while he walked around to the driver's side. The truck's interior smelled faintly of his cologne and coffee, scents that were becoming associated with Matt's presence in her life.

"Nervous?" Matt asked as he started the engine, his tone gentle and understanding.

"A little," Megan admitted honestly. "It's been a while since I've done this."

"Me too, actually. Dating hasn't exactly been a priority in my life. But I'm looking forward to spending time with you without competing with plumbing disasters or community service projects for your attention."

Sue's Pizza occupied a converted house on the edge of downtown, its warm yellow lights spilling onto the front porch where several small tables were arranged for outdoor dining. The autumn evening was perfect for eating outside, with temperatures cool enough to be comfortable but warm enough not to require jackets.

"Matt!" A petite woman with dark hair pulled back in a ponytail emerged from the restaurant with genuine enthusiasm. "I was wondering when you'd stop by. I heard from your mama that you moved back to town."

"Sue, it's good to see you. It's been quite a few years," Matt said as he hugged her. "This is Megan... but I'm sure you two already know each other."

"We do," Sue said warmly. "Evenin' Megan. I've been meaning to get over to the library and pick up those books you have on hold for me. It's... nice to see you two together."

"Hi, Sue," Megan said.

"I've got the perfect table for you," Sue announced, leading them toward a cozy spot on the porch where string lights overhead created a soft ambiance.

As they settled at the small table with its red-and-white checkered cloth and flickering candle, Megan felt her nervousness begin to ease.

"So," Matt said after they'd ordered. "Tell me something I don't know about Megan Miller."

The question was playful but genuine, and Megan laughed despite her earlier nervousness. "That's a dangerous request. There might not be anything particularly interesting to discover."

"I doubt that very seriously." Matt's eyes held a warm attention that made her feel like the most important person in the world. "For instance, I know you're an excellent librarian and devoted mother, but what do you do when you're not working or taking care of Lauren? What makes Megan happy?"

The question was simple but surprisingly difficult to answer, forcing her to think beyond the roles that had defined her life for so long. "I love to read, obviously. Mystery novels when I want to escape, biography when I'm feeling ambitious, poetry when I need beauty."

"Poetry?" Matt's eyebrows rose with interest. "What kind?"

"Nothing too academic. Mary Oliver, mostly. She writes about nature and faith in ways that make ordinary moments feel sacred." Megan surprised herself by admitting something so personal. "I read her work when I need reminding that there's still wonder in the world."

"I'd like to read some of her poems sometime, if you'd recommend a few."

"I could do that. What about you? What makes Matt Smith happy besides fixing things and helping people?"

"Woodworking," Matt replied immediately. "I've got a workshop in the basement of the hardware store where I've started building furniture and small projects again. There's something peaceful about creating something beautiful and functional with your hands."

"What kind of furniture?"

"Mostly practical stuff. I've made a couple of small end tables so far, bookshelves, and storage pieces. Though I've been wanting to try something more challenging—maybe a rocking chair or a hope chest."

"That does sound challenging, but I'm sure you can handle it."

Their conversation was interrupted by Sue's arrival with their pizza, the thin crust perfectly golden and the cheese bubbling with an appetizing aroma. As they ate, their discussion ranged across topics both serious and silly—favorite movies, most embarrassing moments, childhood dreams that had or hadn't come true.

"Okay," Megan said during a lull in conversation, feeling bold enough to ask something she'd been wondering about. "Most unusual place you've ever been stationed?"

"Okinawa," Matt replied without hesitation. "Beautiful island, incredible people, but I once had to explain to a local shopkeeper why I needed seventeen different types of screws for a repair project. The language barrier made it... interesting."

"Did you succeed?"

"Eventually. Though I'm pretty sure he thought all Americans were completely insane." Matt grinned at the memory. "Your turn. Most unusual library patron request?"

"A gentleman once asked me to help him find books on time travel because he was convinced his deceased wife was sending him messages from the future through the library's card catalog system." Megan couldn't help smiling at the memory. "Sweetest man, completely serious about his request."

"What did you do?"

"I found him some gentle books on grief and healing, along with a few harmless science fiction novels. Sometimes people need stories that help them process their feelings, even if the stories involve impossible things."

"Wise. And kind."

Their eyes met across the table.

"I have a confession," Matt said as they enjoyed the last slices of pizza. "I was terrified you'd say no when I asked you to dinner."

"I almost did," Megan admitted honestly. "Not because I didn't want to, but because I've gotten very good at avoiding situations that feel... risky."

"And this feels risky?"

"This feels like it matters. And things that matter can hurt you."

Matt was silent for a moment, his expression growing more serious. "They can also heal you."

The simple statement hung between them, loaded with meaning that went beyond casual dinner conversation. Megan studied his face in the candlelight—the way his blue-gray eyes reflected genuine care, the slight lines around them that spoke of experience and wisdom, the mouth that had been nothing but kind since he'd returned to her life.

"More coffee?" Sue appeared beside their table with perfect timing, breaking the intensity of the moment. "Or are you ready for dessert? I've got fresh apple turnovers that are still warm from the oven."

"Turnovers sound perfect," Matt said, glancing at Megan for confirmation.

"Definitely," Megan agreed, grateful for the interruption that allowed her racing heart to settle.

As they shared dessert, and conversation gradually returned to lighter topics. Matt's easy humor and genuine interest in her thoughts made her feel like the interesting, attractive woman she'd forgotten she could be when she wasn't focused entirely on being a mother.

"This has been wonderful," she said as they prepared to leave, meaning it completely.

"Even though I made you leave your comfortable Friday night routine?" Matt asked as he helped her with her cardigan.

"Especially because of that."

Outside Sue's Pizza, under the glow of the string lights and the emerging stars, Matt opened the passenger door of his truck with the same courtesy he'd shown all evening. But instead of immediately climbing in, Megan paused, looking up at him.

Something had shifted during the evening—not just her nervousness dissolving, but a deeper recognition of what was happening between them. The careful boundaries she'd maintained for years felt less like protection and more like barriers preventing her from something good.

"Matt. I like this thing that's happening between us."

His expression grew still and very focused. "Yeah?"

"It feels right," she continued, the words emerging with surprising certainty. "Scary, but right."

Matt's smile started slowly, then spread across his features like sunrise. "I was hoping you'd say something like that."

"Were you?"

"I've been hoping since the moment you walked into the hardware store and I remembered what it felt like to want to impress someone." His voice was warm with honesty. "You make me want to be the kind of man who deserves your attention."

"You already are that man."

Standing in the parking lot of Sue's Pizza under the autumn stars, with the sound of distant laughter drifting from the restaurant and the scent of the night air carrying promises of changing seasons, Megan felt like she was stepping across a threshold into territory she'd avoided for far too long.

"So what happens now?" she asked.

"Now I take you home," Matt said with gentle humor. "And then, if you're willing, I'd like to keep doing this. Dinner, conversation, getting to know each other again. Seeing where this thing between us might lead."

"I'd like that too."

Chapter 14

Megan knelt in her front flower bed, carefully pulling weeds from around the existing perennials and making room for the fall mums she'd picked up in town at the farmer's market. The burgundy, orange, and golden flowers would provide color through October and November, bridging the gap between summer's fading blooms and winter's dormancy.

Saturday mornings were typically reserved for household projects that couldn't be accomplished during the week, and today's perfect weather made outdoor work appealing. The sun warmed her shoulders through her old gardening shirt while a gentle breeze carried the scent of clean, fresh autumn air.

Lauren had claimed the front porch as her outdoor art studio, spreading a blanket on the wooden boards and arranging her crayons and coloring books with the serious precision of someone preparing for important work. She hummed contentedly as she colored, occasionally offering commentary on Megan's gardening progress or sharing updates about her artistic decisions.

"The butterfly I'm drawing has purple wings with silver dots," Lauren announced from her spot near the porch steps. "Miss Rodriguez said butterflies can be any color we want in our imagination."

"That sounds beautiful, sweetheart." Megan said as she worked rich gardening soil around the base of a robust mum plant, enjoying the satisfying rhythm of outdoor work. "Silver dots will make it sparkle."

"Like jewelry wings."

The morning felt perfectly ordinary and wonderfully peaceful—exactly the kind of Saturday Megan had come to treasure over the years. But underneath the familiar comfort was a warm undercurrent of happiness, a lightness that had everything to do with last night's dinner and the way Matt had looked at her when she'd admitted their connection felt right.

The sound of a truck engine turning into her driveway interrupted her gardening meditation, and Megan looked up with surprise to see Matt's pickup pulling to a stop behind her SUV. She rocked back on her heels, brushing dirt from her hands as she watched him emerge from the truck with a toolbag slung over his shoulder and the kind of purposeful expression that suggested he'd arrived with a specific mission in mind.

"Matt!" Lauren called from the porch, abandoning her coloring project to wave enthusiastically. "Did you come to see me?"

"I did," Matt confirmed, approaching with the easy smile that had been affecting Megan's composure since his return to Laurel Ridge. "And I came to fix something that's been bothering me."

"What's broken?" Lauren asked.

"Your porch railings are a little loose," Matt explained, setting his tool bag down near the front steps. "I noticed it the other times I've been here, and I thought I should take care of it before someone gets hurt."

Megan pushed herself to her feet, suddenly conscious of her appearance—dirt-stained jeans, an old West Virginia University t-shirt, and gardening gloves that had seen better days. "Matt, you don't need to spend your Saturday morning on my home repairs. I was planning to call someone about that."

"No need to call anyone when I'm right here," he said with a boyish grin that made him look exactly like the teenager she'd known in high school. "Besides, it won't take long, and I'd feel better knowing your porch is safe for Lauren to play on."

The thoughtfulness of his motivation—concern for Lauren's safety rather than just general helpfulness—sent warmth spreading through Megan's chest. She nodded in agreement despite her automatic instinct to handle things on her own.

"If you're sure you don't mind," she said. "Can I get you something to drink? Coffee? Sweet tea?"

"Coffee would be great." Matt said as he examined the railing posts. "This shouldn't take more than an hour or so. Just needs some new screws and maybe a bracket or two."

As Megan headed inside, she could hear Matt explaining his repair plan to Lauren in the patient, detailed way that had become his standard approach to her endless questions. Through the living room window, she watched him show how the loose railing moved when pressure was applied, showing Lauren why it needed to be fixed.

This was what Saturday mornings could look like—shared projects, comfortable conversation, and easy collaboration of two adults maintaining a home together while a child played safely nearby. Not that she needed help with her household responsibilities, but she had to admit the partnership aspect was appealing.

When she returned outside with Matt's coffee in one of her better mugs, he was already measuring and marking screw placements.

"Thank you," he said.

"How bad is it?" Megan asked, settling back into her gardening work.

"Not bad at all. Just normal settling and weather exposure. The wood is still solid—it just needs new hardware." Matt took a sip of coffee and then pulled his drill from the toolbag. "Your home is actually in excellent condition for its age. Someone's been taking good care of it."

"My grandmother always said a house would take care of you if you took care of it first." Megan positioned another mum plant in the prepared hole, enjoying the way the golden petals caught the morning light. "Though I have to admit, some maintenance tasks are beyond my skill set."

"That's what neighbors are for," Matt said, beginning to drill pilot holes for the new screws.

The sound of his work provided a pleasant background rhythm as Megan continued planting, both of them working on their respective projects while maintaining the simple conversation that had become natural between them. Lauren moved between them like a small supervisor, offering encouragement to her mother's gardening efforts and asking Matt questions about power tool safety.

"The drill makes holes the right size?" Lauren asked, peering closely at Matt's work.

"That's the idea. If the holes are too small, the screws won't go in the right way. If they're too big, they won't hold tight." Matt showed the concept. "When you work with wood, everything is about getting the measurements exactly right."

"Like when Mom measures stuff to make cookies?"

"Yep. Just like that."

Megan smiled at the comparison.

"I'll be right back," Lauren announced after watching Matt install several new brackets. "I have an important job to do."

She disappeared into the house with the determined stride of someone on a mission.

"She's a character," Matt said, testing the newly secured railing with gentle pressure. "Curious about everything."

"She's always been interested in how things work," Megan agreed, applying mulch around her newly planted flowers. "Sometimes I think she inherited her father's mechanical mind along with his stubborn cowlick."

Lauren emerged from the house carrying a juice box and a chocolate chip cookie on one of Megan's good plates, her face bright with purpose.

"Snack time, Matt," she announced, approaching the porch steps with careful attention to her precious cargo.

Matt stopped his work immediately and accepted the offering that made Lauren beam with pride. "This is exactly what I needed," he said seriously. "Hard work makes a man hungry and thirsty."

"That's what Mom says too." Lauren settled cross-legged on the porch to watch him enjoy her refreshments. "She always has snacks when she's working in the yard."

"That was really thoughtful, sweetheart," Megan said, touched by her daughter's instinctive hospitality. "Matt's been working hard to keep our porch safe."

As Matt ate the cookie and drank the juice box with obvious enjoyment, Lauren peppered him with more questions. Megan listened to their conversation while finishing her planting.

"All finished," Matt announced an hour later, giving the repaired railing a last test. "Solid as a rock now."

"Thank you," Megan said, rising from her garden work and surveying the results of their combined efforts. The front yard looked welcoming and well-maintained, with colorful mums providing autumn cheer and the porch restored to complete safety. "You didn't need to spend your morning on this."

"I wanted to." Matt said as he gathered his tools. "Besides, it gives me peace of mind knowing Lauren can play out safely. Plus... I got to spend time with you."

The simple statement made Megan smile.

"Would you like more coffee before you go?" Megan asked, reluctant to see the morning end.

"I should probably head back and help Dad with some inventory work at the store," Matt said with obvious reluctance. "But I had a really good time this morning. There's something satisfying about working on projects that make daily life better for people you care about."

People you care about. The phrase settled around Megan's heart like a warm blanket.

"Oh, before you leave," Megan said, remembering something important. "There's a Hands of Grace Ministry planning meeting Wednesday evening at church. We're finalizing details for the Fall Festival booth and discussing upcoming service projects. I hope you'll come."

"Wouldn't miss it," Matt replied with a grin that made her pulse quicken.

As he loaded his tools into his truck and prepared to leave, Megan found herself already looking forward to Wednesday evening—not just for the ministry planning, but for the simple pleasure of seeing Matt again.

"See you Wednesday," she called as he backed out of the driveway.

"Looking forward to it," Matt replied through his open truck window.

Chapter 15

Megan arrived at the Laurel Ridge Public Library an hour before opening time on Monday morning, her usual practice for catching up on administrative tasks in the peaceful quiet before patrons began arriving. She unlocked her office door, settled at her desk with a fresh cup of coffee, and hummed while she reviewed the weekend reports.

She was still humming when Heather arrived a few minutes later.

"Well, well," Heather said, settling at her desk across from her with obvious interest. "Someone sounds remarkably cheerful for a Monday morning. Did you win the lottery over the weekend?"

"Just in a good mood, I suppose."

"A good mood," Heather repeated slowly, as if tasting the words. "On a Monday. Before nine AM. While doing paperwork." She leaned back in her chair with the satisfied expression of someone who'd just solved a particularly interesting puzzle. "This has to do with Matt, doesn't it?"

"I don't know what you're talking about."

"Oh, you absolutely do. And unless you've discovered some amazing new moisturizer, I'm guessing this glow has everything to do with a certain hardware store owner who took you to dinner Friday night."

"Our dinner date was lovely, as you already know."

"Lovely," Heather echoed with clear dissatisfaction. "That's all I get? Lovely? Come on. Details. I want more than the few things you told me on Friday after your date. How was the conversation? Are you going to see him again?"

"You're worse than Lauren when she wants to know about something."

"Lauren gets results through persistence, and so do I. Talk."

"It was wonderful, actually. Better than I'd expected."

"Now we're getting somewhere." Heather's voice carried the satisfaction of someone making progress on an important project. "What made it wonderful?"

"He's such a good conversationalist. We talked about everything—books, childhood memories, what we want for the future. He has this way of listening that makes you feel like you're the only person in the world who matters." Megan paused, recognizing how revealing her words were becoming. "And he's funny. He makes me laugh."

"And?" Heather prompted.

"And what?"

"And there's obviously more. You look like someone who's discovered something beautiful and surprising and slightly terrifying all at the same time."

Megan was quiet for a moment. "He came by Saturday morning to fix my porch railings."

"Came by? As in, showed up at your house without being asked?"

"He said he'd noticed they were loose during his previous visits and wanted to take care of it before someone got hurt. Before Lauren got hurt. He spent his Saturday morning making sure our front porch was safe."

"Oh, Megan." Heather's expression grew softer, more understanding. "That's not just helpful neighbor behavior. That's someone who's thinking about you and Lauren and putting you both high on his priority list."

"I know. And that's what scares me."

"Scares you how?"

Megan stood up and walked to the office window that looked out onto Main Street, where early morning shoppers were beginning their weekly routines. The familiar rhythm of small-town life felt comforting and stable, a reminder of the carefully constructed world she'd built for herself and Lauren.

"Lauren has never had a father figure in her life," she said finally. "She's never experienced having a man who cares about her daily safety and happiness."

"Those sound like good things."

"They are good things. But they're also dangerous things." Megan turned back to face her friend. "Lauren is already attached to Matt. I can see it in the way she lights up when he arrives, how she seeks his attention, the way she talks about him throughout the week. She's starting to depend on his presence in ways that could devastate her if he changes his mind about us."

Heather was quiet for a moment. "What makes you think he might change his mind?"

"I don't know that he will. But I don't know that he won't, either." Megan returned to her desk but remained standing, too restless to sit. "He's just settling back into civilian life. He's taking over a business, figuring out what he wants his future to look like. How can I know if what he feels for us is genuine long-term interest or just... nostalgia? Loneliness? The appeal of an instant family?"

"Has he given you any reason to doubt his sincerity?"

"No," Megan admitted. "He's been nothing but consistent and kind and genuine. But Heather, Lauren has never lost someone she counts on. She doesn't remember David, so she's never experienced the devastation of having someone important disappear from her life. If Matt decides this is too complicated, or if he realizes he's not ready for the responsibility of caring about a child..."

"You're protecting her from potential heartbreak."

"I'm trying to. But I'm also starting to wonder if I'm protecting myself just as much." Megan finally sat down, her voice growing quieter. "And then I feel guilty about that too."

"Guilty about what?"

"About wanting this for myself, not just for Lauren. About enjoying his attention and his company and the way he makes me feel like an interesting, attractive woman instead of just a mom and a librarian." Megan's words came out in a rush, carrying confessions she'd barely admitted to herself. "Is it selfish to want time when I'm just Megan instead of always being Mom first? Does wanting that make me a terrible mother?"

"Oh, honey." Heather's voice was gentle but firm. "Wanting your own happiness doesn't make you a terrible mother. It makes you a human being."

"But my choices affect Lauren directly. If I pursue something with Matt and it doesn't work out, she's the one who gets hurt by my decision to take that risk."

"And if you don't pursue it, she misses out on the possibility of having someone wonderful in her life who could love and care for both of you."

Megan was quiet, staring at her hands folded on the desk. The argument felt familiar—the same internal debate she'd been having since Matt's return to her life, weighing the potential for happiness against the risk of loss.

"What does your heart tell you about Matt?" Heather asked.

"My heart tells me he's a good man who genuinely cares about us. My heart tells me Lauren needs someone like him in her life, and that I'm happier when he's around than I've been in years." Megan looked up to meet her friend's eyes. "My heart tells me I'm falling for him in ways that terrify me because they matter so much."

"And your head?"

"My head tells me to be careful. To protect Lauren. To remember that loving someone means risking the possibility of losing them, and that I've already survived that devastation once." She paused. "My head tells me that maybe it's safer to keep things casual and friendly instead of letting myself want something that could change everything."

Heather was quiet for several moments, clearly choosing her words carefully. "Can I ask you something?"

"Of course."

"I'll ask you this question again... just as I have before, because it's important. What would David want for you and Lauren?"

"He'd want us to be happy. He'd want Lauren to have a father figure who loved her, and he'd want me to find love again."

"Do you think he'd want you to choose safety over the possibility of the kind of love that could heal both your hearts?"

"No, David was never someone who chose the safe path when something important was at stake."

"Then maybe the question isn't whether loving Matt is risky. Maybe the question is whether the risk is worth the possibility of the life you and Lauren could have with someone who clearly adores you both."

"But what if—"

"Megan. Stop. Just stop it." Heather's voice was kind but firm. "Don't deny yourself and Lauren this beautiful possibility because you're too afraid to trust that you deserve it."

Megan stared out the window again, watching the familiar rhythms of Monday morning in Laurel Ridge—shoppers heading to Martha's Diner for coffee, schoolchildren walking past with backpacks, the comfortable predictability of a community where everyone looked out for each other.

"I don't know how to do this. I don't know how to be brave enough to want something this much."

"You've already been brave enough. You went to dinner with him. You let him fix your porch. You admitted to both of us that your feelings for him are real and growing. You're already taking the risk, Megan. The question is whether you're going to let yourself enjoy the possibility or spend all your time worrying about what could go wrong."

As the morning sunlight slanted through the office window, Megan realized her friend was right. She could no longer deny her growing feelings for Matt or pretend that what was happening between them was casual friendship.

She was falling in love with him. Despite her fears, despite her protective instincts, despite every rational argument for maintaining a safe emotional distance and taking things slow, she was falling in love with Matt Smith in ways that made her want to believe in the possibility of happily ever after.

"I'm scared, Heather."

"Love is terrifying under the best circumstances, and your circumstances are pretty complicated. But being scared isn't a good enough reason to close your heart to something that could be wonderful."

Chapter 16

Matt arrived ten minutes before the scheduled start of the Wednesday evening Hands of Grace ministry meeting. The church's recreation room buzzed with conversation as volunteers arranged folding chairs in a circle and set up a small table with coffee, sweet tea, and the homemade cookies that seemed to appear at every church gathering. Matt paused in the doorway, taking in the familiar faces of people who'd become important parts of his reintegration into Laurel Ridge life—his parents Earl and Sylvia chatting with Pastor Andrew near the refreshment table, his brother Graham examining project blueprints with two other men Matt didn't recognize, and Helen and Bill Houser were already seated.

But it was Megan who immediately drew his attention, seated in the circle of chairs with an empty seat beside her with a manila folder sitting in her lap. She looked up after he spotted her; her face brightening with a smile.

"Matt!" she called, gesturing toward the vacant chair. "I saved you a seat."

"Thanks," he said, settling into the folding chair and accepting the meeting agenda she handed him. "I've been looking forward to this all week."

"Really?"

"Of course," Matt replied honestly. "I get to see you again."

Pastor Andrew Whitman approached the center of the circle.

"Good evening, everyone," Pastor Andrew said as conversations gradually quieted and attention focused on him. "Thank you all for making time in your schedules to gather for ministry planning. Before we dive into the practical details, let's begin with prayer."

The group joined hands naturally, creating a circle of connection that reinforced the collaborative spirit of their shared work. Matt held Megan's hand on one side and his mother's on the other.

"Heavenly Father," Pastor Andrew began, "we thank You for the opportunity to serve our community through the gifts and abilities You've given us. Guide our planning tonight, help us listen for Your direction, and bless the work we'll do in Your name. In Jesus's name we pray, Amen."

"Amen," the group responded in unison.

"Our primary agenda item tonight is planning our next major service project," Pastor Andrew continued, consulting notes written on index cards. "As many of you know, our brother Harold Brooks will be having hip replacement surgery next week, and his recovery will require the use of a wheelchair and eventually a walker for several weeks."

Matt glanced around the circle, noting heads nodding with understanding and concern for someone clearly valued within their church family.

"Harold's home sits up on a tall foundation, which means he has several front steps that will make it difficult for him once he's released from the hospital after his surgery," Pastor Andrew explained. "His daughter Susan has asked if Hands of Grace might help construct a wheelchair ramp that would allow him to return home from rehabilitation instead of needing extended care facility placement."

"When would he need this completed?" asked Earl.

"Ideally, within the next two to three weeks. His surgery is scheduled for Friday of next week, and depending on his recovery progress, he could be ready to come home as early as two weeks from now."

Matt studied the project details Pastor Andrew distributed, assessing the scope of work involved. A residential wheelchair ramp would require careful planning for proper slope ratios, sturdy construction to support mobility equipment, and weatherproofing for long-term durability.

"This is definitely manageable," Matt said. "I've built similar accessibility modifications during my service years. The key factors are calculating the correct rise-to-run ratio and ensuring the foundation is solid enough to support both the ramp structure and the weight of users with equipment."

"Excellent," Pastor Andrew said with obvious relief. "Would you be willing to take a leadership role in the construction planning?"

"Absolutely." Matt accepted the responsibility without hesitation, already mentally organizing the project into manageable phases. "I'd like to visit Harold's property soon to take measurements and assess the existing structure, then create a materials list and construction timeline."

"I'll go with you, son," Earl volunteered immediately. "Two sets of eyes are better than one for this kind of planning. Plus, we have a few suppliers who might donate materials for a project like this."

The discussion continued for another twenty minutes, covering volunteer scheduling, permit requirements, and coordination with

Harold's family. Matt naturally took notes and asked practical questions, slipping into the organizational mindset that had served him well during military project management.

"Our second major agenda item," Pastor Andrew said as the ramp discussion concluded, "is coordinating our participation in this year's Laurel Ridge Fall Festival. Megan, would you like to update everyone on our fundraising booth plans?"

"The Fall Festival runs Friday through Sunday, October first through third, with activities centered around the town square and Main Street. Hands of Grace has been assigned a booth space near the gazebo, which should give us excellent visibility for both fundraising and community outreach."

Matt listened as she outlined their plans with impressive attention to detail—donation collection strategies, volunteer scheduling, coordination with other church ministries, and promotional materials to explain their service work to festival visitors.

"Our goal is to raise funds for ongoing ministry projects, while also collecting non-perishable food items for families in need during the winter months," Megan continued. "The booth will feature information about our past projects, sign-up opportunities for new volunteers, and activities for children to keep families engaged while parents learn about our work."

"What kind of volunteer help do you need?" asked Heather, who'd been taking notes throughout Megan's presentation.

"I'll be managing the booth on Friday, but I need at least two other people to help with setup, donation collection, and visitor interaction. On Saturday and Sunday, I'll need different volunteers to staff the booth on those days."

"I'd like to help on Friday, if that works for you," Matt said.

Megan's smile carried warmth that made the entire room feel brighter. "That would be wonderful."

"Count me in too," Graham said from across the circle. "Friday works well with my schedule."

"And your mom and I can take Saturday," offered Bill, Megan's father.

As volunteers claimed various time slots and responsibilities, Matt was looking forward to spending six hours working closely with Megan on something that mattered to both of them.

The rest of the meeting covered administrative details—budget updates, various other service opportunities, and coordination with other church ministries. Matt took part actively in discussions, offering insights from his military experience while learning about the specific needs and dynamics of the Laurel Ridge community.

"Before we close," Pastor Andrew said as the agenda neared completion, "I want to remind everyone that our ministry work is most effective when it comes from hearts committed to serving God through serving others. The projects we undertake and the relationships we build through this work are opportunities to show Christ's love in practical, meaningful ways. Let's close in prayer."

This time, Matt was hyperaware of the warmth of Megan's hand in his, the way her fingers felt both delicate and strong, the comfortable way their hands fit together as if designed for exactly this kind of connection.

Pastor Andrew offered a closing prayer of gratitude and blessing, asking for wisdom in their upcoming projects and safety for all their volunteers. But Matt found his attention divided between the spoken words and the simple pleasure of holding Megan's hand, the way her thumb rested lightly against his knuckles and how natural the contact felt.

As the prayer concluded, and conversations resumed, people began gathering their materials and preparing to leave. Matt reluctantly released Megan's hand to help stack chairs and collect coffee cups, but stayed close to her as they completed cleanup tasks.

"Thanks for volunteering to help with the booth," Megan said as they worked together to wipe down the refreshment table. "I was hoping you'd be available, but I didn't want to assume."

"I can't think of anywhere I'd rather spend that Friday," Matt replied honestly. "I'm looking forward to it."

"Me too."

After the cleanup of the recreation room was finished and the last folding chair stored away, the remaining volunteers began making their way toward the exit. In the gentle bustle of people gathering purses and saying goodnights, Megan moved closer to Matt's side. Without a word, she reached for his hand.

Matt smiled as her fingers slipped between his, the gesture both bold and tender. He accepted the contact without hesitation, his thumb stroking gently across her knuckles as their fingers intertwined in a way that felt both natural and significant. Around them, other ministry members called out farewells and car doors began closing in the church parking lot, but Matt was aware only of the warmth of Megan's hand in his and the way she stayed close to his side as they walked.

The September evening had settled into full darkness, with stars visible above the glow of the church's exterior lights. The air carried the scent of cooling earth and the faint smoke of distant fireplaces, while the sound of engines starting and conversations fading created a peaceful backdrop to their quiet walk across the parking lot.

They moved slowly, neither in any hurry to end the evening, walking past his parents, who were deep in conversation with the Housers about weekend plans. Other volunteers waved goodnight as they departed.

When they reached Megan's Ford SUV near the far edge of the parking lot, they stopped walking but neither made any move to separate. The church building behind them glowed softly in the darkness, its white clapboard walls and tall steeple creating a peaceful backdrop, while the sounds of the last few departing cars grew distant.

They stood together in comfortable silence, hands still joined, both seeming to understand that something significant was happening in this quiet moment. Matt could feel the warmth of Megan's fingers intertwined with his, could sense her contentment in the way she remained close to his side despite the cooling night air.

"I should probably head home," Megan said finally, though she made no move to withdraw her hand, and her voice held reluctance rather than urgency.

Matt felt the same reluctance to end this perfect evening, this simple pleasure of standing together under the stars with their hands joined and their hearts full of shared purpose and growing connection. "Of course," he replied gently, finally releasing her hand to open her car door.

As Megan settled behind the steering wheel and started the engine, she rolled down her window and looked up at him with an expression that made his heart race. In the soft glow of the dome light, her face held warmth and something deeper—affection, maybe, or the recognition that whatever was growing between them was worth nurturing.

"See you Friday?" Matt asked.

"Friday."

As Matt watched her drive away, her taillights disappearing down the street, he remained standing in the now-empty parking lot with the warmth of her hand still seeming to linger in his palm and the certainty growing in his heart that Megan Miller was becoming essential to his vision of home.

Chapter 17

The scent of candied apples and fresh funnel cake drifted across Main Street as Megan adjusted the bright blue tablecloth that covered the table in the Hands of Grace ministry booth. The annual Laurel Ridge Fall Festival was already transforming the heart of downtown into something magical—vendor booths lined both sides of Main Street and spilled onto Church and Oak Street, while colorful banners stretched between old-fashioned lampposts and the sound of carnival rides being tested echoed from down the street.

"Hand me that banner, would you?" Matt called from where he stood on a stepladder, securing one end of their ministry sign to the booth's frame.

Megan passed him the vinyl banner that read "Hands of Grace Ministry - Building Hope, One Project at a Time" in cheerful gold lettering against a deep green background. She watched his steady hands work, noting the way his flannel shirt emphasized his broad shoulders and how the early morning sunlight caught the lighter strands in his brown hair.

"Perfect," he said, stepping down from the ladder and surveying their setup with satisfaction. "Looks good."

"Thanks to your engineering skills," Megan replied with a smile. "I never would have figured out how to hang that banner level."

Their booth occupied a prime location near the gazebo, with a clear view of Main Street. The space included two six-foot tables arranged in an L-shape, folding chairs positioned strategically for both volunteers and visitors, and several large cardboard boxes waiting to be filled with donated food items.

Graham approached their booth carrying a steaming cup of coffee and wearing the kind of easy grin that ran in the Smith family. "Morning, you two. Ready to charm the community into opening their wallets for a good cause?"

"Ready as we'll ever be," Megan said, accepting the hug Graham offered. "Thank you for volunteering your day to help us."

"Are you kidding? Everybody deserves a day off from the everyday grind of their job now and then." Graham set his coffee on the corner of their table and began unpacking the informational displays Megan had prepared. "Plus, I get to watch my big brother try to impress the town librarian."

"Graham," Matt warned with a brotherly look that carried no real threat.

"What? It's obvious you two have a thing going—" Graham's teasing was interrupted by the arrival of their first visitors.

"Good morning!" called Janet Dillard, a woman in her fifties who taught third grade at Laurel Ridge Elementary. She approached with her husband, Rex, in tow, both carrying the kind of determined expressions that suggested they'd come specifically to support the ministry.

"Janet, Rex, how wonderful to see you," Megan said, immediately shifting into her welcoming hostess mode. "Thank you for stopping by our booth."

"We wouldn't miss it," Janet replied warmly. "The work you all did on Mrs. Simmons' porch was just beautiful. Rex and I want to contribute to whatever project you're planning next."

As Matt explained their upcoming wheelchair ramp project while Rex examined the photo displays of their previous work, Megan observed the easy way Matt engaged with community members. He had a natural gift for making people feel heard and valued, asking thoughtful questions about their own home maintenance needs while sharing information about the ministry's mission.

"Here's twenty dollars for your general fund," Janet said, tucking the bills into their donation jar, "and I'll be bringing a bag of canned goods from our pantry later this afternoon."

"That's incredibly generous," Megan said. "Every donation helps us serve more families."

As the Dillards moved on toward the apple cider stand, Graham whistled softly. "Twenty dollars before ten o'clock. You two have definitely found your calling."

The morning progressed with a steady stream of visitors—church members offering enthusiastic support, neighbors curious about their upcoming projects, and families attracted by the children's coloring station Graham had improvised using paper and crayons from the church supplies. Megan and Matt developed a natural rhythm of collaboration, with one of them engaging visitors in conversation while the other organized donations or updated their volunteer sign-up sheets.

"Tell me about this wheelchair ramp project," said a woman Megan didn't recognize, studying the project description Matt had posted on their information board.

"We're building an accessibility ramp for Harold Brooks, one of our church members who's having hip surgery next week," Matt explained. "The ramp will allow him to return home safely instead of needing extended care facility placement."

"How long will something like that take to build?"

"With enough volunteers, we can complete it in one Saturday," Matt said. "The key is having the materials ready, and the work organized efficiently."

"My husband is retired, and he'd love to help with a project like that," the woman said, writing her contact information on their volunteer sheet. "He was a carpenter for forty years."

As she walked away, Megan touched Matt's arm gently. "You're really good at this."

"Good at what?"

"Talking to people about the ministry. Making them understand why the work matters." Megan arranged the growing pile of food donations with careful attention to organization. "You have a gift for helping people see how they can make a difference."

Matt's smile made her pulse quicken. "I learned from watching you. You make everyone feel needed and welcomed."

The festival atmosphere grew more festive as the morning progressed. The carousel near the town square began playing cheerful music, the scent of barbecue smoke drifted from food trucks, and children's laughter echoed from the pumpkin painting station that had been set up in the library's front yard. Megan stole glances at Matt throughout the morning, watching the way he interacted with their visitors, the careful attention he paid to Graham's stories about their childhood, and the gentle way he helped elderly visitors navigate around their booth setup.

"Megan! Matt!"

Megan turned at the familiar sound of Ruthanne's voice and saw David's parents walking toward the booth, Lauren skipping happily between them. Ruthanne's silver hair framed her face in a neat bob, and her cardigan—rich in autumn shades—made her look every bit the picture of fall comfort. Beside her, Henry stood tall and steady, his kind eyes glinting behind wire-rimmed glasses.

"Henry, Ruthanne," Megan said warmly, stepping around the table to greet them. "I didn't expect to see you until later this afternoon."

"We couldn't resist bringing this young lady by a little early," Ruthanne said with a grandmother's twinkle in her gaze. "She's been talking about the carnival rides since breakfast."

"Mommy!" Lauren launched herself into Megan's arms, nearly breathless with excitement. "Grandma made pancakes shaped like pumpkins, and Grandpa taught me a new card game, and we saw the Ferris wheel, and there's a booth with cotton candy that looks like pink and purple clouds!"

"Sounds like you've had quite an adventurous day already," Megan said, smoothing Lauren's hair with maternal affection. "Are you having fun with Grandma and Grandpa?"

"The best fun!" Lauren grinned, then turned her bright gaze toward Matt. "Hi, Matt! Are you helping Mommy with her church work?"

"I am," Matt said, his voice steady but gentle. "We're collecting donations to help families in town."

Henry reached for Matt's hand, his grip firm. "That's good work, son. It's been too long since we've seen you."

"Yes, sir," Matt replied with quiet respect. "It's good to be home—and good to see you both."

"We've heard quite a lot about you from this little chatterbox," Ruthanne said with a knowing smile, placing her hand on Lauren's shoulder. "She talks about your visits and the stories you tell and how you fixed Mommy's sink."

Megan felt a flush rise in her cheeks under their careful, knowing glances. She cleared her throat softly. "Matt's been a real blessing to our ministry team since moving back."

Henry nodded. "David always spoke highly of his friends—especially you, Matt."

"I'm sure he has," Henry said. "David always spoke highly of his close friends, especially you, Matt."

At the mention of David, a hush seemed to settle over the group. Matt's expression grew more thoughtful, his voice low but sure. "David was the best man I ever knew. I miss him every day."

Ruthanne's face softened, her eyes misting with both sorrow and peace. "We miss him too. His absence will always leave a space... but I believe God called him home in His time. That truth has carried us."

"Can we ride the Ferris wheel now?" Lauren asked brightly, her child's heart untouched by the heaviness.

"Of course, sweetheart," Ruthanne said, her voice warm again. She looked back at Matt and Megan. "We just wanted to stop by, welcome Matt home, and check on your booth."

"It's doing great," Graham chimed in, his tone proud. "We've already raised over a hundred dollars so far."

"Excellent." Henry pulled his wallet from his pocket and slipped two twenty-dollar bills free. "Add this to the total."

"Thank you," Megan said, accepting the donation with heartfelt gratitude. "Your support means the world to our ministry."

Ruthanne lingered for a moment beside Matt. Her gaze was steady, kind but unflinching.

"Young man," she said softly, "David would want the people he loved to be happy. That includes you. Remember that."

Matt's throat tightened. He inclined his head with quiet respect. "Yes, ma'am."

"Have fun, sweetheart," Megan called after Lauren, who waved before the trio disappeared into the crowd.

"That went well," Graham said, breaking the thoughtful silence. A grin tugged at the corner of his mouth as he nudged Matt. "Face it—Ruthanne Miller just gave you her blessing, big brother. And trust me, I know what family approval looks like."

The afternoon slipped by in a blur as the festival swelled with people. Their booth saw a steady stream of visitors—some dropped coins and bills into the donation jar, others carried bags of canned goods, and many lingered simply to chat about upcoming projects and community needs.

Megan became more and more aware of Matt's nearness—the way their hands brushed when they both reached for an envelope, the quiet rhythm they had fallen into as they managed the booth side by side, and the easy laughter that rose whenever Graham added his wry observations about festivalgoers.

"Five minutes until four o'clock," Matt announced after glancing at his watch, just as a group of teenagers walked off, leaving behind an armful of canned vegetables.

"I can't believe how quickly the day has gone," Megan said, her eyes sweeping over the growing stack of boxes with a sense of wonder. "We've collected more than I ever hoped."

"That's because you two make an excellent team," Graham said as he straightened items on the table. "You complement each other's strengths."

Before Megan could reply, Pastor Andrew and Lily Whitman approached, their purposeful stride carrying the ease of people ready to step in without missing a beat.

"Good afternoon," Pastor Andrew greeted, his warm smile as steady as ever. "Looks like you've had a fruitful day."

"Beyond our expectations," Megan said, gesturing toward the full collection boxes. "The community's response has been incredible."

As they wrapped up the handover—walking the Whitmans through the system, pointing out the sign-up sheets, and reviewing the informational flyers—Megan felt a flutter of anticipation in her chest. The official work of the day was over, and for the first time she realized she and Matt could enjoy the festival as participants instead of volunteers.

"Thank you for serving today," Pastor Andrew said as Graham gathered his things. "The ministry is blessed through your dedication."

"Our pleasure," Matt replied. But even as he spoke, his gaze had drifted to Megan, who was tugging off her "Volunteer" badge and smoothing a stray lock of hair.

With the booth safely in evening hands, Megan found herself at a crossroads. She could say goodbye to Matt, collect Lauren from her grandparents, and slip into the familiar rhythm of mother-and-daughter festival fun. Or she could take a risk and suggest they explore the festival together.

"Matt," she said, her voice catching just slightly. "Would you walk around the festival with me?"

"I thought you'd never ask."

Without overthinking, she reached for his hand.

His fingers closed around hers immediately, warm and strong and exactly right.

"Come on," she said, grinning back at him as she pulled him away from the Hands of Grace booth and into the crowd of festival-goers. "Let's see what we've been missing."

Chapter 18

The evening air had grown crisp as Matt and Megan walked around the festival; her hand felt warm and sure in his. String lights began to twinkle to life above the vendor booths, casting everything in a warm glow that made the autumn decorations look like something from a storybook. The scent of pumpkin donuts and caramel apples scented the air from nearby food stands.

"Where to next?" Megan asked, her face tilted up toward his with an expression of pure delight that made Matt's chest tighten with something he hadn't felt in years.

"Wherever you want," he said, meaning it completely. "I'm just happy to be here with you."

She squeezed his hand, and Matt felt the simple gesture all the way to his heart. Around them, families strolled between booths while children darted ahead with sticky fingers and bright laughter, their parents calling gentle warnings about staying close. The carousel played its cheerful melody, and somewhere in the distance, Matt could hear the beginning notes of live music drifting from the direction of the town square.

"Candied apples," Megan announced suddenly, pointing toward a booth decorated with orange and red streamers where a vendor was dipping fresh apples into glossy caramel. "I haven't had one in years."

"Since high school?" Matt asked, guiding her toward the stand.

"Probably. Remember when we used to come to these festivals when we were teenagers? You, David, Heather, and I would spend our allowance money on the most ridiculous carnival food."

"David always got those enormous turkey legs, and you always went straight for anything involving caramel or chocolate."

"And you always went for--"

"Funnel cakes, every single time."

Megan laughed, the sound bright and unguarded. "I bet you still have a weakness for funnel cake."

"Guilty as charged," Matt admitted as they reached the candied apple vendor, a cheerful woman in her sixties wearing an apron decorated with autumn leaves.

"Evening, folks," the vendor called. "What can I get you? We've got traditional caramel, chocolate-dipped, or caramel with crushed peanuts."

"Two caramels, please," Matt said, reaching for his wallet.

"Make mine chocolate," Megan corrected with a grin. "I'm feeling adventurous tonight."

As the vendor prepared their apples, Matt studied Megan's profile in the warm light from the booth's lanterns. Her cheeks were pink from the cool air, and her eyes sparkled with the kind of joy he'd forgotten existed until she'd walked back into his life. She looked younger somehow, less careful, as if the evening had given her permission to set aside her usual responsibilities and simply enjoy herself.

"Here you go," the vendor said, handing them their treats wrapped in wax paper. "Beautiful evening for the festival."

"Perfect evening," Matt agreed, accepting the change and guiding Megan away from the booth.

They found a quiet spot near the edge of the square, away from the heaviest foot traffic but still close enough to watch the festival activity swirl around them. Megan took a careful bite of her chocolate-covered apple, closing her eyes in exaggerated bliss.

"Oh, this is exactly as wonderful as I remembered," she said, offering Matt a taste. "Try it."

Matt leaned forward and took a small bite of her apple. The chocolate was rich and sweet, but he barely noticed. What held his attention was Megan—cheeks pink from the cool air, eyes sparkling with unguarded joy.

"Good?" she asked.

"Perfect," Matt said, his eyes meeting hers.

The moment stretched between them, charged with possibilities and the kind of awareness that made Matt's pulse quicken. Around them, the festival continued its cheerful chaos, but for a few heartbeats, it felt like they were the only two people in the world.

"Matt! Megan!"

The spell broke as Graham approached with his cousin Sue from the pizza restaurant, both of them carrying corn dogs and wearing the satisfied expressions of people enjoying a night away from work responsibilities.

"Look at you two," Graham said with obvious delight, "acting like teenagers on their first date."

"Graham," Matt warned, but his tone held no real irritation.

"What? It's adorable," Sue said with a grin. "The whole town's been rooting for you two."

"The whole town?" Megan asked.

"Honey, did you forget where you live? This is Laurel Ridge," Sue said.

They chatted for a few more minutes, catching up on Sue's plans for expanding her restaurant's menu, before they moved on toward the ring toss game. Matt watched them go, then turned back to Megan with an expression of amused resignation.

"Small-town life takes some getting used to when you've been away for twelve years. Nothing slips past anyone." Matt said.

"I don't mind," Megan said. "It's actually kind of sweet, knowing people care enough to want us to be happy."

They resumed their leisurely stroll through the festival, sharing bites of their apples and pointing out booth displays that caught their attention. In the craft section, Megan admired hand-knitted scarves in jewel tones while Matt examined woodworking demonstrations. They stopped to watch children try their luck at a duck pond game, laughing at the determined concentration on youthful faces as small hands maneuvered plastic hooks toward floating prizes.

"Remember when we were their age?" Megan asked as they moved away from the game booth. "Everything seemed so important, so urgent. Getting the prize was a matter of life and death."

"Some things never change," Matt observed. "Just look at how seriously that little boy is approaching the ring toss."

"True. But I think we understand now that the fun is in the trying, not just the winning."

Matt glanced at her sideways. "Is that what this is between you and me? Trying?"

Megan's step faltered slightly, and she looked up at him with eyes that held hope. "Yes. And so far... it feels like winning."

They'd wandered toward the town square, where a small stage had been set up for live music. A local country band was performing versions of popular songs, their voices harmonizing beautifully in the crisp evening air. Couples swayed together in the open space in front of the stage while children chased each other between the dancers, and families sat on blankets spread across the grass.

"This is nice," Megan said, settling onto an empty bench at the edge of the square. "I love watching people enjoy themselves."

Matt sat beside her, close enough that their shoulders touched. "You're good at that."

"Good at what?"

"Finding joy in other people's happiness. It's one of the things I've always admired about you."

"Always?" Megan turned to face him more fully. "Even back in high school?"

"Especially back in high school. You had this way of making everyone around you feel included, valued. David used to say you could make friends with a fence post if you set your mind to it."

At the mention of David, Megan's expression grew more thoughtful, but not sad. "He was the same way. Maybe that's why you two got along so well."

"Maybe. Though I think my reasons for appreciating your kindness have changed over the years."

"How so?"

Matt took a breath, choosing his words carefully. "In high school, I appreciated it because it made you a good friend to have around. Now... now I appreciate it because it makes you the kind of woman a man could build a life with."

Megan's eyes widened, and Matt wondered if he'd pushed too hard, revealed too much too soon.

"Matt," she said softly, "that's... that's a beautiful thing to say."

"It's true."

"I know. That's what makes it beautiful."

They sat in comfortable silence for a while, watching the festival activity swirl around them. The music drifted over from the stage—gentle country ballads that spoke of love and home and second chances.

"Megan," Matt said suddenly, the idea forming as he spoke, "would you and Lauren like to go to Whitaker Farms next Friday? They have pumpkin picking, hayrides, and a corn maze. All the traditional fall activities."

Megan's face lit up. "Lauren would love that. She's been talking about wanting to pick our own pumpkins for Halloween."

"Then it's a date," Matt said, then caught himself. "I mean, if you want it to be a date. Or it could just be... friends spending time together. Whatever you're comfortable with."

"Matt," Megan said, reaching over to cover his hand with hers, "I'd like it to be a date. I think we're in the solid dating phase now."

The relief that washed over him was almost overwhelming. "Good. Great. I'll pick you both up Friday evening after I close the store."

"We'll be ready."

As they sat together, planning their upcoming outing and watching families enjoy the surrounding festival, Matt felt a deep contentment that came from being exactly where he belonged, with exactly the right person.

The band on the stage transitioned into a slower song, something tender and romantic that made several couples stand up and move closer to dance. Matt watched them with interest, remembering high school dances and the awkward, wonderful ritual of asking girls to dance.

He was still lost in memory when Megan suddenly stood up, startling him.

"What—" he began, turning to look at her.

"I love this song. Dance with me."

She held out her hand, and Matt felt his heart do something complicated in his chest. Around them, other couples swayed together under flickering string lights, but all he could see was Megan standing there with her hand extended, asking him to dance as if it were the most natural thing in the world.

He stood and took her hand, allowing her to lead him toward the other dancers. She stepped into his arms with a grace that took his breath away, her hand settling on his shoulder while his found the small of her back. They began to move together to the gentle rhythm of the music, and Matt was amazed at how perfectly they fit together, how natural it felt to hold her this way.

"Thank you," Megan murmured against his ear as they swayed together.

"For what?"

"For coming back home. For being patient with me. For making me remember what it feels like to be young again and wanted."

Matt closed his eyes, breathing in the scent of her perfume. As they danced together under the autumn stars, surrounded by the gentle sounds of their community enjoying the festival, he sent up a silent prayer of thanks to God for the beautiful, kind woman He had placed back in his life.

Chapter 19

"This one's too lumpy," Lauren announced, abandoning her third potential pumpkin candidate and skipping ahead through the sprawling pumpkin patch at Whitaker Farms. "I want one that's round and not all bumpy for my jack-o'-lantern face."

Megan laughed as she watched her daughter dart between the orange spheres scattered across the field, her small hands testing each possibility with the serious consideration of someone making a life-altering decision. The late afternoon September sun cast everything in golden light, and the air carried the sweet scent of hay and the crisp promise of autumn evenings ahead.

"She's very particular about her pumpkins," Matt observed, his warm hand finding Megan's as they followed Lauren's zigzag path through the patch.

"She gets that from me," Megan admitted. "I was the same way when I was her age. My parents used to spend hours at pumpkin patches while I searched for the perfect one."

"And did you ever find it?"

"Every single year," Megan said with a grin. "Though looking back, I'm pretty sure my dad helped by steering me toward the ones he knew would be easiest to carve."

They'd been at Whitaker Farms for over an hour already, having arrived just after school let out for the day.

"Matt!" Lauren called from where she'd discovered a promising cluster of pumpkins near a weathered fence post. "Come help me decide!"

Matt squeezed Megan's hand before releasing it, jogging toward Lauren. Megan watched him crouch down beside her daughter, giving serious consideration to Lauren's detailed comparison of two nearly identical pumpkins.

"This one has a better stem," Lauren explained, pointing to the pumpkin on her left, "but this pumpkin is more orange."

"And which one do you think would be better for carving?"

"The stem, one. You need a good handle to take the top on and off."

"Excellent logic. I think the left one wins."

Lauren beamed at his approval, then reached up for Matt's hand as she stood up.

"Will you carry it?" she asked. "It looks heavy."

"Of course," Matt said, bending to scoop up the pumpkin while keeping hold of Lauren's small hand.

When Megan approached, Lauren immediately reached for her hand as well, creating a chain of connection that made Megan smile. Here they were—the three of them holding hands in a pumpkin patch, looking for all the world like a family that had always belonged together.

"Now we need to find pumpkins for you and Mommy," Lauren declared, swinging their joined hands as they walked deeper into the patch.

"What kind should we look for?" Matt asked.

"Big ones. And maybe... some little ones for decorating the front porch."

As they wandered through the field, testing pumpkins and debating the merits of various shapes and sizes, Megan smiled as she watched Lauren and Matt debating pumpkins like seasoned experts. When Lauren declared that, as a grown-up, he needed a "really, really big one," Matt spent ten patient minutes helping her find the largest pumpkin in the patch.

"This one is perfect!" Lauren announced, patting a pumpkin that was indeed impressively large. "It's huge!"

"It's definitely going to make a spectacular jack-o'-lantern," Megan agreed, watching Matt test the weight of Lauren's selection.

"It's substantial," he said with mock seriousness. "I think we'll need the wagon to get this one back to the truck."

They collected two more medium-sized pumpkins and several smaller decorative ones before loading everything into the red wagon Lauren had spotted that had been left nearby. As Matt pulled the wagon with Lauren skipping happily at his side, Megan felt a wave of contentment so deep it nearly stole her breath.

This was what she'd imagined during those lonely evenings when Lauren was smaller and she wished for someone to share the parenting moments with. Matt wasn't just being polite; he was engaged—asking about her friends at school, nodding along to her grand Halloween decorating ideas, and giving her the kind of attention that made her entire face light up.

"Hayride next?" Matt suggested as they deposited their pumpkins in his truck after paying for them.

"Yes!" Lauren bounced on her toes. "Can we sit in the front of the wagon?"

"We can sit wherever you want," Matt assured her.

Once they boarded, Lauren scrambled onto Matt's lap without hesitation, tucking herself against his chest as if she'd always belonged there. Megan settled beside them on the hay bale, and Matt slipped his free arm around her shoulders, drawing her gently against his side.

The wagon jolted forward, pulled by a vintage red tractor that chugged along winding dirt paths through fields of corn and pastures dotted with grazing cattle. Lauren's excited chatter spilled over to the families around them as she pointed out the cows and the blaze of color in the trees edging the path.

"Comfortable?" Matt murmured near Megan's ear, his breath warm against her skin.

"Perfect," she answered, and she meant it.

The ride bumped steadily along as the driver called out landmarks and shared bits of farm history. Lauren peppered him with questions about everything they passed—from the horses grazing in a distant field to the weathered old barn and silo. Matt answered what he could and encouraged her curiosity when he didn't know, drawing the other riders easily into the conversation.

"Look at those trees," Megan said softly, pointing toward a grove of maples that blazed brilliant red against the blue sky. "I never get tired of autumn in West Virginia."

"It's beautiful," Matt agreed, his arm tightening gently around her shoulders. "I missed this when I was in the service, especially overseas."

"Did you miss home a lot?" Lauren asked, tilting her face up toward him.

"Every day," Matt answered honestly. "But especially in autumn. Fall was always my favorite season growing up."

"It's my favorite too," Lauren said with great satisfaction. "Because of Halloween, and pumpkins, and candy, and pretty leaves."

"All excellent reasons," Matt said with a smile.

As the hayride rolled on, Megan let herself sink fully into the comfort of Matt's arm. Her head rested easily against his shoulder while Lauren pointed at cloud shapes and peppered the driver with questions about the tractor. The afternoon sun was warm on her face, and the gentle motion of the wagon combined with Matt's steady presence created a sense of peace that wrapped around her like a favorite old quilt.

And in that quiet, Megan realized—this was happiness. Not the cautious contentment she had carefully pieced together over the past few years, but genuine joy. The kind that welled up from deep inside and made her believe, for the first time in a long time, that anything was possible.

"Corn maze time!" Lauren announced as they climbed down from the wagon twenty minutes later.

The corn maze spread across several acres, with paths winding through tall stalks that towered over their heads. A sign at the entrance warned that it typically took between thirty and forty-five minutes to find the exit, depending on problem-solving skills and luck.

"Stay together," Megan cautioned as they entered the maze. "It's easy to get separated in here."

"I'll keep track of both my girls," Matt said with a grin that made Megan's pulse quicken.

His girls. The casual possessiveness in those words sent warmth spreading through her chest.

The maze was designed with clever dead ends and false paths that had them doubling back multiple times. Lauren treated it like the greatest adventure imaginable, running ahead to scout upcoming turns and reporting back on what she could see. At one point, Matt hoisted her onto his shoulders without being asked, letting her serve as their lookout.

"Left," Lauren instructed from her perch. "And then it gets twisty."

"You're an excellent navigator," Matt told her, steadying her with careful hands as they walked.

They fell into an easy rhythm: Megan tracked their attempted routes, Matt provided Lauren with a higher vantage point, and Lauren offered enthusiastic commentary on everything they passed. At each tricky intersection, the three of them huddled together to debate their options, letting Lauren cast the deciding vote.

"This way!" she declared at one especially confusing junction, pointing confidently down a path that looked identical to the others.

"You sure?" Matt teased.

"Yep," Lauren said with seven-year-old certainty.

Fifteen minutes later, her confidence was rewarded. They stepped into the central clearing, where picnic tables and a small concession stand welcomed successful navigators. Matt eased Lauren down from his shoulders, and she immediately flung her arms around both of them.

"We did it!" she cheered. "We're the best mazers ever!"

"Absolutely the best," Matt agreed, returning her hug while his eyes met Megan's.

"Apple cider?" Megan suggested, nodding toward the concession stand.

"With cinnamon?" Lauren asked hopefully.

"Definitely with cinnamon."

They settled at one of the picnic tables with steaming cups of cider and warm apple cider donuts, watching new families disappear into the maze. The sun sagged lower in the sky, stretching long shadows across the farm and bathing everything in the golden glow that made autumn evenings feel touched with magic.

"Can we come back here again?" Lauren asked around a bite of donut. "And maybe bring Grandma and Grandpa? And Heather?"

"We'll have to see what everyone's schedule looks like," Megan said.

"Matt, will you come back with us?" Lauren asked directly.

"I'd love to," he said without hesitation.

As they finished their cider and gathered their things, Megan felt a bittersweet tug in her chest. She leaned closer as Matt slipped his arm around her shoulders on the walk back toward the truck.

"Thank you," she said softly.

"For what?"

"For this. For being so good to Lauren. For making today perfect."

Matt's answering smile held a warmth that made her feel like the most cherished woman in the world. "No thanks needed... all I want is to make you and Lauren happy. Your smiles are enough."

As they climbed into the truck for the drive back to town, with Lauren already chattering about her pumpkin-carving plans and the Halloween decorations they could make together, Megan let herself imagine a future where days like this weren't special occasions, but simply the rhythm of their life together.

The thought filled her with such deep happiness that she couldn't stop smiling.

Chapter 20

The sound of hammers and cordless drills filled the crisp late September morning as Matt knelt beside the freshly constructed frame of Harold Brooks' wheelchair ramp, checking the alignment of the support joists one final time. Around him, a dozen Hands of Grace volunteers worked together, their voices mixing with the mechanical sounds of construction in a symphony of purposeful activity.

"How's the spacing on those joists?" Earl called from where he was cutting lumber on the portable table saw they'd set up in Harold's driveway.

"Perfect dad," Matt replied, running his hands along the smooth wood. "Sixteen inches on center, just like the plan."

"Good man. Your military precision is showing."

Matt smiled at his father's approval, then glanced over to where Megan was carefully measuring the next section of decking boards. She had a pencil tucked behind her ear and wore work gloves that were slightly too big for her hands.

"Need help with those measurements?" he asked, moving to crouch beside her.

"I think I've got it," Megan said, double-checking her marks against the measuring tape. "Twelve feet, six inches for this section, right?"

"Right. Good work. Want me to show you how to make the cut?"

Her eyes lit with curiosity. "With the circular saw?"

Matt nodded. "Yep. It's quicker and cleaner for boards this size, as long as you set it up right."

He showed her how to steady the board on sawhorses, clamp it in place, and line up the saw with her pencil mark. "Keep a firm grip, but don't fight it," he explained. "Let the saw do the work. And always check where your cord is before you start."

Megan listened intently, nodding as she absorbed each instruction.

"Like this?" she asked, mimicking his stance as she placed her hands on the saw's handle.

"Exactly." He adjusted her elbow slightly. "That'll give you more control. You're a natural."

She laughed. "Hardly. But I like learning new things—especially when they're useful."

"Most people are nervous around power tools," Matt said.

"Most people didn't grow up with a father who believed daughters should know how to fix whatever breaks," Megan replied, brushing sawdust from her jeans. "Though I'll admit—circular saws still make me nervous."

"Want me to walk you through it? It's not as scary once you know the safety basics."

"You wouldn't mind?"

"Are you kidding? I love teaching this stuff. And you've got steady hands."

Together they went through the process—checking the blade depth, sighting along the guide, practicing the trigger and guard release. Matt stood close as he talked her through the cut, his hand briefly covering hers to adjust her grip.

When the blade bit smoothly through the board and Megan lifted the finished piece away, her face broke into a triumphant smile. "It's straight!"

"Perfect cut. But the best part is seeing that smile," Matt said with a grin. What struck him most, though, wasn't the cut itself—it was the way she'd trusted him completely, the way her confidence had grown under his guidance, and the quiet satisfaction in her voice that made the moment feel far more significant than just sawing a board.

They worked steadily for the next hour, cutting and fitting decking boards while other volunteers focused on the railing and handrail installation. Pastor Andrew had arrived with his toolkit and was working alongside Earl to anchor the bolts that would secure the ramp to Harold's front steps.

"How's our patient doing?" Pastor Andrew asked during a quick break, wiping sweat from his brow despite the cool morning air.

"Susan called this morning," Sylvia replied, referring to Harold's daughter. "The hip replacement went well, and he's already ahead of schedule in therapy. If he keeps improving, he could be home by Tuesday."

"Then we timed this project perfectly," Megan said with satisfaction.

"He's going to be amazed," Matt added, surveying their progress. "This will give him real independence getting in and out of the house."

"That's the goal," Pastor Andrew agreed. "Harold's been worried about being a burden to Susan. This should give him peace of mind that he can still manage on his own."

As they settled back into work, Matt stole glances at Megan throughout the morning. She'd fallen into a rhythm of measuring, marking, and cutting that dovetailed with his own. When he needed someone to hold the far end of a board, she was there. When she struggled with a heavier piece, he stepped in without being asked. They moved around each other with an ease that surprised him.

"You two work well together," Earl observed approvingly as they fastened the last section of decking. "Takes most couples years to build that kind of unspoken communication."

Heat crept up Matt's neck at the word couples, but when he glanced at Megan, she was smiling.

"We do," she said simply.

"You do," Sylvia agreed, arriving with a cooler of cold drinks. "Watching you is like seeing two pieces of a puzzle fit together."

At lunch, spread out on lawn chairs and tailgates with the sandwiches the church women had provided, Matt turned his mother's words over in his mind. The puzzle piece analogy fit all too well. Working with Megan didn't just feel natural—it felt right. As if they were meant to tackle projects together, to solve problems side by side, to build things that mattered.

"Penny for your thoughts," Megan said quietly, settling into the chair beside his with a sandwich and a bottle of water.

"Just thinking about the project. Harold's going to love this ramp."

"He is. Though I suspect you were thinking about more than the ramp."

Matt studied her face, noting the gentle curiosity in her expression. "Maybe."

"Care to share?"

Matt weighed his words. "I was just thinking about how good it feels to do something that matters. To build something that'll actually help somebody."

"It does feel good," Megan agreed.

He nodded, his gaze lingering on her. "And when you're doing it with the right person..."

Megan tilted her head, finishing softly, "It doesn't feel like work at all."

Their eyes held, and that familiar tightness pressed in Matt's chest with the quiet certainty that she saw him. Really saw him. Not just the Marine who'd come home, or the man running a hardware store, but the deeper part of him—the one that needed to be useful, to serve, to build something that lasted.

The afternoon flew by as they completed the ramp installation, adding final touches like grip tape on the deck surface to prevent slipping in wet weather.

"Harold's going to think professionals did all this," Pastor Andrew said, stepping back to survey their completed work.

"It looks good," Earl agreed, hands on his hips as he studied the finished ramp. "Solid construction, clean finish, properly engineered for the load. Harold will be using this for years to come."

Matt felt a surge of pride at his father's assessment.

As he watched Megan packing up tools, listened to his parents admiring the workmanship, and saw Pastor Andrew snapping photos to show Harold at the hospital tomorrow, Matt was struck by how perfectly this moment captured the life he wanted.

This was community. This was meaningful work. And this—standing beside Megan, surrounded by family and friends—this was love in its truest form, moving past attraction into something deeper and more enduring.

The clarity startled him. He wasn't simply drawn to Megan anymore, or grateful for her friendship and kindness. He loved her. He was in love with the woman now laughing at something his mother had said.

Watching her interact with his family, seeing how naturally she fit into their rhythm, Matt couldn't help imagining what it might look like to keep building a future with her. Marriage, maybe. Lauren calling him Dad. Holiday dinners with Megan at his side.

The images came so vividly that for a moment Matt could almost see it all laid out before him like a blueprint for happiness. But into that clarity intruded another image he hadn't expected.

David.

His friend's face flashed into his mind with startling force—David as a teenager, young and brimming with plans, talking excitedly about the future. David at twenty, certain he'd marry Megan and settle in Laurel Ridge after the service. David at twenty-one, grinning through a computer screen as he told Matt he was going to be a father. David, who never got the chance to hold his daughter, who never came home to build the life he'd dreamed of with the woman he loved.

What would their lives have been if David had lived?

The thought hit Matt like a punch to the chest. Was he building something beautiful, or was he constructing his happiness on the foundation of his best friend's tragedy?

"Matt?"

The voice seemed far away, though he knew Megan was right beside him.

"Matt, are you all right?"

He blinked, awareness returning all at once—Megan's hand resting lightly on his arm, the sounds of cleanup around Harold's yard, the warmth of late-afternoon sun.

"Sorry," he said, shaking his head. "What were you saying?"

"I asked if you'd help me load the leftover lumber into your dad's truck, but you seemed... somewhere else." Her blue eyes searched his face with a tenderness that saw more than he wanted her to. "Are you okay?"

Matt forced a smile he didn't feel. "I'm fine. Just thinking."

"About anything you want to share?"

"Nothing important," he lied. Even as the words left his mouth, he knew the truth: the questions David's memory had stirred were among the most important he'd ever face.

Chapter 21

The food pantry room in the recreation hall behind the Laurel Ridge Community Church hummed with chatter as Megan checked items off her inventory list, surrounded by volunteers sorting donations into carefully organized categories.

The pantry took up the entire back room now—three long rows of steel shelving, two folding tables for sorting, and a hand-lettered sign that read "Hands of Grace" in cheerful block letters. Someone from the youth group had drawn vines of morning glories curling around the edges. It made the whole place feel like hope on a budget.

"Canned vegetables by expiration date," Megan called, as volunteers gathered around. "Green beans and corn together, tomatoes on their own. Pasta and rice go on the second table. If you're not sure where something goes, ask me or Heather."

"Yes, ma'am," Graham said, saluting her with a bag of elbow macaroni. "Captain of carbohydrates reporting for duty."

"Go sort," Megan said, fighting a smile.

Matt had come early. He'd carried in two cases of peanut butter from the truck without being asked and, in classic Matt fashion, set the boxes exactly where she would've wanted them—out of everyone's way but close to the shelf where they belonged. Now he stood with a shy teenager from the youth group, showing her how to line up labels so they faced the same direction. He didn't rush her. He didn't do it for her. He just stood steady at her elbow, letting his quiet presence say, You've got this.

The girl looked up once, uncertain. Matt gave a small nod and a half-smile. She kept going.

Megan felt her heart tug in that now-familiar way, equal parts admiration and something deeper she tried not to name too soon. It would be so easy to fall in love with the way he treated people. It was already happening, if she was honest.

By nine-thirty the room had found its rhythm—paper rustling, cans thudding softly onto metal shelves, the low hum of conversation. Pastor Andrew circulated with a clipboard, checking inventory, jotting down needs. Heather and two ladies from the women's ministry created an assembly line for care packages: pasta, sauce, vegetables, tuna, oatmeal, a bag of flour, a roll of paper towels, bars of soap, and a note card with a handwritten prayer.

Across the room, Matt and Graham were debating whether dinosaur-shaped macaroni counted as protein. Megan rolled her eyes, but her smile lingered. She kept sorting while stealing glances at Matt. He moved with such ease among the volunteers—lifting the heavy boxes, handling the hard tasks as if they were simple, making space for others to shine. His presence lightened the work in ways he probably didn't even notice.

By late morning, the shelves stood full and orderly, a picture of abundance. Pastor Andrew clapped his hands once, drawing the room's attention.

"All right, team," he said. "We've got five food basket deliveries today—two in town, two out on Oak Hollow, and one on Dry Creek Road. Who can help?"

"I can take both on Oak Hollow," Heather offered.

"Graham and I will do the two in town," one deacon volunteered.

Megan scanned the list and lifted her hand. "I'll take the Carter home on Dry Creek Road. She's been on my heart ever since we first heard about her situation."

The young widow had come to the church's attention through the elementary school counselor. Her husband's sudden death in a car accident had left her alone in an unfamiliar town, struggling to pay rent and keep food on the table for two small children. It was exactly the kind of circumstance that reminded Megan why Hands of Grace mattered so deeply—practical service that carried hope right to a doorstep.

"I'll go with you," Matt said.

A smile broke easily across her face. "I was hoping you would."

An hour later, Matt's truck wound along the narrow country roads that twisted upward through the mountains. The food basket rode in the backseat of Matt's truck, filled with shelf-staples—canned vegetables, pasta, rice, oatmeal and snacks kids would enjoy—along with fresh items like milk, bread, and fresh produce that would help stretch a tight grocery budget.

"Lisa's about my age," Megan said quietly as they turned onto the gravel drive. "I can't imagine trying to carry everything alone with two little ones."

"You did it with Lauren," Matt reminded her gently.

Megan shook her head. "I had help—my parents, David's parents, this whole church community. Lisa doesn't have any of that. She's completely on her own in a new town."

The front door opened as they approached the porch, revealing a petite woman with dark circles under her eyes and the kind of weariness that spoke of sleepless nights and constant worry. Two children—a boy who looked about six and a girl perhaps three—clung to her legs, peeking out with shy curiosity.

"Mrs. Carter?" Megan offered a warm smile. "I'm Megan Miller from Laurel Ridge Community Church, and this is Matt Smith. We brought a basket of groceries for you and the kids."

"Please call me Lisa," the woman replied, her voice tired but kind. "This is so generous. You didn't have to come all this way."

"It's our privilege," Matt said, crouching until he was eye-level with the children. "I'm Matt. What are your names?"

The little boy whispered something that sounded like "Tommy," while his sister pressed her face deeper into her mother's skirt.

"Tommy's a good name," Matt said with quiet seriousness. "And I bet your sister has a wonderful name too. She's just being careful with strangers—that's a smart thing."

A flicker of brightness crossed Lisa's face. "Emma's usually our chatterbox. She just needs a little time."

As they carried the food basket inside, Megan observed the small details that told the story of their circumstances—furniture that looked secondhand but was carefully maintained, children's drawings taped to the refrigerator beside a chart tracking expenses, and the kind of careful organization that came from making every dollar count. Lisa had created a home for her children despite the challenges, and Megan felt deep respect for the strength that required.

"This is wonderful," Lisa said as they unpacked the groceries, her voice thick with emotion. "The children have been asking for fresh fruit, and I just couldn't..." She stopped, clearly fighting tears.

"You're doing an amazing job," Matt said quietly, and something in his tone made Megan glance at him. His jaw had tightened slightly, and for a moment his easy smile faltered before returning. "Taking care of your family in difficult circumstances isn't easy."

"Thank you," Lisa whispered. "Both of you. I don't know how to repay this kindness."

A shadow flickered across Matt's expression—so brief Megan almost doubted she'd seen it. His shoulders stiffened, then eased as he answered.

"You don't need to repay a thing," he said. "This is what neighbors do for one another."

While Lisa tucked items into the cupboard, Tommy edged closer to Matt, clutching a toy car in his small hand. "Wanna see my race car?"

"Absolutely," Matt said, lowering himself to the floor without hesitation. Cross-legged, he leaned in as Tommy showed off the car's wheels and sound effects with the eager enthusiasm only a six-year-old could muster. Before long, Emma slipped out from behind her mother's legs, bringing her own treasures to share.

Megan's heart swelled as she watched the scene unfold. Matt didn't just tolerate their chatter—he welcomed it. Somehow he carved out a little pocket of joy in the middle of a weary home.

"Will Daddy be proud of us for sharing our toys with you?" Tommy asked suddenly, the innocent question hitting the room like a stone dropped into still water.

Matt's answer came gently, his voice thick but steady. "I'm sure he would be very proud. You're both brave, and you're both kind. Those are the things that matter most."

He cleared his throat, and Megan sensed the tenderness beneath his calm exterior. The boy's words had touched something deep in him.

Megan turned to Lisa, easing the moment with practical concern. "Do you need anything for winter? Warm coats for the children, or help with heating?"

"We're managing," Lisa replied with the careful pride of someone determined not to ask for more help than absolutely necessary. "The landlord says the heating system works well."

Matt rose to his feet and slipped a card from his pocket. "If you need anything, here's my card. I run Earl's Hardware in town. Don't hesitate to call if you need anything fixed."

Lisa accepted the card as though it were a lifeline. "You're both too kind. I can't tell you what it means—to know people care."

As they prepared to leave, the children wrapped their arms around both Megan and Matt with the uninhibited affection of little ones who had felt safe for a moment. Megan's eyes stung when Tommy whispered, "Thank you for the apples," into her ear. Emma, shy but determined, pressed a crayon drawing of flowers into Matt's hand.

"I'll treasure this," Matt told her with quiet sincerity. For just an instant, Megan caught the same shadow flicker across his eyes as Lisa thanked them once more, her voice unsteady with gratitude.

The ride back to town settled into silence. Matt's hands rested firmly on the steering wheel, his knuckles tight, his gaze fixed on the winding road. Megan studied his profile—the powerful line of his jaw, the way his brow furrowed as though he were carrying something heavy that no one else could see.

"Are you alright?" she asked softly.

He startled slightly, as if he had forgotten she was there. "Yeah," he said, managing a smile that didn't quite reach his eyes. "Just thinking."

"About Lisa and the children?"

His shoulders lifted and fell. "Among other things."

The careful deflection hung between them, leaving a quiet that spoke louder than words. Megan had noticed it all afternoon—tiny pauses, a shift in his voice, the flicker of pain when Tommy had asked about his father. Whatever Matt carried, it wasn't something he was ready to lie down yet.

Her chest ached with a mixture of concern and something deeper. She was falling in love with this man—not only with his steady competence or his kindness, but with the quiet strength that allowed him to hold others up even while he bore his own hidden weight. Watching him with Lisa's children, seeing how he protected their mother's dignity while offering real help, witnessing the way he carved joy out of hardship—it had crystallized into a truth she could no longer ignore.

Her heart had opened fully to Matt Smith.

But love came with awareness too. She could sense the shadows in him, the burdens he carried alone, the unspoken grief that gratitude sometimes seemed to sharpen instead of ease. As the truck wound its way back toward Laurel Ridge, the autumn hills bathed in gold and russet light, Megan sat quietly beside him. She longed to reach across the space between them, not with answers, but with presence. For now, all she could do was pray for the strength to walk beside him when he was ready to share whatever weighed so heavily on his heart.

<h1 style="text-align:center">Chapter 22</h1>

"Any chance the head librarian is free for lunch?" Matt's voice carried the hint of a smile as Megan looked up from the returned books she'd been checking in at the circulation desk.

He stood just inside the library's oak doors, hands tucked into the pockets of his work jacket. The spontaneous nature of his appearance sent a flutter of warmth through Megan's chest.

"That depends," she replied, setting down her date stamp. "What did you have in mind?"

"Martha's Diner. Just thought you might be hungry... and I wanted to spend time with you."

"She's absolutely free," Heather said as she walked toward them.

"Heather—" Megan began.

"Go," Heather insisted, practically shooing them toward the door. "Take a long lunch. The library will survive without its fearless leader."

Matt's grin widened. "I think that's what they call administrative support."

"That's what they call meddling," Megan replied, but she was already reaching for her sweater from behind the desk.

The October afternoon wrapped around them as they stepped outside, crisp and bright with a golden light that made every autumn day feel precious. Maple leaves drifted down from the trees lining Main Street, creating a carpet of red and gold that rustled under their feet as they walked.

"Beautiful day," Matt observed, matching his stride to hers as they headed toward the diner.

"Perfect weather. Lauren's been collecting leaves for a school project, and this morning she announced we have the most beautiful yard in Laurel Ridge because of all the colors."

"She's not wrong. Your oak trees are spectacular this year."

They walked in comfortable quiet for a few steps, and Megan studied Matt's profile, remembering the shadows she'd glimpsed during their visit to Lisa Carter's home. The memory of his troubled expression in the truck afterward had stayed with her for days.

She slipped her hand around his arm and drew a little closer. "Matt," she said softly, "if something's been weighing on your heart, I hope you know you can share it with me. I don't want to pry, but I've sensed that something's been troubling you."

Matt's step faltered slightly, and Megan felt the muscles in his arm tense beneath her touch. For a moment, his easy smile faded, replaced by something more vulnerable and uncertain.

"I appreciate that," he said finally, his voice gentle but careful. "There are just some things I need to work through on my own, you know? But thank you for caring enough to ask."

The deflection was kind but firm, and Megan recognized the boundary he was drawing even as her heart ached to cross it. She squeezed his arm gently, letting him know she understood without pushing for more.

"Always," she said simply.

Martha's Diner buzzed with the comfortable energy of the lunch crowd as they settled into one of the red vinyl booths near the front windows. The familiar surroundings—chrome fixtures, black-and-white photographs, the scent of coffee and home cooking—created an atmosphere of small-town comfort.

"Well, look what the cat dragged in," Martha announced as she approached their table with menus and a knowing smile. "Afternoon, you two. Sweet tea?"

"Please," Megan replied, settling back against the vinyl cushions.

"Make mine coffee," Matt added. "Black."

"Coming right up. And might I suggest the chicken salad sandwich? Made it fresh this morning with grapes and pecans."

As Martha bustled away, Matt leaned back in the booth and let out a contented sigh. "I have to admit, playing hooky from work for a little bit feels pretty good."

"Rough morning?" Megan asked.

"Actually, no. Entertaining, though. Mrs. Andrews came in looking for a specific type of doorknob that she couldn't describe except to say it was 'like the one her grandmother had, but shinier.' Took us twenty minutes and half the hardware aisle to figure out she wanted brushed nickel instead of brass."

Megan laughed, imagining the patient way Matt would have worked through the puzzle with an older adult customer. "Did you find what she needed?"

"Eventually. Though I think she bought three other things, she didn't come in for just because she enjoyed the conversation."

"That's the Earl's Hardware experience. Your dad always says people come for the nails and stay for the therapy."

"Dad's not wrong. Some days I feel like I'm running a counseling service that happens to sell hardware."

Their drinks arrived, followed shortly by Martha herself taking their order rather than sending one of the other servers. Megan relaxed into the easy rhythm of simple conversation—the kind of comfortable exchange that felt both intimate and effortless.

"How was your morning?" Matt asked after they'd ordered their sandwiches.

"Delightful, actually. Mrs. McMahon's first-grade class came for story time, and they were absolutely enchanted by a picture book I read to them about a little owl who was afraid of the dark. Twenty-two six-year-olds hung on every word."

"I can picture that. You probably had them eating out of your hand."

"By the end, they were all making owl sounds and flapping their wings around the children's section. Very dignified library behavior." Megan grinned at the memory. "Though I have to admit, seeing them discover the magic of stories never gets old."

Matt reached across the table, covering her hand with his. "It shows, you know. The way you light up when you talk about the kids and the library."

The simple contact sent warmth through Megan's entire body, and she turned her palm up to intertwine their fingers. This was what she'd been recognizing more clearly each day—not just her growing love for Matt, but her longing for exactly this kind of ordinary everyday interaction. Holding hands across a diner table while talking about work and daily life felt more precious than any fancy dinner could have been.

"Speaking of the library," she said, "I'm deep in planning mode for our fall fundraiser. Stories for Tomorrow—it's our biggest event of the year. I'll be holding a volunteer meeting in a couple of weeks if you'd be interested in helping."

"Of course," Matt replied without hesitation. "Whatever you need."

"I haven't even told you what it involves yet."

"Doesn't matter. If it's important to you, it's important to me."

The simple declaration made Megan's breath catch slightly. She studied his face, noting the sincerity in his blue-gray eyes, the way his thumb traced gentle circles across her knuckles.

"It's not glamorous work," she warned. "Mostly setup, serving refreshments, helping with the silent auction."

"I'm perfectly fine with all of that."

Their sandwiches arrived, temporarily interrupting their conversation as Martha set down plates and refilled their drinks with the practiced efficiency of someone who'd been serving the community for decades.

"You two look mighty content," she observed with obvious approval. "Nothing better than seeing two young people happy together."

"Martha," Megan said with mock exasperation, though her smile betrayed her pleasure at the comment.

"What? I'm just speakin' the truth. The whole town's rootin' for you two. Seeing couples like you just makes my heart happy. Keep it up... I have faith in you both."

As Martha moved on to check other tables, Matt shook his head with amused resignation. "I'm still getting used to small-town life where everyone knows everyone else's business."

"And has opinions about it," Megan added. "But the nice thing is that those opinions usually come from people who genuinely care about your happiness."

"True. Though it's a little unsettling to think Martha's been keeping tabs on us."

"Oh, she's probably been keeping a detailed log."

They ate their sandwiches and talked about everything and nothing—Lauren's upcoming school Halloween party, Matt's plans to winterize his apartment above the hardware store, Megan's ongoing battle with the library's temperamental heating system. The conversation flowed with the kind of ease that made an hour and a half pass like ten minutes, each ordinary topic made special by the simple fact of sharing it together.

When Martha brought their check, Matt insisted on paying despite Megan's protests, and she found herself not arguing too hard. There was something sweetly old-fashioned about the gesture that made her feel cherished in a way she thoroughly enjoyed.

The walk back to the library felt too short, their joined hands swinging gently between them as they strolled down the tree-lined sidewalk. Other pedestrians nodded and smiled as they passed, and Megan realized with a start that she and Matt had become part of the fabric of the town's daily life—a couple people expected to see together, walking hand in hand through the golden autumn afternoon.

"Thanks for lunch," she said as they paused outside the library's brick steps.

"I'm glad you joined me. I know it was spontaneous... I just really wanted to be with you."

"You know... you are just the sweetness man... don't ever stop being like this."

Matt lifted their joined hands and pressed a gentle kiss to her knuckles, the gesture so tender and natural that it made Megan's heart flutter like a teenager's.

"I should let you get back to work," he said, though he made no move to release her hand.

"Probably. Heather's going to want a full report on our lunch date."

"Tell her the chicken salad was excellent, and the company was even better."

As they stood together on the library steps, surrounded by the peaceful afternoon sounds of their small town, Megan felt a deep sense of rightness about everything in her world. Whatever had been troubling Matt over the past few days seemed lighter now, and the easy affection between them felt stronger than ever. Looking into his eyes, she could almost see the future they might build together—more spontaneous lunches, more ordinary conversations that felt extraordinarily simple because they were shared.

The October breeze stirred the surrounding leaves, and Megan reluctantly stepped back toward the library doors, knowing that this perfect moment would carry her through the rest of her workday.

Chapter 23

The afternoon lull at Earl's Hardware had settled into the kind of comfortable quiet that Matt had come to appreciate during his first months back in civilian life. Outside, the October wind rustled through the maple trees lining Main Street, occasionally sending bright leaves spiraling past the front windows. Inside the store, inventory spreadsheets waited on the counter beside his half-empty coffee cup, but Matt found himself staring out at the street instead of focusing on the numbers.

"Son, you okay?" Earl asked from where he sat behind the register, his coffee steaming in the afternoon light.

"Sure, Dad,... I'm fine," Matt turned away from the window, genuinely surprised.

"You've seemed pretty happy these past few weeks. I noticed you've been quieter, though, for the past couple of days."

"Really, Dad. I'm good." Matt abandoned the inventory paperwork and moved to lean against the counter, accepting the conversation his father was offering. "Things have been... good lately."

"Good, how?"

"Just good. Work, life, settling back into civilian routines." Matt took a sip of his coffee. "I'm finally finding my place here again."

Earl studied his son's face. "This wouldn't have anything to do with Megan Miller, would it?"

"Maybe," Matt admitted.

"Maybe's not much of an answer, son."

Matt set down his coffee cup and looked directly at his father. "All right. Yes. It has everything to do with Megan."

"Go on."

"I feel like I'm seventeen again and discovering what it means to want to impress someone. I feel like I've been sleepwalking for twelve years and I'm finally awake. I feel like..." He paused, searching for words adequate to describe the transformation Megan had brought to his daily life. "I feel like I understand why people write songs about falling in love."

Earl's smile started slowly, spreading across his features with obvious satisfaction. "That's a powerful feeling."

"It is. And it terrifies me."

"Why?"

Matt ran his hands through his hair. "Because she was David's wife."

The admission hung between them like a bridge neither of them was sure they should cross. Earl was quiet for a long moment, his expression growing more serious as he processed the complexity his son had just revealed.

"David's been gone seven years," Earl said finally.

"I know that. But knowing it and feeling right about it are two different things." Matt pushed away from the counter, beginning to pace the narrow space behind the register. "He was my best friend,

Dad. My brother in every way that mattered. We were supposed to come home together, supposed to raise our kids as cousins, supposed to--"

"But that's not how life worked out."

"No. Life worked out with David dying in a training accident while I was half a world away, safe on a different base. Life worked out with me coming home to the future he was supposed to have."

Earl was silent, letting his son work through the words that had clearly been building pressure for weeks.

"And now," Matt continued, "I'm in love with his widow. I'm becoming a father figure to his daughter. I'm taking over the life he should have lived." His voice cracked slightly. "How is that not a betrayal of everything our friendship meant?"

"Is that what you think you're doing? Taking over David's life?"

"Aren't I? That's what it feels like." Matt stopped pacing, facing his father with eyes that held genuine anguish. "Megan, Lauren, this town, this community—they were all supposed to be his. He made plans, Dad. He talked about coming home and raising his family here, about working with you and me here at the store, about coaching Lauren's softball team when she got old enough. Everything I'm doing now, everything I want for my future, was supposed to be his future."

Earl stood slowly, moving to stand beside his son with the steady presence that had anchored Matt through every crisis of his childhood. "Son, you're thinking about this all wrong."

"How should I be thinking about it?"

"Like a man who understands the difference between honoring someone's memory and limiting his own life in their honor."

Matt stared at his father, processing words that carried more weight than their simplicity suggested.

Earl continued, his voice gentle but firm. "David Miller was a good man who loved his wife and daughter more than his own life. You know what he'd want for them?"

"What?"

"He'd want them to be happy. He'd want Megan to find love again with someone who would treasure her and Lauren both. He'd want his daughter to have a father figure who would love her unconditionally." Earl placed a weathered hand on Matt's shoulder. "And if that man happened to be his best friend—someone he trusted completely, someone he knew would honor his memory while building something new—don't you think that would give him peace rather than pain?"

The logic was sound, but Matt's heart continued to wrestle with doubts that felt bone deep. "What if I'm just... convenient? What if she's choosing me because I'm familiar, because I remind her of him?"

"Do you honestly believe that, son?"

Matt thought about Megan's face when she laughed at his jokes, the way she listened to his stories about adjusting to civilian life, the careful attention she paid when he talked about his hopes for the future. He thought about the trust in her eyes when she let him teach her to use the circular saw, the warmth in her voice when she'd told him he was the sweetest man she knew.

"No," he said quietly.

"Then what's really bothering you?"

Matt was quiet for a long moment, staring out the front window at the autumn afternoon while he tried to name the fear that had been growing alongside his happiness.

"I think I'm afraid that if I let myself love her completely, if I let myself want the life we could have together, then David really will be gone forever. Like accepting happiness means forgetting him."

Earl nodded slowly. "Matt, a man can fix a lot with his hands, but some things only God can mend. Your heart's been broken since David died, and healing that kind of hurt isn't something you can accomplish with willpower and good intentions."

"Then how?"

"By trusting that God's grace is big enough to include second chances. By believing that healing doesn't mean forgetting, and that honoring David's memory might mean living fully rather than limiting yourself." Earl's voice carried the quiet authority of someone who'd walked through his own valleys of loss and doubt. "David would want you to be happy, son. The question is whether you're going to let yourself believe that."

Matt stared into his coffee cup, watching the dark surface reflect the overhead lights. His father's words made sense intellectually, but the guilt in his chest felt heavier than logic could lift.

"I love her, Dad," he said finally, the admission coming out rough and honest. "I love Megan in ways that scare me because they feel so... permanent. So serious. And I love Lauren like she's my daughter. But every time I let myself imagine the life we could have together, I feel like I'm stepping into shoes that were never meant for me."

"Those shoes don't belong to David anymore," Earl said gently. "They belong to whoever's brave enough to fill them with his own love, his own commitment, and his own way of caring for those girls."

The bell above the front door chimed, announcing the arrival of a customer, and Earl rose to help them with the courtesy that had made Earl's Hardware a community institution. Matt watched his father engage with the customer—answering questions about winterizing outdoor faucets, offering advice about pipe insulation, providing exactly the kind of practical wisdom that people had come to depend on.

As the customer left with his purchases and words of thanks, Matt realized that his father had spent most of his life building something that mattered to people, creating a business that served the community's needs while supporting his own family. Earl had figured out how to balance loyalty to tradition with openness to change, how to honor the past while building something meaningful for the future.

Maybe that was what Matt needed to learn—not how to choose between David's memory and his own happiness, but how to hold both with open hands and trust that love could multiply rather than diminish when it was shared freely.

But as he returned to his inventory spreadsheets while Earl helped another customer, Matt carried with him the weight of unresolved questions that felt too important to answer hastily. His father's wisdom offered direction, but the final steps of the journey were one's Matt would have to take alone, in his own time, with his own courage.

Chapter 24

"Knock, knock." Matt said as he tapped on the frame of Megan's open office door.

She looked up from the stack of book orders spread across her desk to find him standing in her doorway with a brown paper bag from Martha's Diner in one hand and a boyish grin on his face. The sight of him there, unexpected and welcome, made her heart lift like a bird taking flight.

"Matt," she said, her face breaking into a smile. "What are you doing here?"

"Thought you might be hungry," he replied, holding up the take-out bag.

"You brought me lunch?"

"I wanted to see you," Matt said with the kind of honesty that still had the power to make Megan's pulse quicken. "And I figured you probably hadn't eaten yet."

Megan glanced at the clock on her wall, surprised to discover it was already past one o'clock. "You're absolutely right. I got caught up in budget reports and completely lost track of time."

She quickly cleared space on her desk, moving the financial paperwork aside to make room for whatever Martha had packed for them. Matt settled into Heather's chair across from her desk.

"Where's Heather?" Matt asked as he unpacked containers of what smelled like Martha's chicken and dumplings along with fresh rolls and two pieces of pie.

"Reference desk duty. Monday afternoons are always busy with students working on research projects." Megan accepted the plastic fork he handed her, touched by the care he'd taken to bring a complete meal. "This smells wonderful."

"Martha said it was your favorite."

As they settled into eating, Megan filled Matt in on Lauren's excitement about finalizing her Halloween costume—a princess dress complete with a glittery tiara that they'd purchased after much deliberation at the department store in town.

"She's been practicing her curtsy constantly," Megan said with a laugh. "And informing everyone who'll listen that princesses wave with their whole hand, not just their fingers."

"Important distinction," Matt observed with a smile, though Megan noticed it didn't quite reach his eyes the way it usually did.

"She's also decided that our front porch needs to be the 'most beautiful Halloween porch in Laurel Ridge,' which means we spent Sunday afternoon after church arranging the pumpkins we picked at Whitaker Farms along with some corn stalks and autumn flowers. The result is... impressive."

"I'd like to see it," Matt said, but there was something distracted in his tone, as if part of his attention was focused elsewhere.

Megan studied his face as they ate, noting the way his responses came just a beat slower than usual, how his laughter felt slightly forced. The easy contentment that had characterized their interactions over the past weeks seemed muted today, replaced by something she couldn't quite identify.

"Are you alright?" she asked finally, setting down her fork. "You seem... quiet today."

Matt's hand stilled halfway to his mouth, and for a moment his expression grew vulnerable before he attempted a reassuring smile. "Just a lot on my mind."

The deflection felt familiar—the same careful boundary he'd drawn during their walk to lunch last week. But today, something in his tone made Megan's concern deepen into genuine worry.

"Matt," she said gently, leaning forward in her chair. "Something's been troubling you. I can see it, and I can feel it. This entire past week, I've sensed that something's weighing on you. Is there... is there something wrong between us that I'm missing?"

The direct question seemed to hit Matt like a physical blow. He set down his fork and stared at his hands for a long moment before looking up to meet her eyes.

"No," he said with quiet intensity. "Nothing's wrong between us. That's... that's actually what's got me so unsettled."

"I don't understand."

Matt took a deep breath, as if gathering courage for something difficult. "Megan, I've fallen in love with you."

The words hit Megan with stunning force, even though part of her had been hoping to hear them for days now. Her heart began racing, and she felt her breath catch as the simple declaration settled between them.

"You have?"

"Completely. Absolutely. In ways that scare me because they feel s o... permanent." Matt's voice carried a raw honesty that made Megan's chest tighten with emotion. "I wake up thinking about you, and I fall asleep hoping you're having sweet dreams. I want to share every ordinary moment of every ordinary day with you and Lauren."

Tears pricked at Megan's eyes as she absorbed the beauty of his confession. "Matt..."

"I know it happened fast," he continued, his words coming in a rush as if he needed to get them all out before he lost his nerve. "I know we've only been... whatever this is... for a few weeks. But I've never felt anything like this before, and it's overwhelming me how much it means."

"Why does that trouble you?" Megan asked softly, though her heart was singing with joy at his admission.

Matt was quiet for a moment, his expression growing complex in ways that made Megan sense deeper currents beneath his confession.

"Because love this big deserves to be given without hesitation," he said finally. "And I want to be the kind of man who can offer you everything—his whole heart, his complete commitment, his absolute certainty. You deserve nothing less than that."

The statement carried a weight that Megan couldn't quite decipher, as if Matt was confessing both his love and his awareness that something was preventing him from offering it freely.

"Matt," she said, reaching across the desk to take his hand. "Love isn't about having all the answers. Sometimes it's about being brave enough to trust what your heart is telling you, even when your head is still catching up."

Her words seemed to provide some comfort, and Matt's smile grew more genuine as he turned his hand palm-up to intertwine their fingers.

"I do love you," he said. "I needed you to know that."

"I'm so glad you told me," Megan replied, meaning it completely. "Because I love you too."

The admission came out easier than she'd expected. Matt's eyes widened, and for a moment his entire expression transformed into something that looked like wonder.

"You do?"

"I do. I love your kindness, your steady strength, the way you make Lauren light up when you walk into a room. I love how you make ordinary moments feel special just by being present for them." Megan squeezed his hand gently. "I love the man you are, Matt Smith."

Matt stood from Heather's chair and moved around the desk to where Megan sat, pulling her to her feet and into his arms. The hug he gave her was fierce and gentle at the same time, as if he were memorizing the feeling of holding her close.

"Thank you," he murmured against her hair. "For saying that. For feeling that."

"I appreciate your being brave enough to tell me how you feel."

When Matt finally stepped back, he reached up to brush a crumb from her cheek with fingertips that lingered against her skin. Megan's breath caught as she saw something shift in his expression, and for a moment she thought he might kiss her. Instead, he lifted her hand to his lips, pressing a soft kiss to her knuckles that was somehow more intimate than a kiss on the mouth might have been.

"I should let you get back to work," he said, though his reluctance was evident in every word.

"I suppose so. Though this has been the best lunch break I've ever had."

As Matt gathered the empty containers and disposed of them in her office wastebasket, Megan studied his profile again. Despite the beauty of what they'd just shared—his love confession, her own admission, the sweet tenderness of holding each other—she couldn't shake the sense that part of him remained elsewhere, wrestling with something he wasn't ready to discuss.

"Matt," she said as he prepared to leave, "don't forget about the library fundraiser planning meeting this Wednesday at four. I'll need all the help I can get."

"I'll be there," he promised.

"And Matt? Whatever's been weighing on your heart, I hope you know that loving each other doesn't mean carrying burdens alone. Sometimes sharing the load makes everything lighter."

Matt's expression grew soft and grateful, though Megan caught a flicker of something that might have been pain before he nodded. "I'll remember that."

After he left, Megan remained standing in her office, surrounded by the lingering scent of Martha's home cooking and the echoing warmth of Matt's embrace. Her heart felt full enough to burst—he loved her, and she loved him, and for a few precious minutes they'd existed in the perfect bubble of mutual recognition and affection.

But underneath the joy was a thread of concern that she couldn't quite dismiss. Even in the moment of confessing his love, even while holding her and accepting her love in return, Matt had carried shadows in his expression that spoke of struggles he wasn't ready to share. Love had been declared between them, but Megan couldn't escape the growing certainty that something important remained unspoken.

Chapter 25

"Thank you all for coming to help plan our biggest fundraiser of the year," Megan said from her position at the head of the library's conference table, her voice carrying the professional warmth that made people want to volunteer for whatever she was organizing. "I know October is busy for everyone with harvest festivals and Halloween preparations, but your support means everything to the children's reading program here at the library."

Matt settled into one of the folding chairs arranged around the table, nodding politely to the other volunteers who'd gathered for the meeting. Heather sat directly across from him with a yellow legal pad, clearly prepared to take detailed notes. Pastor Andrew had claimed the chair to Megan's right, while several other church members and community supporters filled the remaining seats.

The library's conference room felt warm and inviting despite its utilitarian purpose, with afternoon sunlight streaming through tall windows and the comforting scent of books drifting in from the main collection area. Matt watched Megan as she organized her materials, noting the careful way she'd prepared for this meeting and the obvious excitement in her voice when she talked about the fundraiser's goals.

"Stories for Tomorrow has been our signature event for five years now," Megan continued, consulting the agenda she'd prepared. "We combine a silent auction with readings by local authors, activities for families, and a community potluck dinner. Last year we raised over six thousand dollars for new children's books and reading programs."

"That's impressive," Pastor Andrew said with obvious admiration. "The reading program serves how many children?"

"Nearly four hundred kids throughout Laurel Ridge and the surrounding areas," Megan replied, her face lighting up with passion. "We provide free books for families who can't afford them, fund after-school reading tutoring, and sponsor the summer reading program that keeps kids engaged when school's out."

As Megan outlined the various aspects of the fundraiser—author readings, silent auction items, food service coordination—Matt tried to focus on the practical details she was sharing.

"The event is scheduled for the last Saturday of October, just as it has been for the past five years," Megan said. "This year, that falls on October 30. We'll start setup at noon, open to the public at five, and run until nine in the evening."

October 30th.

The date hit Matt like a punch to the chest, driving the air from his lungs with such force that he gripped the edge of the conference table to steady himself. Around him, the planning conversation continued, but the voices seemed to come from very far away as the significance of that date crashed over him in waves.

October 30th was the anniversary of David's death.

Seven years ago on that exact date, David Miller had died during a routine training exercise when an equipment malfunction had caused a fatal accident. Matt had been stationed half a world away, sleeping peacefully in his bunk while his best friend's life ended in a moment of mechanical failure and terrible timing.

The irony was too brutal to process. Here he was, planning a community celebration with the woman David had loved, getting ready to help raise money for programs that would benefit David's daughter, sitting in a room full of people who remembered David and had watched his widow rebuild her life with quiet dignity. And he was doing it all with growing certainty that he was in love with Megan in ways that felt like stealing something that had never been his to take.

"Matt?" Megan's voice penetrated his spiraling thoughts. "Did you want to help with setup on the day of the event?"

He looked up to find everyone at the table watching him expectantly, clearly waiting for his response to a question he hadn't heard. Megan's expression held gentle concern, and Matt realized his distraction had become obvious.

"Yes," he managed, his voice sounding strange to his own ears. "Whatever you need."

But even as he agreed to help, Matt's mind was reeling with the implications of what he'd just committed to.

How had he not realized the date before now? How had he been so caught up in his growing relationship with Megan that he'd almost forgotten the most significant date of loss in both their lives?

The meeting continued around him, but Matt felt increasingly disconnected from the planning conversation. Instead, his thoughts were pulled inexorably toward memories of David—their high school friendship, their shared military service, the plans David had made for his life with Megan and his future daughter.

I'm going to marry her, Matt. I know we're young, but I know she's the one. When we get back from deployment, I'm going to ask her to marry me properly, with a ring and everything.

David's voice echoed in Matt's memory with painful clarity. They'd been sitting in their barracks overseas, sharing pictures from home and talking about their futures with the kind of certainty that only twenty-year-olds could muster.

And when we have kids, I want you to be their Uncle Matt. You're going to be the best uncle in the world.

Uncle Matt. Not father. Not the man who would teach Lauren to ride bicycles or help her with homework or walk her down the aisle someday. Uncle Matt—the honorary family member who would visit on holidays and birthdays, who would be important but not central to their lives.

Instead, here he was, falling in love with David's widow and developing genuine paternal feelings for David's daughter. The child, who was supposed to call him Uncle Matt, now lit up whenever he walked into a room and had begun seeking his guidance on everything from pumpkin selection to toy preferences.

"For the auction items," Heather was saying, "we've got commitments for artwork, gift baskets, and several dinner certificates from local restaurants. Matt, would Earl's Hardware be able to donate something? Maybe a tool set or home improvement gift card?"

"I'd be happy to contribute," Matt replied automatically.

What would David think if he could see this meeting? Would he be grateful that his best friend was helping to raise money for his daughter's education, or would he be hurt to see Matt sitting in his place, planning community events that he should have been organizing himself?

Promise me something, Matt. If anything ever happens to me, make sure Megan knows how much I loved her. And make sure my kid knows I wanted to be the best father in the world.

The memory of David's voice was so clear it made Matt's hands shake slightly. They'd been having one of those late-night video conference conversations that soldiers sometimes had when deployment stretched long and dangerous, when thoughts turned to home and the people they might never see again.

Matt had promised, of course. He'd promised to deliver messages of love, to offer comfort, to ensure that David's family knew how deeply they'd been cherished. But he'd never promised to fall in love with David's widow. He'd never promised to want to be Lauren's father. He'd never promised to build his future happiness on the foundation of his best friend's truncated dreams.

"The setup crew will need to arrive by noon to arrange tables and chairs," Megan was explaining, her voice carrying the kind of organized enthusiasm that made complex projects seem manageable. "We'll need people to help with decorations, arrange the auction display, and coordinate with the caterers."

October 30th. Setup at noon. Matt tried to imagine himself arriving at the library that day, carrying tables and hanging decorations while internally marking the anniversary of the day his best friend had died. The prospect felt not just difficult but somehow wrong, as if he would be celebrating his own happiness on the very date that had destroyed David's future.

"Any questions about the timeline or volunteer responsibilities?" Megan asked, scanning the faces around the table.

Matt opened his mouth to speak, then closed it again. What could he say? That he'd just realized their community celebration fell on one of the most painful dates of his life? That the joyful event Megan had been planning for months was scheduled for the anniversary of the accident that had made his current happiness possible? Surely she remembered the date, and its significance.

The questions he wanted to ask had no place in a public planning meeting: *How do I help celebrate when I should be mourning? How do I smile and serve dinner when all I can think about is how David should be here instead of me? How do I participate in something meant to benefit his daughter when I'm in love with his wife?*

"Matt?" Megan's voice was gentle, concerned. "You've been quiet. Is everything all right? Do you have any other commitments that day?"

Other commitments. The phrase would have been laughable if it weren't so painful. His only commitment on October 30th was to remember David, to sit with his grief, to acknowledge the anniversary that marked the end of his best friend's dreams and the beginning of the survivor's guilt that had shadowed Matt's life for seven years.

"No other commitments," he said, his voice sounding hollow to his own ears. "The date is... fine."

But it wasn't fine. Nothing about October 30th was fine, and the more Matt thought about it, the less he understood how he'd allowed himself to almost forget the significance of that date. His growing happiness with Megan had created a kind of fog that had obscured his memory, making him believe he could move forward without carrying the weight of the past.

"Wonderful," Megan said with relief.

Matt managed what he hoped was an encouraging smile, but inside his chest, everything felt like it was collapsing. The woman he loved was counting on him to help create a celebration on the anniversary of the tragedy that had made their love possible. The child he adored would benefit from funds raised on the date her father had died. The community that was beginning to accept him as Megan's partner would gather on October 30th to support a cause that David should have been championing himself.

The meeting concluded with task assignments and timeline confirmations, but Matt barely registered the specific details. His signature appeared on volunteer sheets, and his voice offered appropriate responses to logistical questions, but his mind remained fixated on the impossible collision of dates that had just been revealed.

As volunteers gathered their materials and prepared to leave, Megan approached him with the kind of careful attention that suggested she'd noticed his withdrawal.

"Thank you for volunteering to help," she said quietly, her blue eyes studying his face with growing concern. "I know it's a lot, but having you there with me on that day will make everything easier."

"Of course," Matt replied, though the words felt like they belonged to someone else.

"Matt," Megan's voice dropped to barely above a whisper, "are you sure you're all right? You seemed... distant during the meeting."

Distant. The word captured exactly what Matt was feeling—not just physically removed from the planning conversation, but emotionally separated from the happiness he'd been building with Megan over the past weeks. The anniversary date had created a chasm between his love for her and his loyalty to David that he didn't know how to bridge.

"Just tired," he lied, hating himself for the deception even as the words left his mouth. "It's been a long week at the store."

Megan's expression suggested she wasn't entirely convinced, but she didn't press him for a more honest explanation. Instead, she reached out to squeeze his hand gently.

"If you need to talk about anything, you know I'm here. It's the date the fundraiser will take place on that's bothering you, and I get that… trust me, it's not easy on me either," she said with the kind of understanding that made Matt's guilt deepen rather than ease.

"I know," Matt said, squeezing her hand in return while struggling to keep his voice steady.

As the library emptied and Matt walked toward the parking area behind the building, his mind raced with calculations that had nothing to do with lumber measurements or hardware inventory. Seven years since David's death. Seven years that Megan had spent building a life as a single mother. Seven years that Matt had spent trying to make peace with surviving when his best friend hadn't.

And now, with just ten days until the anniversary, Matt was forced to confront the truth: his growing love for Megan and Lauren wasn't just complicated by his history with David—it was built on it. If David hadn't died, Matt would never have had the chance to fall in love with Megan. If that training accident hadn't happened, Lauren would have grown up with her father.

The realization that his happiness was directly connected to David's tragedy felt like carrying lead in his chest. Every smile Lauren gave him, every moment of domestic contentment he shared with Megan, every community celebration where people accepted him as part of their family—all of it was made possible by the accident that had ended David's life.

As Matt climbed into his truck and sat in the library parking lot, surrounded by the golden light of an October afternoon, he felt the weight of an impossible choice settling onto his shoulders. He could continue building toward a future with Megan and Lauren, accepting the happiness they offered while trying to ignore the guilt that came with it. Or he could step back, protecting David's memory by refusing to take what should have been his friend's place in their lives.

The truck engine turned over with reliable efficiency, but Matt remained motionless in the driver's seat, staring through the windshield at the brick building where the woman he loved was probably returning to her office with plans for a celebration that would fall on the worst day of both of their lives.

For the first time since Megan had walked into Earl's Hardware with her plumbing disaster, Matt wondered if some things were too complicated to fix, even with the best intentions and the strongest love.

The October wind stirred the leaves in the parking lot, and Matt finally shifted the truck into drive, carrying with him the knowledge that everything had just become much more difficult than he'd ever imagined it could be.

Chapter 26

The jingle of the bell above the door at Martha's Diner announced Megan's arrival as she scanned the lunch crowd for Heather. She found her friend already settled in their favorite booth near the front windows, two glasses of sweet tea waiting.

"There's my favorite librarian," Heather called with a grin, standing to wrap Megan in a hug. "I was beginning to think you'd gotten lost."

"Sorry I'm a few minutes late," Megan said, sliding into the booth across from her friend. "Mrs. Gallagher called right as I was trying to leave the library with a very important question about whether the library had any books on training pet parrots."

"Pet parrots?"

"Apparently her grandson convinced her to adopt one, and she's discovered that Charlie has quite a vocabulary. Most of it inappropriate."

Heather laughed, the sound bright and infectious in the warm diner atmosphere. Around them, the Saturday lunch crowd created a comfortable buzz of conversation, punctuated by the clink of dishes and Martha's voice calling orders to the kitchen.

"Well, I need all the girlfriend time I can get today," Heather declared, settling back into her seat with obvious satisfaction. "Between work, dating, and that new mystery novel I can't put down, I feel like I haven't had good girl-time chat in ages."

"How is the mystery novel?"

"Terrible and addictive. The detective makes the most illogical decisions, but somehow I have to know if he catches the killer." Heather said as she picked up her menu. "How are things with your hardware store hero?"

Megan felt her cheeks warm slightly. "Things are... good."

"Just good?" Heather's eyebrow arched with the kind of skeptical expression that suggested she expected much more detailed information. "That's all I get?"

Before Megan could formulate a more informative response, Martha appeared beside their table with her order pad and a smile.

"Afternoon, girls," Martha said warmly. "Interested in the lunch special today?"

"Please," Megan confirmed. "Tomato soup and grilled cheese."

"Same for me," Heather added. "And Martha, could we get two pieces of whatever pie is calling your name today?"

"Dutch apple pie, fresh from the oven," Martha replied with obvious pride.

As Martha bustled away toward the kitchen, Heather leaned forward across the table with an intense focus that meant serious girlfriend conversation was about to begin.

"Now," she said expectantly. "Details. Real details about you and Matt."

Megan glanced around the diner, noting the other diners who were close enough to overhear before leaning closer to her friend. "I've been holding this in for a few days, but I have to tell you what happened."

"I'm listening."

"Matt came by during lunch hour with takeout from here, just showed up at my office door with food because he wanted to see me during the day." Megan felt her smile spreading as she remembered the sweetness of the gesture. "We were eating in my office, talking about Lauren's Halloween costume and everyday things, when he got quiet and seemed troubled about something."

"Troubled how?"

"Just... distant. Like part of him was somewhere else." Megan took a sip of her sweet tea. "So I asked him what was wrong, and after some hesitation, he looked me straight in the eye and told me he'd fallen in love with me."

Heather's squeal of delight was loud enough to attract glances from neighboring tables. "Megan! He said, he loved you?"

"Completely and absolutely, in his words." Megan couldn't contain her grin at the memory. "And I told him I loved him too."

"This is wonderful!" Heather reached across the table to squeeze Megan's hands with obvious excitement. "How do you feel? Are you floating on air? Are you planning your wedding?"

"I feel... happy. Really, truly happy in ways I'd forgotten were possible." Megan's expression grew more thoughtful. "But also worried."

"Worried about what?"

"About Matt. Even when he was telling me he loved me, even when we were having this beautiful, special moment, I could sense something was troubling him. And since the fundraiser planning meeting, he's been even quieter."

Their lunch arrived with Martha's usual efficient timing, and Megan found herself grateful for the brief interruption as she tried to organize her thoughts about Matt's recent behavior.

"What happened at the fundraiser meeting? I must have missed something." Heather said after Martha had departed.

"Nothing obvious to most people. He volunteered to help, agreed to everything I asked, and was perfectly polite and supportive." Megan stirred her soup thoughtfully. "But he was distant the entire time. Like he was physically present but emotionally somewhere else."

"Any idea what might have caused that?"

"I think it's the date."

"The date?"

"October 30th. The fundraiser falls on October 30th this year." Megan's voice grew quieter as she voiced what she'd been suspecting for days. "It's the anniversary of David's death."

Heather's expression immediately grew more serious and understanding. "Oh, Megan. I didn't realize that. I'm so sorry."

"I've been thinking about it ever since the meeting. The way Matt's face changed when I mentioned the date, how he's been withdrawn since then and well... he's seemed a bit off prior to that as well." Megan met her friend's eyes with a mixture of sadness and determination. "That date will always matter to me, Heather. David was my husband, and losing him changed everything about my life. October 30th will never be just another day."

"But?"

"But I've learned to trust that God's timing includes both beginnings and endings. David's death was devastating, and I'll always carry love for him in my heart. But that doesn't mean my life stopped when his did." Megan's voice carried a quiet strength that had sustained her through seven years of rebuilding. "I believe God can use our grief to teach us about love, and our healing to help others find hope."

Heather was quiet for a moment, processing Megan's words with the careful attention she gave to complex situations. "And you think Matt is struggling with that or something else?"

"I think Matt might still be grieving and possibly feeling some guilt. Maybe he's feeling as if he's stepping into David's place. Not because anyone else sees it that way, of course... and I could be wrong about that. I've been trying to think all of this through from his perspective. Different things that he might be thinking or feeling that could have him acting... well, just different. A little off."

"That would make sense," Heather said gently. "Matt knew David, loved him as a friend. From his perspective, he might feel like he's taking something that wasn't meant for him. Maybe stopping and questioning things."

"But that's not how it is. David is gone, and while I'll always love him, Lauren and I are still here. We're still living, still needing love and companionship and family. If God has brought Matt back into our lives, if He's opened our hearts to love again, then that's not a betrayal of David's memory—it's a testament to how love can multiply rather than diminish when we're brave enough to trust His plan."

"You sound very certain about that."

"I am certain. My faith tells me that honoring David doesn't mean freezing our lives at the moment he died. It means living fully enough to make his sacrifice meaningful, loving deeply enough to show Lauren that her father's love created something beautiful in the world."

Heather smiled. "That's a beautiful way to think about it."

"It's taken me years to understand it that way," Megan admitted. "And there are still moments when I wonder if I'm being selfish, wanting happiness again. But when I pray about it, when I really listen for God's voice, I feel peace about moving forward."

"What about Matt? Do you think he's found that same peace?"

Megan was quiet for a long moment, thinking about Matt's withdrawal during the fundraiser meeting, the way his smiles hadn't quite reached his eyes, the careful distance he'd maintained even while expressing his love.

"I don't think so," she said finally. "I think Matt is wrestling with questions I've already worked through, and I'm not sure how to help him find the answers without pushing him to talk before he's ready."

"Men process things differently than we do. Sometimes they need to work through their feelings internally before they can share them, even with people they love."

"I understand that. But I also can't ignore the fact that he's been pulling away from me, even while saying he loves me." Megan finally took a spoonful of soup, though her appetite had diminished with her growing concern. "It's like he's afraid of his own feelings, afraid of what loving us might mean."

"What do you think it means to him?"

"I think it means he's terrified of dishonoring David by taking his place in our lives. I think he feels guilty for surviving when David didn't, and now that guilt is extending to his feelings for Lauren and me." Megan set down her spoon, her voice growing softer. "I think Matt believes that loving us means betraying his friendship with David."

"And you don't believe that?"

"I believe David would want Lauren to have a father figure who loved her unconditionally. I believe he'd want me to find love again with someone who would treasure us both." Megan's words carried the quiet conviction of someone who'd thought deeply about these questions. "And if that someone happened to be his best friend—someone he trusted completely—I think that would give David peace, not pain."

Heather nodded slowly, clearly moved by Megan's perspective. "Have you tried talking to Matt about any of this?"

"I've tried to let him know I'm available to listen, but he keeps deflecting. Says he needs to work through some things on his own. I want to respect that, but I also can't pretend I don't see him struggling."

"So what are you going to do?"

"I'm going to keep loving him and praying for him. I'm going to trust that God's timing includes both Matt's healing and our relationship." Megan met Heather's eyes with determination that masked her underlying worry. "But I'm also going to try to find a way to let him know that he doesn't have to carry this burden alone."

Their Dutch apple pie arrived warm and fragrant, providing a sweet punctuation to their serious conversation. As they shared bites and talked about lighter topics—Lauren's excitement about Halloween, Heather's latest dating adventures, the library's upcoming winter programs—Megan felt grateful for her friend's listening ear and supportive presence.

But underneath the comfortable friendship conversation, her concern for Matt continued to grow. She'd seen the shadows in his eyes during the fundraiser meeting, felt the careful distance he'd maintained even while expressing his love, noticed the way he seemed to be wrestling with questions he wasn't ready to voice.

"Thank you," she said as they prepared to leave the diner. "For listening, for understanding, for not trying to solve everything with easy answers."

"That's what friends are for," Heather replied, gathering her purse. "And Megan? Whatever Matt is working through, it's obvious he loves you and Lauren. Sometimes love just takes time to find its courage."

Chapter 27

The fellowship hall buzzed with the comfortable chaos of Sunday after-service gathering—children weaving between clusters of adults, the gentle clatter of coffee cups against saucers, and the warm hum of conversation that had become as familiar to Matt as the hymns they'd just finished singing. Lauren darted past him toward the children's activity corner, her Sunday dress a flash of pink against the autumn decorations that adorned the walls.

"Matt!" Earl's voice called from across the room. "Son, come settle a debate about the best wood stain for outdoor furniture."

Matt managed what he hoped was an appropriate smile and raised his hand in acknowledgment, but made no move toward the group of men gathered near the coffee station. Around him, the fellowship swirled with the kind of easy warmth that had once felt welcoming but now pressed against his chest like a weight he couldn't bear.

"There's our girl," Ruthanne Miller's voice carried across the room as she wrapped Megan in an affectionate embrace that spoke of years of shared history. Henry stood beside his wife, his weathered hands gentle as he smoothed Lauren's hair and listened to her excited chatter about the morning's Sunday school lesson.

Matt felt his breath catch as he watched the scene unfold. David's parents loved their granddaughter, cared for his widow, and provided the grandparental warmth that Lauren had never known from her biological father. The sight should have brought him joy—evidence that Lauren was surrounded by love, that Megan had found her place in this community after years of rebuilding.

Instead, it felt like watching a life that had been stolen and redistributed, with himself cast as the unwitting thief.

"Matt!" Lauren's voice pierced through his spiraling thoughts as she bounded toward him, clutching a piece of construction paper covered in crayon drawings. "Look what I made in Sunday school!"

Matt. Not Dad. Not the man who would help with homework and teach her to drive and walk her down the aisle someday. Matt—the beloved family friend who would visit on holidays and special occasions, important but not central to her daily life.

"It's beautiful, Lauren," Matt said, crouching down to study Lauren's artwork. The drawing showed three stick figures holding hands in front of a house, with a large tree beside them and a smiling sun overhead. "Tell me about it."

"That's you and Mommy and me," Lauren explained with seven-year-old pride, pointing to each figure. "And that's our house, and that's the big oak tree in our yard. See how happy we all look?"

The innocence in her voice hit Matt like a physical blow. Here was David's daughter, drawing pictures of herself with the man who should have been her uncle, imagining a family life that was built on the foundation of her father's death. Every smile she gave him, every moment of trust and affection, was possible only because David wasn't there to claim his rightful place.

"It's perfect," Matt managed, though his voice sounded hollow to his own ears.

Lauren beamed at the praise and skipped back toward her grandparents, leaving Matt holding her drawing like evidence of his own unworthiness. The stick figures stared back at him with their simple crayon smiles, a mockery of the happiness he'd been building while David lay in a grave.

"You look like you've seen a ghost," Megan's voice was soft beside him.

Matt looked up to find her blue eyes studying his face with growing worry. She'd apparently extracted herself from her conversation with the Millers and approached him while he was lost in his self-recrimination.

"Just thinking," he said, forcing what he hoped was a reassuring smile.

"About anything you want to share?"

The question was familiar—Megan's patient way of offering him space to talk without pushing him beyond his comfort zone. But today, surrounded by the warm fellowship of people who remembered David, who had watched Megan rebuild her life, who were accepting Matt as part of her future, the careful boundary felt more like a barrier between him and the honesty he owed her.

"Would you..." Matt glanced around the crowded fellowship hall, noting how many people were close enough to overhear their conversation. "Could we step outside for a minute?"

Concern flickered across Megan's features, but she nodded immediately. "Of course."

They made their way through the mingling congregation, past groups of people who smiled and nodded, past children playing games in corners, past the coffee station where his dad was still expounding on wood stain techniques. Matt felt hyperaware of every greeting, every warm glance, every indication that the community had accepted him as Megan's partner and Lauren's father figure.

David's partner. David's daughter.

The October afternoon was crisp and bright as they walked toward the church and finally came to the church's front steps, the autumn air carrying the scent of the changing season and the distant sound of leaves rustling in the breeze. For a moment, Matt just stood there, breathing deeply and trying to organize the chaos of guilt and grief that had been building in his chest for days.

"Talk to me," Megan said quietly, settling beside him on the wide stone steps. "You've been carrying something heavy, and I can see it's getting harder to bear alone."

Matt stared out at the street, watching cars pass and people walk by, ordinary Sunday afternoon life continuing around them while his world felt like it was collapsing inward.

"The date," he said finally, his voice barely above a whisper. "October 30th. It's hitting me harder this year than it has since..." He paused, struggling to find words for feelings that seemed too large and complex for language. "Since I got back from overseas."

"Because of the fundraiser?"

"Because of everything." Matt turned to face her, knowing she deserved honesty even if it revealed things about himself that he'd rather keep hidden. "Because I'm in love with you, and I'm in love with Lauren, and I feel like I'm betraying David every time I let myself be happy about it."

Megan's expression grew soft with understanding, but she didn't interrupt, giving him space to continue working through thoughts he'd been wrestling with alone.

"I keep thinking about what David planned for your lives," Matt continued, his words coming faster as the dam finally broke. "He was going to be the best father in the world to his daughter. He was going to settle in Laurel Ridge and be part of this community after he left the service, coach Lauren's softball team, help with church functions, grow old with you."

"Matt—"

"Everything I want now," Matt's voice cracked slightly, "everything I love about this life we're building together, was supposed to be David's. I'm sitting in his place at fellowship, helping plan fundraisers he should be organizing, falling asleep thinking about a future with his wife and daughter." He buried his face in his hands. "How is that not a betrayal of everything our friendship meant?"

The silence stretched between them for a long moment, filled only by the distant sounds of fellowship continuing inside the recreation hall behind the church and the whisper of autumn wind through the trees that lined the parking area.

"Matt," Megan said finally, her voice carrying the gentle strength that had sustained her through seven years of rebuilding, "that date means everything to me too. October 30th will never be just another day, because that's when I lost the first great love of my life. David's death changed everything—my plans, my dreams, my understanding of how unpredictable and precious life can be."

Matt looked up to find her eyes bright with unshed tears, but her expression held steady resolve.

"But I've learned something through all these years of grief and healing," she continued. "Honoring David doesn't mean freezing our lives at the moment he died. It means living fully enough to make his sacrifice meaningful. It means loving deeply enough to show Lauren that her father's love created something beautiful in the world."

"But I'm not just anyone," Matt protested. "I'm his best friend. I'm the person who promised to make sure you knew how much he loved you. I was supposed to be Uncle Matt, not..." He gestured helplessly between them.

"Not what?"

"Not the man who wants to marry you. Not the man Lauren draws pictures of as her father figure. Not the person who gets to have the life David dreamed about."

Megan was quiet for a moment, clearly choosing her words with care. "Do you think David would want Lauren to grow up without a father figure who loved her unconditionally?"

"That's not the point."

"That is exactly the point." Megan's voice held quiet conviction. "Do you think David would want me to spend the rest of my life alone, never allowing myself to love again, never giving Lauren the chance to experience the kind of family life she deserves?"

Matt stared at his hands, unable to meet her eyes. "No. But he'd want you to find that with someone else. Not with me."

"Why?"

"Because I was his friend. Because I survived when he didn't. Because every moment of happiness I have with you and Lauren is a moment he'll never get to experience."

"Matt." Megan's voice was so gentle it made his chest ache. "Survivor guilt is normal. It's part of how we process loss when someone we love dies and we don't. But letting that guilt control your life doesn't honor David—it diminishes the gift you've been given by surviving."

The words hit Matt like someone had punched him in the chest and knocked the wind out of him, each one carrying a truth he wasn't ready to accept. Gift. As if David's death was something that had benefited him rather than devastated both their lives in different ways.

"I don't deserve this," he said quietly. "I don't deserve to have what he can't have."

"That's not how love works," Megan replied with patient firmness. "Love isn't a zero-sum game where someone else's loss becomes your gain. Love multiplies when we're brave enough to let it grow."

But instead of comfort, Megan's words only deepened the terrible certainty that had been building in Matt's chest. She was so good, so full of faith and wisdom and hope. She deserved someone who could love her without reservation, someone who could build a future with her and Lauren without constantly looking over his shoulder at the ghost of what should have been.

She deserved better than a man whose love for her was tainted by guilt and grief and the constant awareness that he was living in his dead friend's place.

"I know you're trying to help," Matt said carefully, "and I appreciate your faith, your perspective. But I think I need some time to work through this on my own."

Something in his tone must have alerted Megan to the deeper meaning behind his words, because her expression grew more concerned. "Matt, what does that mean?"

"It means maybe I should step back for a while. Give you and Lauren space. Let you focus on the fundraiser and the anniversary without having to worry about my feelings."

"That's not what I want."

"But it might be what's best." Matt said as he stood up. "I love you, Megan. I love Lauren. But maybe that love is selfish. Maybe the most loving thing I can do is remove myself from the equation so you can honor David's memory without having to navigate my guilt."

"You're not making sense." Megan stood as well, reaching toward him with hands that he couldn't bring himself to take. "Matt, running away from what we have doesn't solve anything."

"I'm not running away. I'm trying to do the right thing."

"The right thing is staying. The right thing is working through this together. The right thing is trusting that God brought us back together for a reason."

But even as Megan spoke with conviction and love, Matt felt himself retreating further into the certainty that had been building for days. Every word of comfort she offered, every expression of faith in their relationship, only reinforced his growing belief that he was unworthy of what she was offering.

She was amazing—strong, faithful, loving, capable of finding meaning in suffering and hope in grief. She deserved someone equally amazing, someone who could love her without reservation, someone who could be a father to Lauren without constantly questioning whether he had the right to fill that role.

"I should get going," Matt said, his voice sounding foreign to his own ears. "I need to think about some things."

"Matt, please." Megan's voice carried a note of panic that made his chest tighten with guilt. "Don't shut me out. Whatever you're working through, we can face it together."

But that was exactly the problem. Megan's faith in them, her willingness to face any obstacle together, her complete acceptance of his struggles—all of it only highlighted how much she was willing to compromise for someone who could never be worthy of her sacrifice.

"I'll call you," he lied, knowing even as he said it that he needed distance to think clearly, to figure out how to love her enough to let her go.

As Matt walked toward his truck in the church parking lot, he couldn't resist one last glance back toward the recreation hall. Through the windows, he could see the warm glow of community continuing inside—people sharing food and conversation, children playing games, families enjoying the simple pleasure of Sunday afternoon together.

And there, stood Henry and Ruthanne Miller with Lauren, the three of them forming a small circle of connection and care. Lauren was with her grandparents, her small hands animated as she explained something.

This is what David should be seeing, Matt thought as he came to stand beside his truck, key in hand but unable to bring himself to drive away from the scene. *His parents loving his daughter, his child growing up surrounded by family and faith and unconditional love.*

Instead, David was buried in a cemetery on the other side of town, while Matt stood in a church parking lot wrestling with guilt over wanting to claim the life his best friend had planned to live.

He glanced toward Megan, who stood on the church steps watching him. Even from a distance, Matt could see the worry in her posture and the concern on her face.

The realization that had been building for days crystallized into painful certainty: the only way to truly honor David's memory was to step back from the life that should have been his. Megan and Lauren would be fine—better than fine. They had community, family, faith, and each other. They didn't need Matt complicating their healing with his guilt and unworthiness.

Matt climbed into his truck and started the engine, but he remained parked for another moment, seeing everything through the front windshield as the life David should have lived continued without him. The October afternoon sun slanted across the scene, making everything look golden and perfect and completely beyond his reach.

As Matt finally shifted into drive and pulled away from Laurel Ridge Community Church, he carried with him the growing conviction that loving Megan and Lauren meant protecting them from his own brokenness. Some wounds were too deep to heal through love alone, and some guilt was too heavy to be lifted by even the most generous heart.

The fundraiser was six days away. October 30th would mark seven years since David's death, and Matt was increasingly certain that the most loving thing he could do was ensure that date wasn't complicated by his presence. Megan deserved to honor her first husband's memory without having to worry about her current boyfriend's struggles with survivor's guilt.

She deserved better than someone who could only love her in the shadow of his dead friend's dreams.

Chapter 28

The October evening had settled into a deep quiet that small towns wore like comfortable old clothes, and Matt found himself driving through Laurel Ridge's empty streets with no clear destination in mind. He'd left his apartment above the hardware store an hour ago, unable to sit still with the weight of Sunday's confrontation pressing against his chest like a physical ache.

The truck's headlights swept across familiar landmarks—Martha's Diner with its red neon sign darkened for the night, City Hall with its Civil War memorial casting long shadows, Earl's Hardware where tomorrow he'd have to pretend again that everything was normal while helping customers choose between different grades of sandpaper and types of wood stain. The ordinary rhythm of his new civilian life felt impossible to navigate when everything inside him churned with guilt and confusion.

Three days had passed since he'd walked away from Megan on the church steps, three days of avoiding her calls and declining his parents' dinner invitations, three days of carrying conversations he couldn't finish and feelings he couldn't reconcile. His father had stopped by his apartment twice in the evenings, with increasingly concerned expressions, and his mother had sent over a casserole he hadn't touched, but Matt couldn't bring himself to explain what he was working through when he didn't understand it himself.

The truck seemed to steer itself toward Church Street, and Matt found himself pulling into the parking lot of Laurel Ridge Community Church. The white clapboard building stood quiet against the star-filled sky, its tall steeple reaching toward heaven like a prayer made tangible. Most of the windows were dark, but warm lamplight spilled from one office window near the back of the building.

Matt sat in his truck for several minutes, engine ticking as it cooled, wondering what he was doing here. Pastor Andrew barely knew him—a few Sunday services, some brief conversations during fellowship time, a handshake and a smile. But something about the man's steady presence and quiet wisdom had impressed Matt during his first weeks back in Laurel Ridge, and right now, Matt desperately needed to talk to someone who might understand the tangle of faith and guilt that was threatening to choke him.

The church doors were unlocked. Inside, the sanctuary stretched before him in peaceful darkness, moonlight filtering through stained glass windows to create pools of colored light across empty pews. The familiar scents of aged wood and fresh flowers lingered in the air, along with furniture polish.

His footsteps echoed softly on the polished wooden floors as he made his way toward the rectangle of light that marked Pastor Andrew's open office door. The sound of a pen scratching against paper drifted into the hallway, accompanied by the quiet hum of an electric heater and the distant tick of a clock somewhere in the building's depths.

Matt paused outside the office, uncertain about interrupting. Through the open doorway, he could see Pastor Andrew bent over his desk, dark hair slightly mussed, sleeves rolled up as he worked on what appeared to be sermon notes or perhaps correspondence. A steaming mug of coffee sat within easy reach, and a small reading lamp cast a warm circle of light across the desk's surface.

The pastor looked up as if sensing his presence, and Matt was struck again by the man's genuine warmth. Pastor Andrew couldn't have been much older than Matt himself, but his eyes held a depth that suggested he'd spent considerable time listening to people's struggles and pointing them toward hope.

"Matt," Pastor Andrew said, setting down his pen with the unhurried grace of someone accustomed to unexpected visitors. "Come in, please. I was just finishing up some notes for Sunday's service."

"I'm sorry to interrupt," Matt began, hovering in the doorway like someone who hadn't quite committed to entering. "I saw your light and thought maybe—"

"No apology necessary." Pastor Andrew gestured toward one of the comfortable chairs positioned across from his desk. "I was hoping for an excuse to take a break anyway. Coffee? I made a fresh pot about an hour ago."

"That would be good, thanks."

Pastor Andrew moved to a small table in the corner, where a coffee maker sat alongside a collection of mismatched mugs that spoke of countless late-evening counseling sessions. As he poured the coffee, Matt settled into the offered chair and tried to organize thoughts that felt like scattered pieces of a puzzle he couldn't solve.

The office felt like a sanctuary within the sanctuary—books lined three walls from floor to ceiling, their spines bearing titles that ranged from ancient theology to contemporary Christian living. A guitar leaned against one corner, and family photos were scattered across the desk alongside prayer request cards and a well-worn Bible bristling with bookmarks.

"Cream and sugar?" Pastor Andrew asked.

"Black is fine."

They settled into their chairs, and Pastor Andrew waited with a patient silence that invited confidences without demanding them. Matt wrapped his hands around the warm mug, grateful for something to do with the restless energy that had been building in his chest for days.

"I don't really know where to start," Matt admitted finally.

"Sometimes the middle is as good a place as any," Pastor Andrew said gently. "Or the end, if that's what's weighing on you most. God's not particular about the order when we're bringing our struggles to Him."

Matt took a sip of coffee, surprised by its quality. "You make good coffee for a preacher."

"Seminary requirement," Pastor Andrew replied with a slight smile. "Right after 'How to Write a Sermon That Doesn't Put Everyone to Sleep' and 'Pastoral Care in the Digital Age.'"

The gentle humor helped ease some of the tension in Matt's shoulders, and he almost smiled in return. Almost.

"Pastor, can I ask you something that might not have a simple answer?"

"Those are usually the most important questions."

Matt set down his coffee and leaned forward, his hands clasped tightly together. "How do you know when something feels like love but might actually be betrayal? When what looks like God's blessing might be your own selfishness dressed up in good intentions?"

Pastor Andrew's expression grew more serious, though his eyes remained kind. "That's a question that could apply to a lot of situations, but I suspect you're talking about something specific. Something that's been weighing on your heart."

"I am." Matt's voice came out rougher than he'd intended. "I'm talking about falling in love with my best friend's widow and her daughter. I'm talking about wanting a life that was supposed to belong to someone else."

The confession hung between them in the warm lamplight, and Matt felt simultaneously relieved and terrified. Pastor Andrew didn't look shocked or disapproving, but Matt could see him processing the complexity of what had been revealed.

"Tell me about your friend," Pastor Andrew said quietly. "And tell me about the love you're afraid might be betrayal."

So Matt did. Starting with David—their friendship, their shared military service, David's plans for the future he'd never get to live. He talked about the training accident, about the years of carrying guilt over surviving when his best friend hadn't, about returning to Laurel Ridge and finding Megan and Lauren living the life David had dreamed about.

"I love them," Matt said, his voice breaking slightly on the admission. "I love Megan in ways that scare me because they feel so permanent, so complete. And I love Lauren like she's my own daughter, which terrifies me because she's not. She's David's daughter, and every moment of happiness I have with her is a moment he'll never experience."

Pastor Andrew listened without interrupting, occasionally nodding or leaning forward when Matt's voice grew quieter. When Matt finally fell silent, the office felt heavy with everything that had been spoken and everything that remained unspoken.

"Matt," Pastor Andrew said finally, "what do you think David would want for Megan and Lauren?"

"He'd want them to be happy. He'd want Lauren to have a father figure who loved her unconditionally, and he'd want Megan to find love again with someone who would treasure them both."

"And if that someone happened to be his best friend—someone he trusted completely—what do you think David's response would be?"

Matt stared at his hands. "I don't know. Maybe he'd be glad they weren't alone. Or maybe he'd feel betrayed that I was taking his place."

"Taking his place, or filling a place that was left empty when he died?"

The question hit Matt hard, and he looked up to find Pastor Andrew watching him with compassionate intensity.

"There's a difference," Pastor Andrew continued gently. "David's place in Megan's heart as her first husband, as Lauren's father—those places belong to him alone, and nothing you do can change or diminish that. But the place in their lives for a husband and father moving forward? That place was empty, Matt. Not taken, not stolen, but empty and waiting for someone worthy to fill it."

"But I'm not worthy." The words came out in a rush of pain Matt hadn't known he was carrying. "I survived when David didn't. I get to come home and fall in love and build a family while he's buried in a cemetery on the other side of town. How is that not a betrayal of everything our friendship meant?"

Pastor Andrew was quiet for a long moment, and when he spoke, his voice carried the authority of someone who'd wrestled with similar questions in his own ministry.

"Matt, can I share something with you that I've learned about guilt and grief and the complicated ways they can tangle up with love?"

Matt nodded.

"Survivor guilt is real, and it's normal, and it's part of how we process losses that make little sense to us. But here's what I've seen over and over again in pastoral care: guilt that keeps us from living fully doesn't honor our loved ones—it wastes the gift of life we've been given. When we refuse joy, refuse love, refuse the possibility of building something beautiful with the days we've been granted, we're not honoring the dead. We're diminishing the value of life itself."

Pastor Andrew reached for his Bible, pages falling open with practiced ease. "Jesus said, 'I have come that they might have life, and have it abundantly.' Not carefully. Not halfway. Not with constant apologies for breathing when others can't. Abundantly."

He flipped to another passage. "Paul tells us to 'bear one another's burdens,' but he doesn't say we should carry burdens that aren't ours to bear. David's death was a tragedy, Matt. But your survival isn't a tragedy. It's a gift. And gifts are meant to be used for good, not buried in guilt."

Matt felt tears threatening and blinked them back. "But what if I'm just telling myself what I want to hear? What if this isn't God's will but my own selfishness?"

"Then let me ask you this: when you're with Megan and Lauren, when you're serving others through the Hands of Grace Ministry, when you're building something meaningful in this community—do those moments feel selfish? Do they feel like you're taking something that doesn't belong to you?"

Matt considered the question honestly. "No. They feel like... like I'm becoming who I was meant to be. Like I'm finally home after years of being lost."

"And when you pull away from them? When you isolate yourself out of guilt?"

"It feels like I'm dying inside. Like I'm choosing emptiness over fullness, fear over faith."

Pastor Andrew leaned back in his chair, his expression gentle but firm. "Matt, I'm going to say something that might be hard to hear, but I need you to consider it carefully. Sometimes what we call loyalty to the dead is actually fear of the living. Sometimes what we call honoring the past is actually refusing the future God has planned for us."

The words settled over Matt like stones dropping into still water, creating ripples of recognition he wasn't sure he was ready to follow.

"David loved Megan and Lauren," Pastor Andrew continued. "That love was real and good and holy. But David is with Jesus now, Matt. His story on Earth is complete. Megan and Lauren's stories are still being written, and so is yours. If God has brought you together, if He's opening doors for love and family and service, then stepping through those doors isn't betrayal—it's faithfulness."

Pastor Andrew opened his Bible again, turning to what appeared to be a well-marked passage. "'To everything there is a season, and a time to every purpose under heaven. A time to be born and a time to die, a time to plant and a time to pluck up what is planted... a time to mourn and a time to dance, a time to weep and a time to laugh.'"

He looked up from the text. "You've had your time to mourn, Matt. You've carried that grief faithfully for seven years. But maybe God is calling you to a new season. Maybe He's calling you to dance again, to laugh again, to love again. Not because the mourning was wrong, but because the dancing is right too."

Matt felt something in his chest, like a knot that had been tied so tightly he'd forgotten it was there beginning to loosen just slightly.

"What if I'm not good enough for them?" he asked quietly. "What if I can't be the husband David would have been, the father Lauren deserves?"

"You're not David," Pastor Andrew said simply. "And God isn't asking you to be. He's asking you to be Matt—the Matt He created you to be, with your own gifts, your own heart, your own way of loving. Megan fell in love with Matt, not with a replacement for David. Lauren lights up when Matt walks into the room, not when she imagines someone else."

Pastor Andrew stood and moved to the window, looking out at the quiet street beyond. "I've been watching you these past few weeks in church, in fellowship, working with the ministry. I've seen how you treat people, how you serve, how you love. And Matt, you're not trying to be someone else. You're just being yourself—and that self is exactly what Megan and Lauren need."

"Then why does it feel so complicated?"

"Because love is complicated when it matters. Because second chances require courage. Because building something beautiful on the foundation of loss takes faith that God can create beauty from ashes." Pastor Andrew returned to his chair. "But complicated doesn't mean wrong, Matt. Sometimes it just means important."

They sat in comfortable silence for several minutes, the weight of the conversation settling between them like something substantial that needed to be acknowledged. Matt felt lighter somehow, as if speaking his fears aloud had robbed them of some of their power over him, but the relief wasn't complete. Understanding something intellectually and feeling it in his heart were two different things.

"Would you pray with me?" Matt asked finally. "I feel like I need help letting go of some things I've been carrying."

Pastor Andrew smiled. "I'd be honored to."

They bowed their heads in the warm lamplight, and Pastor Andrew's voice became intimate and reverent as he addressed God on Matt's behalf.

"Heavenly Father, we come before You tonight with hearts that are heavy with questions and complicated with love. You see Matt's struggle, Lord. You understand his desire to honor his friend's memory while also embracing the gifts You've placed in his life. We thank You for David's friendship, for the love he shared with Megan and Lauren, for the sacrifice he made in service to others. And we thank You for Matt's survival, for bringing him home safely, for opening his heart to love again.

"Lord, we ask You to lift the burden of guilt that Matt has been carrying. Help him to understand that survivor's guilt is not from You—that You delight in life, in love, in the courage to build something beautiful even after loss. Give him peace about loving Megan and Lauren. Help him to see that honoring David doesn't mean limiting his own life, but living it fully enough to justify the gift of breath he's been given.

"We pray for wisdom as Matt navigates this relationship. We pray for Megan's heart as she waits for him to work through his struggle. We pray for Lauren, that she might continue to feel secure in the love of both her mother and this man who's learning to be a father to her. And we pray for David's memory to be a blessing rather than a burden, a foundation rather than a barrier.

"Help Matt to trust Your timing, Your plan, Your grace. Help him to accept that second chances are gifts from You, not betrayals of the past. And help him to move forward in faith, knowing that You make all things work together for good for those who love You.

"In Jesus' name we pray, Amen."

"Amen," Matt echoed, his voice rough with emotion.

When they raised their heads, Matt felt as if something fundamental had shifted inside him. Not a complete transformation—the guilt and confusion were still there, still tangled around his heart like thorns. But the edges felt softer somehow, less sharp, more manageable.

"Thank you," he said simply.

"Thank you for trusting me with something so important to you," Pastor Andrew replied. "And Matt? This isn't the kind of thing you work through in one conversation. If you need to talk again, if you need someone to help you process what God is saying to your heart, I'm here."

"I appreciate that. And Pastor?"

"Yeah?"

"What you said about David's story being complete while mine is still being written—I think I need to sit with that for a while. Let it really sink in."

Pastor Andrew nodded. "Sometimes the most important truths take time to travel from our heads to our hearts. Be patient with yourself in the process."

Matt stood to leave, feeling both lighter and somehow more substantial at the same time. The conversation had given him tools to work with, perspectives to consider, and Scripture to meditate on. But it hadn't magically erased the complexity of loving Megan while missing David, of wanting to be Lauren's father while honoring the father she'd never known.

"One more thing," Pastor Andrew said as Matt reached the office door. "I want you to consider something this week. Instead of asking, 'What would David think about me loving his family,' try asking, 'How can I love his family in a way that honors the love he showed them?' See if that changes how the question feels."

Matt paused in the doorway, struck by the subtle but significant difference in framing. "I'll think about that."

"Good. And Matt? The fundraiser is this Saturday, on the anniversary. That's going to be a difficult day no matter what, but it might also be an opportunity. Sometimes God uses the hardest days to show us the most important truths."

"Yeah. Maybe."

Matt made his way back through the quiet church. The October night air hit him as he stepped outside, crisp and clean and full of stars that seemed brighter than they had when he'd arrived.

He climbed into his truck and sat for a moment before starting the engine, looking up at the church steeple reaching toward heaven. Somewhere in that building, Pastor Andrew was probably returning to his sermon notes, carrying Matt's struggle in his prayers. Somewhere across town, Megan was probably helping Lauren with homework or reading bedtime stories, wondering why the man she'd grown to love had suddenly pulled away. And somewhere beyond the stars, David was... what? Waiting? Watching? At peace in ways that transcended earthly concerns about who loved whom and why?

Matt started the truck and pulled out of the parking lot, carrying with him the faint but persistent hope that maybe, just maybe, love could be larger than guilt, and grace more powerful than fear. The October night felt less heavy somehow, though he couldn't say exactly why.

Chapter 29

The digital clock on Matt's nightstand glowed 10:17 PM when he finally gave up on the pretense of trying to sleep. He'd been lying in the darkness of his apartment for nearly an hour, staring at the ceiling and replaying his conversation with Pastor Andrew, but rest felt as distant as it had for the past several days. The pastor's words had planted something in his mind—seeds of possibility, different ways of thinking about guilt and love and the complicated territory between them—but they hadn't yet grown into anything resembling peace.

Matt sat up and switched on the small lamp beside his bed, its warm light pushing back the shadows that seemed to mirror the confusion still churning in his chest. The apartment was quiet around him. Outside, Laurel Ridge slept under its blanket of October stars, while inside, Matt wrestled with questions that felt too large for the confines of his living space.

He padded barefoot to the kitchen and put on a pot of coffee, knowing that caffeine was probably the last thing his restless system needed but craving the familiar sounds and scents that might ground him. While the coffee brewed, Matt was drawn to the small bookshelf in his living room, where his Bible sat alongside a handful of novels, some military history texts, and a collection of woodworking magazines.

The Bible was well-worn, a gift from his parents when he'd left for boot camp twelve years ago. Its leather cover was scarred from deployment, marked by desert sand and humidity, water stains and the accumulated weight of years spent in duffel bags and footlockers. Matt had read it sporadically during his service—more often during the difficult times, the dangerous deployments, the long nights when home felt like something he might never see again.

Now he carried it to his kitchen table and opened it randomly, letting the pages fall where they would. The words that greeted him were from Ecclesiastes, verses he recognized from Pastor Andrew's earlier quotation: "To everything there is a season, and a time to every purpose under heaven..."

Matt read the familiar passage slowly, letting each phrase settle in his mind. A time to be born and a time to die. A time to plant and a time to pluck up what is planted. A time to mourn and a time to dance.

"A time to mourn and a time to dance," he repeated aloud, his voice barely above a whisper in the quiet apartment.

He'd had his time to mourn. Seven years of carrying David's death like a weight around his neck, seven years of survivor's guilt and questions about why he'd been spared when his friend hadn't. Seven years of believing that happiness somehow dishonored the dead, that moving forward meant leaving David behind.

But what if Pastor Andrew was right? What if there really was a time for mourning and a separate time for dancing? What if the dancing didn't diminish the mourning but built on it, transformed it into something that honored rather than buried what had been lost?

Matt poured himself coffee and returned to the Bible, this time turning pages with more purpose. In Isaiah, he found words about God doing "a new thing,": "Behold, I will do a new thing; now it shall spring forth; shall ye not know it? I will even make a way in the wilderness, and rivers in the desert."

A new thing. Not a replacement for what had been, but something entirely different, something that could exist alongside memory and loss without canceling them out.

In Galatians, Paul's words about bearing one another's burdens jumped off the page. Matt had been carrying David's burden—the burden of an unfinished life, unlived dreams, the weight of a family left behind. But what if that wasn't his burden to carry? What if his real burden was the responsibility to live fully with the life he'd been given?

Finally, he turned to John's Gospel, finding the verse Pastor Andrew had quoted: "I am come that they might have life, and that they might have it more abundantly."

Abundantly. Not carefully. Not apologetically. Not halfway.

Matt closed the Bible and wrapped his hands around his coffee mug, feeling the warmth seep through the ceramic into his palms. The apartment was so quiet he could hear the refrigerator humming, the distant sound of a car passing on Main Street, and the settling sounds of the old building around him. In that stillness, he prayed—not with the formal language of church services, but with the raw honesty that came in the middle of sleepless nights.

"God," he said aloud, his voice rough in the quiet room, "I don't know if You're listening, or if You care about the mess I've made of trying to figure this out. But I'm tired. I'm tired of carrying this guilt. I'm tired of feeling like loving Megan and Lauren means betraying David."

The words came slowly at first, then with gathering momentum as he finally gave voice to thoughts he'd been afraid to speak even to himself.

"I love them. I love Megan in ways that terrify me because they feel so permanent, so complete. I love Lauren like she's my own daughter, and maybe that should scare me more than it does, but it doesn't. It feels right. It feels like I was meant to be part of their lives."

He paused, taking a sip of coffee and listening to the silence that followed his confession.

"I think David would want them to be happy. I think he'd want Lauren to have a father who loved her unconditionally, and I think he'd want Megan to find someone who would treasure her the way she deserves to be treasured. And if that someone is me... if You brought me back to Laurel Ridge not just to run the hardware store but to love David's family..."

Matt's voice broke slightly, and he had to stop for a moment to collect himself.

"Then help me believe that's okay. Help me believe that love can multiply instead of diminish. Help me believe that honoring David doesn't mean limiting my own life, but living it fully enough to justify the gift of still being here."

The prayer continued, wordless now, more feeling than language. Matt sat with his Bible and his coffee and his heart wide open, letting the peace that Pastor Andrew had spoken about begin to settle around him like a blanket. It wasn't the absence of grief—David's death would always be a wound in his heart, a loss that had shaped him in ways he was still discovering. But grief didn't have to mean guilt. Missing David didn't have to mean avoiding happiness.

For the first time in days, Matt felt something like clarity beginning to emerge from the chaos in his chest. Not complete understanding—the situation was still complicated, still required courage and faith and the willingness to risk his heart. But the crushing weight of betrayal was lifting, replaced by something that felt like hope.

Loving Megan didn't diminish his friendship with David.

Wanting to be a father to Lauren didn't dishonor the father she'd never known.

Instead, Matt realized with growing certainty, his love for them was a continuation of David's own love, a way of ensuring that David's sacrifice had meaning beyond the grave.

The clock showed 11:30 PM when Matt finally felt ready to move. But instead of returning to bed, he pulled on jeans and a flannel shirt; he needed something to do while his mind continued processing the breakthrough he'd experienced. The apartment felt too small suddenly, too confining for the energy that was building in his chest.

He made his way downstairs to the workshop in the basement, using his key to let himself into the darkened space. The familiar scents of wood and metal and honest work greeted him, and Matt felt his shoulders relax as he moved through the space.

His father had set up the workshop years ago as a place to repair tools and build custom pieces for customers who needed something specific. It was well-equipped with a table saw, drill press, sanders, and all the hand tools a craftsman could want. Matt had spent countless hours here as a teenager, learning from his father the satisfaction that came from creating something useful with his own hands.

Now he looked around the space with fresh eyes. Wood of various types was stored in neat racks along one wall—oak and pine, maple and cherry, some pieces rough-cut and others already planed smooth. A selection of hardware filled organized bins, while plans and sketches for various projects covered one corner of the workbench.

Matt pulled out a piece of paper and began sketching, letting his hands translate the thoughts that had been forming in his mind during his prayer. A bench. Simple but elegant, sturdy enough to last for years, beautiful enough to honor the memory it would carry.

The measurements came naturally—he'd built similar pieces before, understood the proportions that would make it both functional and pleasing to the eye. But as he sketched, Matt added details that spoke to something deeper than mere craftsmanship. The bench would be made of oak, strong and enduring. The back would feature gentle curves that invited people to linger, to sit and read and think. And across the top rail, carved letters would spell out words that connected past and future in a declaration of love that honored both.

In Memory of Corporal David Miller, who believed in stories worth living and lives worth loving.

The inscription came to him completely, and Matt wrote it carefully across the top of his sketch. This bench would be his gift to Megan and Lauren, but more than that, it would be his gift to the community, to the library where children like Lauren would discover the joy of reading. It would be a memorial that celebrated life instead of mourning death, a reminder that love multiplied when it was shared rather than hoarded.

Matt selected his wood carefully, running his hands over the boards to feel for imperfections, checking the grain for strength and beauty. Oak for the frame and seat, with contrasting cherry accents for the armrests and back slats. The wood was seasoned, dry, ready to be shaped into something permanent and beautiful.

He began with rough cuts, measuring twice and cutting once according to the carpenter's wisdom his father had drilled into him years ago. The saw's clean bite through the wood felt satisfying, each cut bringing the vision in his mind closer to reality. As he worked, Matt found his thoughts settling into a rhythm that matched the steady progress of his hands.

This wasn't betrayal. This was love made tangible, grief transformed into something useful and beautiful. Every measurement was a prayer, every cut a declaration that life could grow from loss, that hope could flourish in the soil of sorrow.

The bench would sit in the library's children's section, where Lauren and her friends would climb onto it to reach books from higher shelves. Parents would use it while reading to their children, creating memories that would last long after the stories ended. And someday, when Lauren was grown with children of her own, she would be able to tell them about the father she'd never met and the man who'd loved her mother enough to build something beautiful in his memory.

Matt worked steadily, losing track of time as the pieces began to take shape. The frame came together first, mortise and tenon joints fitting with the precision that spoke of careful measurement and patient craftsmanship. The seat followed, boards edge-glued and planed smooth, the surface inviting touch.

It was nearly four in the morning when he stepped back to survey his progress. The basic structure was complete, awaiting the detail work that would transform it from functional furniture into something special. Tomorrow he would begin the carving, the careful shaping of letters and curves that would make this bench unique.

But already, Matt could see the finished piece in his mind, could imagine it in place at the library, could picture Megan's face when she saw it and understood what it represented. Not an apology for loving her, but a declaration that love could be larger than guilt, that honoring the past could coexist with embracing the future.

He gathered his tools and swept up the sawdust, preparing the workshop for tomorrow's continued work. As he prepared to turn off the lights and return to his apartment, Matt felt something he hadn't experienced in days: peace. Not the absence of complexity—his feelings for Megan and Lauren were still complicated by history and loss and the delicate work of building a family from the pieces of broken dreams. But peace nonetheless, the kind that came from aligning action with conviction, from choosing faith over fear.

The bench stood in the workshop like a promise, solid and real and full of possibility. Matt turned off the lights and locked the door behind him, carrying with him the certainty that had settled into his heart during the hours of prayer and work.

This wasn't betrayal. This was love—multiplied, not diminished.

Chapter 30

"Okay, so Janet Dillard is handling the children's craft station from five to seven," Megan said, checking names off her master volunteer list with mechanical precision. "Then Rebecca Martinez takes over from seven to nine, and Sarah Thompson will be our floater volunteer, allowing a break to each of these volunteers at the top of each hour."

"Got it," Heather replied, adding notes to her own copy. "And the book sale volunteers?"

"Mrs. Porter and her book club are covering that completely. They've been sorting donations all week." Megan moved on to the next item on her checklist. "Face painting is handled by the high school art class, the bake sale committee has everything under control, and Pastor Andrew confirmed the church youth group will help with setup starting at noon."

Heather looked up from her notes, studying Megan's profile as she bent over her paperwork. "You know, for someone who's pulled off the library event of the decade, you look like you're carrying the weight of ten fundraisers instead of one."

"It's a big day tomorrow," Megan replied without lifting her eyes from the schedule grid she was reviewing. "Lots of moving parts, lots of ways things could go wrong. I just want to make sure we've thought of everything."

"Megan."

Something in Heather's tone made Megan finally look up, meeting her friend's concerned gaze across their shared workspace.

"Talk to me."

For a moment, Megan considered deflecting with another comment about logistics or volunteer coordination. She'd been doing it all week, burying her personal concerns under layers of responsibility, using the demands of event planning to avoid thinking about the silence that had stretched between her and Matt since Sunday afternoon's painful conversation on the church steps.

"He hasn't called," she said quietly, setting down her pen and leaning back in her chair. "It's been five days, and he hasn't called or stopped by or... anything. I've left a message for him every day. I've sent a text every day, and nothing."

"You said he was struggling with guilt about David, about feeling like he was somehow betraying his memory by loving you and Lauren. That's complicated territory for anyone, but especially for someone who's spent years in the military where loyalty and brotherhood mean everything."

Megan nodded, acknowledging the logic of Heather's words while still feeling the ache of Matt's absence in her chest. "I know that. I do. And I've been trying to be patient, trying to trust that if he needs space to work things out, then that's what I should give him. But, Heather, he looked so… resolved when he walked away from me on Sunday. Like he'd made up his mind that what we had was wrong somehow."

"And you think he's decided to end things?"

"I don't know what to think anymore. Part of me wants to believe he'll come back, that whatever he's working through will lead him back to us. But another part of me wonders if I was foolish to think love was possible again, if maybe I pushed too hard or expected too much too soon."

Heather set aside her own paperwork and gave Megan her full attention. "Can I remind you of something?"

"What?"

"Men process emotional things differently than women do. That's not weakness or anything to diminish—it's just different. When we're hurting or confused, we tend to talk it out, seek advice, and process things with our friends. But men, especially men who've been trained to handle things on their own, sometimes need to work through complicated feelings internally before they can share them with anyone else, even people they love."

Megan considered this, remembering Matt's tendency toward measured responses, his way of thinking before speaking, his comfort with silences that might feel awkward to others.

"You might be right," she admitted. "But it doesn't make the silence any easier to live with, especially when I don't know if he's working toward coming back to us or working toward convincing himself to stay away."

"What does your heart tell you when you pray about it?"

Over the past few days, between the demands of fundraiser preparation and the challenge of keeping Lauren's spirits up despite Matt's absence, she'd turned to prayer more frequently, seeking peace in the familiar rhythm of bringing her concerns to God.

"My heart tells me to trust," she said. "To trust that what Matt and I shared was real, that the way he looked at Lauren wasn't pretense, that the love I felt from him wasn't something I imagined. But my head keeps whispering that maybe I was naïve, that maybe second chances are just stories we tell ourselves because the alternative is too lonely to bear."

Heather leaned forward. "Megan, listen to me. I watched you and Matt together for weeks. I saw the way he looked at you when he thought no one was paying attention. I saw him with Lauren, the way he listened to her chatter about school and friends like every word was precious. I saw him bringing you coffee at work just because he wanted to brighten your day."

Megan felt tears threatening and blinked them back, not wanting to lose her composure completely.

"That wasn't pretense," Heather continued firmly. "That wasn't someone playing a role or testing the waters. That was a man who'd found something he treasured and was trying to figure out how to hold on to it without breaking it."

"Then why hasn't he called?"

"Because sometimes the things that matter most to us are the things that scare us most deeply. Because Matt's probably wrestling with questions about worthiness and loyalty and whether he deserves happiness when his best friend never got the chance to experience it. Because grief is complicated, and guilt can be louder than love if we let it be."

Heather reached across the desk and took Megan's hand. "But here's what I know about God's gifts, Megan. He doesn't give them to us just to snatch them away. He doesn't open our hearts to love and then punish us for being brave enough to receive it. What you and Matt found together—that was a gift. And gifts are meant to be embraced, not rejected out of fear."

"But what if he can't get past the guilt? What if he's decided that loving us means betraying David's memory, and he can't live with that?"

"Then he'll miss out on one of the greatest blessings God could offer him," Heather said simply. "But that doesn't mean the gift wasn't real, or that you were wrong to accept it when it was offered."

Megan sat quietly for a moment, letting Heather's words settle in her heart alongside the doubts and fears she'd been carrying. Outside, the October afternoon was growing longer, shadows shifting across the library floor as the sun moved toward evening. Tomorrow would bring the fundraiser, the anniversary of David's death, and a day that would require every ounce of strength and grace she could muster.

"I've been preparing myself to face tomorrow alone," Megan said finally. "To stand up in front of the community and celebrate this accomplishment, to honor David's memory and support Lauren and be the librarian everyone expects me to be, even if my heart is breaking underneath it all."

"That's what strong women do," Heather said gently. "We show up and do what needs to be done, even when it hurts. But Megan, strength doesn't mean you have to face life alone forever. It just means you're capable of surviving whatever comes, whether you're alone or surrounded by love."

"I know that. Intellectually, I know that. But right now, it feels safer to expect nothing and hope for everything than to expect Matt to walk through those doors tomorrow and tell me he's figured it out."

Heather squeezed her hand. "Safe isn't always the same as faithful. Sometimes faith means hoping for things we can't see, believing in love even when circumstances make it seem impossible."

They returned to their planning work, but Heather's words had planted something in Megan's chest that she couldn't quite dismiss. Not certainty—she was far from certain about anything regarding Matt and their future. But possibility, perhaps. The recognition that her story with Matt might not be finished, even if the current chapter felt incomplete.

As the day wore on, they finalized the last details of the next day's event. Volunteer phone trees were activated, supply lists were double-checked, and timeline contingencies were established for everything from unexpected rain to equipment failures. By the time they finished, the library was preparing to close, and Megan felt as ready as she could be for whatever tomorrow might bring.

"You know what I'm going to do tonight?" Heather said as she gathered her purse and jacket. "I'm going to pray specifically that God's timing in all of this will be revealed tomorrow. That whatever He has planned for you and Matt and Lauren, it will unfold in a way that brings glory to Him and healing to your hearts."

"Thank you," Megan said, meaning it more than she could express. "For the prayers, for the encouragement, for helping me see things from different angles when I get stuck in my own perspective."

"That's what friends do. And Megan? I still believe your story with Matt isn't finished. Call it intuition, call it faith, call it stubborn optimism—but I don't think this silence is the end of anything. I think it's just the pause before something beautiful."

After Heather left, Megan remained in the office for another hour, reviewing the checklist one final time and making last-minute phone calls to key volunteers. The library grew quiet around her as evening settled over Laurel Ridge, and she found comfort in the familiar surroundings that had become such a central part of her identity over the years.

This building had been her refuge, the place where she'd rebuilt her sense of purpose and competence. Tomorrow it would host a celebration that honored both the past and the future, a fundraiser that would ensure children like Lauren had access to stories that could transport them beyond the boundaries of their daily lives.

She could face tomorrow alone if she had to. She'd faced harder things by herself and survived, even thrived. Lauren would be proud of her mother's accomplishment, the community would benefit from the resources raised, and life would continue moving forward as it always had.

But as Megan turned off her office light and locked the library doors, she carried with her something she hadn't expected: a flicker of hope that refused to be extinguished. Heather's words about God's gifts and timing echoed in her mind, mixing with memories of Matt's gentle hands fixing her sink, his patient voice reading to Lauren, his eyes full of love when he'd told her how he felt about both of them.

Standing on the library steps on the crisp October evening, surrounded by the quiet streets of the town that had held her together through loss and healing, Megan whispered a prayer.

"God, I don't know what tomorrow holds, and I'm trying to trust Your timing even when I can't see where this path is leading. If Matt is meant to be part of our story, help him find his way back to us. Help him understand that love can honor the past while embracing the future. And if he's not... help me accept that with grace and continue building the life You've given Lauren and me."

Chapter 31

"Careful with that banner; it tears easily," Megan called out as Janet Dillard and Rebecca Martinez maneuvered the large "Stories for Tomorrow" sign toward the library's front entrance. "Perfect. Right there above the main doors."

The Laurel Ridge Library buzzed with a dozen volunteers transforming the space for the evening's fundraiser. Folding tables appeared as if by magic, carried in by the church youth group exactly at noon as promised. Boxes of donated books created temporary towers in the main circulation area while Mrs. Porter and her book club members sorted titles with practiced efficiency. The scent of fresh-baked goods drifted from the community room, where the bake sale committee had already begun arranging their contributions on checkered tablecloths.

Megan moved through the organized disorder with her clipboard, checking items off her master list while directing traffic with the calm authority that came from weeks of planning. Today was the day she'd been preparing for—a celebration of stories and community, and a fundraiser that would benefit children for years to come.

She was doing this, just as she'd steeled herself to do. The thought had carried her through a restless night and the morning's preparations, giving her the strength to smile at volunteers and coordinate logistics even as she privately braced her heart against the significance of the date and Matt's absence in her life.

"Megan, where do you want the face-painting station?" called Sarah Thompson, gesturing toward a card table and folding chairs. "Near the children's section or closer to the main entrance?"

"Children's section, please. That way, parents can browse while their kids get painted." Megan made a note on her clipboard and moved toward the community room to check on the silent auction display. "And Sarah, thank you again for being our floater today. Having someone available to give our volunteers breaks will make all the difference."

The activity felt good—purposeful, meaningful, busy enough to keep her mind occupied and her hands moving. This was what she did well: organize, coordinate, serve the community through the work she loved. She could focus on the tasks at hand and let the deeper currents of grief and hope flow beneath the surface without drowning her.

Heather appeared at her elbow, her own clipboard in hand and a concerned expression on her face. "The church youth group brought more tables than we needed. Do you want them to set up the extras in the reading nook, or should we store them?"

"Reading nook, definitely. We'll need the extra space for the storytelling sessions this afternoon." Megan glanced around the main floor, mentally calculating traffic flow and volunteer coverage. "This is coming together better than I had hoped."

"It's going to be wonderful," Heather agreed. "The entire community's been looking forward to this. And Megan—"

Her friend's words were interrupted by the sound of the front door opening and heavy footsteps crossing the threshold. Megan looked up automatically, expecting to see another volunteer or perhaps an early visitor, and felt the world shift slightly on its axis.

Matt stood at the library entrance, carrying a large cardboard box marked "Book Donations" in black marker. He wore jeans and a navy flannel shirt, his hair slightly mussed as if he'd been working, and his eyes found hers immediately across the busy space.

Megan's clipboard nearly slipped from her fingers.

For a moment, neither of them moved. Volunteers continued their work around them—hanging decorations, arranging tables, sorting books—but Megan felt as if the entire scene had suddenly been placed under glass, muffled and distant. Matt was here. After days of silence and preparing herself for this day alone, he was standing in her library holding a box of books and looking at her with an expression she couldn't quite read.

"I'll be right back," she managed to say to Heather, her voice sounding strange to her own ears.

Matt set the box down near the book-sale area and walked toward her, his steps deliberate but unhurried. When he stopped in front of her, close enough that she could catch the familiar scent of his after-shave, Megan felt her carefully constructed composure threatening to crack.

"Hi," he said quietly.

"Hi." The word came out smaller than she'd intended.

For several heartbeats, they stood facing each other in the middle of the busy library with volunteers working around them. Megan searched Matt's face, looking for clues about why he was here, what his presence meant, and whether she dared to hope it signaled something more than simple community support for the fundraiser.

"I haven't been myself these past days," Matt said, his voice pitched low enough that only she could hear. "I'm sorry for that. I'm sorry for the silence, for leaving you to wonder, for not being the man you deserved."

Megan felt tears threatening and blinked them back. "Matt—"

"I'm figuring things out," he continued, taking a small step closer. "Moving forward in ways that feel right, that honor everyone involved. I can't explain it all right now, not here, but I want you to know that I'm here. I want to be here with you, helping make today everything you've planned it to be."

He reached out and took her hand, his fingers warm and calloused and achingly familiar. The simple contact sent relief flooding through her chest, followed immediately by caution. His words were hopeful, but they weren't promises. His presence was reassuring, but it didn't answer the deeper questions about their future.

"Can you give me a little more patience?" Matt asked, his thumb brushing across her knuckles in a gesture so gentle it made her heart ache. "We'll talk more later, when we have the time and space to do it properly. If that's okay with you?"

Megan nodded, not trusting her voice to remain steady.

Matt's expression relaxed into something approaching a smile. "Now, where do you need me? I'm here to work."

"Megan!" Heather's voice cut through the moment, and Megan turned to see her friend approaching with a clipboard and a question about table arrangements that required immediate attention.

As she dealt with the logistics, Megan felt Matt step back to give her space, but his presence remained like a steady anchor in her peripheral vision. He moved toward the book-sale area and began unpacking his donation box, sorting titles and helping Mrs. Porter arrange display tables.

The afternoon progressed with the steady rhythm of community effort. Matt worked alongside the other volunteers with the same humble competence Megan remembered from the Hands of Grace projects—carrying heavy boxes without being asked, steadying ladders while others hung decorations, fixing a wobbly display shelf with tools he'd brought from the hardware store. He spoke when spoken to, smiled at the right moments, and served with an unobtrusive helpfulness that made everything run more smoothly.

But he didn't presume. He didn't position himself as Megan's co-organizer or insert himself into leadership roles. Instead, he found ways to be useful without being intrusive, helpful without being presumptuous. Watching him work, Megan felt some of the tension in her shoulders begin to ease.

The internal struggle Matt had been wrestling with seemed to have settled into something more peaceful. He looked... lighter, somehow. Less burdened. The shadows that had clouded his expression during their last conversation appeared to have lifted, replaced by something that looked like quiet resolution.

"He's different," Heather murmured during a brief lull in the activity, appearing beside Megan as they watched Matt help Pastor Andrew arrange chairs in the community room.

"Different how?"

"Settled. More himself. Like he's made peace with something that was eating at him. I can't even imagine everything that he's had to work through, but I think he's found his answer."

Megan hoped her friend was right, but she kept her own counsel, focusing on the final preparations for the fundraiser's five o'clock opening. Tables were arranged, decorations were hung, baked goods were displayed, and the silent auction items created an impressive array of community generosity. The library looked festive and welcoming, ready to host what promised to be one of Laurel Ridge's most successful fundraising events.

At three o'clock, Megan stepped outside to check the exterior setup and make sure the welcome signs were properly positioned. Matt followed her onto the library's front steps, and they stood together in the October afternoon air, surveying the street where community members would later arrive for the celebration.

"It's going to be wonderful," Matt said, his hands in his pockets as he looked out at the quiet street. "You've created something special here, Megan. The whole community's been talking."

Before Megan could respond, the familiar rumble of the school bus engine filled the air, and the yellow vehicle rounded the corner. Megan felt her heart lift as she saw Lauren's face pressed against one of the windows, scanning her surroundings with the eager anticipation of a seven-year-old looking for familiar faces.

The bus pulled to a stop in front of the library, and Lauren practically bounced down the steps, her backpack bouncing behind her and her face bright with excitement. She spotted her mother immediately and started to wave, but then her eyes fell on Matt standing beside Megan on the library steps.

"Matt!" Lauren's shriek of delight could probably be heard three blocks away. She dropped her backpack where she stood and ran toward them, her sneakers slapping against the sidewalk and her arms outstretched.

Matt's face transformed as he saw her running toward him. The careful restraint he'd maintained all afternoon melted away, replaced by pure joy as he stepped down from the library entrance to meet her. Lauren launched herself into his arms with the complete trust of a child who'd never doubted she'd be caught, and Matt lifted her up, spinning her once before settling her against his chest.

"I missed you," Lauren said, her arms tight around his neck. "Where have you been? Mommy said you were busy with work stuff, but I thought maybe you forgot about us."

"I would never forget about you," Matt said, his voice rough with emotion. "Never. I've been working through some things that grown-ups sometimes have to figure out, but I'm here now."

"Are you coming to the fundraiser tonight? Mommy's been planning it forever, and there's going to be face painting and stories and everything."

"I wouldn't miss it," Matt promised, meeting Megan's eyes over Lauren's head. "I'm here to help your mom with whatever she needs."

Lauren pulled back to look at his face, her expression serious. "Good. Because today's kind of a sad day too? Because of my daddy?"

Matt's expression grew gentle. "Yes, it is. But you know what I think your daddy would say if he could see what your mom has organized today?"

"What?"

"I think he'd say he was proud of her for turning a sad day into a day that helps other children. I think he'd be amazed at how smart and strong and beautiful you've grown up to be. And I think he'd be happy that you and your mom have so many people who love you."

Lauren considered this with the seriousness of someone processing complex emotions. "I think so too," she agreed. "I'm really glad you're here."

"So am I, sweetheart."

Megan watched this exchange with her heart in her throat, seeing in Matt's face the same natural affection for Lauren that had drawn her to him weeks ago. His absence hadn't changed that. The struggle he'd been fighting hadn't diminished his love for her daughter.

As Matt set Lauren down and she retrieved her abandoned backpack, chattering about her day at school and the Halloween party they'd had in her classroom, Megan felt everything might work out after all.

Matt hadn't explained everything yet. He hadn't answered the deeper questions about their future or resolved the guilt that had driven him away. But he was here, holding Lauren's hand as she told him about her spelling test and the art project she'd completed that morning, looking at Megan with eyes that held warmth instead of conflict.

As they prepared to go back inside and make final preparations for the evening ahead, Megan whispered a prayer of gratitude. She didn't know what the night would bring, didn't know if Matt's presence signaled complete reconciliation or simply a temporary truce. But for the first time in days, she wasn't facing the anniversary of David's death entirely alone.

God's timing remained mysterious, but His faithfulness was becoming increasingly clear.

Chapter 32

"—and so we gather tonight to invest in our children's futures, to ensure that every young person in Laurel Ridge has access to the books and programs that will expand their horizons and nurture their dreams. Our children are our community's greatest treasure, and supporting their love of reading is one of the most important investments we can make." Megan's voice carried clearly through the library's main floor as she concluded her welcome speech, looking out at the sea of familiar faces that filled every available space.

Pastor Andrew stepped forward with his gentle smile. "Before we officially begin this wonderful evening, let's bow our heads in prayer." The crowd quieted, and his voice took on the reverent tone Megan had come to appreciate. "Heavenly Father, we thank You for this community and for the love that brings us together in support of our children. Bless this fundraiser and all who have worked so tirelessly to make it possible. We pray for the young minds who will benefit from these programs, that they might discover joy in reading and find their imaginations expanded through the power of stories. Help us to be faithful stewards of the gifts You've given us, using them to nurture the next generation. In Your name, Amen."

"Amen," the crowd echoed, and then the evening truly began.

The Laurel Ridge Library had been transformed into something magical. Strings of fairy lights cast a warm sparkle across familiar faces, while the scent of Martha's apple cider mingled with potluck casseroles and fresh-baked pies. Children's laughter bubbled from the craft tables, where Janet guided small hands in making bookmarks with faux autumn leaves. Nearby, the silent auction buzzed with friendly rivalry as neighbors discovered who had outbid them for Rebecca Martinez's donated quilt.

Megan moved through the library with ease, her clipboard forgotten as she allowed herself to simply be present in the moment. Mrs. Porter's book club had outdone themselves with the used book sale, arranging displays that might have impressed a professional bookstore. At the face-painting station, a line of children stretched six deep, high school volunteers wielding brushes like artists while parents waited with patient smiles. Everywhere she looked, the library reflected community care—donated goods, volunteer hours, and the kind of generous spirit that made a small-town feel like one big extended family.

And through it all, Matt worked beside her with the same quiet competence that had drawn her to him weeks ago. He carried heavy items without being asked, refilled the cider dispenser when it ran low, and helped elderly community members navigate between the crowded tables. His presence anchored her in a way she was only beginning to understand—not because she needed rescuing, but because having someone to share the load made every task feel lighter.

"Megan, this is incredible," Ruthanne Miller said, appearing at her elbow with Henry close behind. David's parents looked both happy and wistful, their eyes carrying the same warmth that had sustained her through those first difficult months of widowhood. "David would be so proud of what you've accomplished here."

"Thank you," Megan replied, her voice soft with sincerity. "Having Lauren surrounded by people who loved her father makes days like this feel less overwhelming."

"She's a remarkable child," Henry said, his gaze following Lauren as she animatedly spoke with one of her classmates. "Strong, bright, and full of joy — just like her parents."

The conversation continued for several more minutes, but Megan found herself only half-listening as her eyes tracked Matt's movements across the room. He was helping Pastor Andrew rearrange some chairs in the community room.

Around six-thirty, as the potluck dinner reached its peak and conversation filled every corner of the library with comfortable noise, Pastor Andrew moved to the center of the main floor and raised his voice above the crowd.

"Friends, if I could have your attention for just a moment," he called out, his words carrying the gentle authority that made people naturally quiet down to listen. "I wonder if everyone could join us in the Children's Section for a special unveiling. There's something I think you'll all want to see."

Megan felt a flutter of confusion in her chest. This wasn't part of the planned program—she had the entire evening's schedule memorized, and there was no "special unveiling" anywhere on her timeline. She looked toward Heather, expecting to see matching puzzlement, but found her friend grinning with barely suppressed excitement.

"Heather," Megan began, but Pastor Andrew was already leading the crowd toward the children's section.

Megan felt a warm hand slip into hers and looked up to find Matt beside her, his expression soft but determined. "Come on," he said quietly, his fingers tightening around hers. "Trust me."

He led her through the moving crowd, past families gathering their children and volunteers pausing their activities to see what was happening. The Children's Section, normally a cozy corner of the library with small chairs and low shelves, had somehow been cleared to create an open space in front of the reading nook. Pastor Andrew positioned himself at the front, while Matt guided Megan to stand beside him, her hand still clasped in his.

"What's going on?" she whispered, but Matt's answer was interrupted by movement near the library's front entrance.

Earl appeared, carrying one end of something large covered by a quilt. Graham held the other end, both men moving with careful precision as they maneuvered their burden through the crowd. Behind them walked Sylvia, her face bright with tears she wasn't bothering to hide.

The object they carried was clearly a piece of furniture—substantial and carefully crafted, judging by the way they handled it. They set it down in the cleared space in front of the assembled crowd, the quilt still concealing its form, and stepped back to join their family.

Pastor Andrew's voice filled the quiet that had settled over the room. "We're gathered here tonight to celebrate stories, and sometimes the most important stories are the ones that help us understand how love can grow from loss, how honoring the past can open doors to the future."

Megan's breath caught as understanding began to dawn. She looked up at Matt, seeing in his face a mixture of nervousness and hope that made her heart race.

"Lauren," Pastor Andrew called, "would you come help us?"

Lauren bounded forward from where she'd been standing with her grandparents, her face bright with curiosity. "What is it?" she asked, reaching toward the quilt with eager hands.

"Something special," Matt said, his voice rough with emotion as he looked down at her. "Something that honors your daddy and celebrates the future at the same time."

Together, Lauren and Pastor Andrew lifted the quilt away.

The bench revealed underneath was beautiful beyond anything Megan could have imagined. Crafted from rich oak with cherry accents, it was clearly the work of skilled hands that had poured love into every joint and curve. The proportions were perfect for the children's section, inviting small bodies to climb up and settle in with beloved books. But it was the inscription carved into the top rail that made Megan's breath catch in her throat:

In Memory of Corporal David Miller, who believed in stories worth living and lives worth loving.

Silence fell over the assembled crowd as the words sank in. Megan felt tears spill over her cheeks as she stared at the bench, seeing in its craftsmanship not just Matt's skill with wood and tools, but his heart laid bare. This wasn't just furniture—it was a declaration, a bridge between past and future, a testament to the possibility that love could multiply rather than diminish when it was shared freely.

The quiet was broken by movement from across the room. Ruthanne and Henry Miller stepped forward, their faces wet with tears, and Henry's voice carried clearly in the hushed space.

"Matt," he said, his words thick with emotion, "this is the most beautiful tribute to our son that anyone could have created. David would be proud to see his family loved like this."

Ruthanne nodded, her hands pressed to her heart. "He would be so grateful to know that Lauren will grow up surrounded by people who choose to love and who understand that honoring his memory means living fully."

A murmur of affirmation rippled through the crowd, and Megan felt the community's blessing wash over them like a tangible force. These people, who had known David, who had watched her struggle through the early years of widowhood, who had seen Lauren grow from infant to bright seven-year-old—they understood what this moment meant.

Matt turned to face her fully, taking both her hands in his, his voice steady despite the emotion that clouded his eyes. "I thought loving you and Lauren meant betraying David," he said, his words carrying clearly through the quiet room. "I thought I had to choose between honoring his memory and embracing the future. But I've learned that loving you is how I honor him. Megan, I love you. I love Lauren. And I don't want to run from that anymore."

The words she'd been longing to hear for days—the declaration that transformed all her hopes into truth. Megan looked into Matt's face and saw there the man who had fixed her sink and read bedtime stories, who had worked beside her in service to others, who had wrestled with guilt and fear because his love for them mattered so much.

"I love you too, Matt," she said, her voice carrying despite the tears that threatened to overwhelm her. "You're not taking David's place. You're building a new life with us—and that's exactly what he would have wanted."

For a moment they simply held each other's gaze, the weight of all they had carried shifting into joy. Then Matt stepped closer, his hands framing her face with gentle reverence as he bent to kiss her.

The kiss was tender, reverent, and exactly right—full of promise and commitment and the kind of love that was meant to last. Around them, the crowd erupted in joyful applause, but Megan heard it as if from a distance, her entire attention focused on the man who had chosen to love her and Lauren despite the complexity, despite the risk, despite the ghosts that would always be a part of their story.

When they finally drew apart, the first voice Megan heard was Lauren's, bright with delight: "Does this mean Matt gets to be my daddy?"

The question sent laughter rippling through the crowd, and Matt dropped to one knee, his smile warm though his tone was serious. "If you and your mom will have me, sweetheart, I'd like that very much."

"I vote yes!" Lauren announced, throwing her arms around Matt's neck with an enthusiasm that made everything she did feel like a celebration.

Over Lauren's head, Matt's eyes found Megan's again, and she saw reflected there the same peace that was settling into her own heart. Not the absence of complexity—their story would always carry threads of memory and loss, and the delicate work of building a family from pieces of other dreams. But peace nonetheless—the kind that comes from choosing love over fear, from trusting that some gifts are meant to be embraced rather than questioned.

The crowd began to disperse, some offering congratulations while others drifted back toward the auction tables and refreshments. Children, however, gravitated instantly to the bench, clambering onto its smooth surface with the delight of young explorers claiming new territory. Megan watched a group of Lauren's friends lean against its back, picture books open in their laps as they began to read aloud in that unselfconscious way children do when joy in a story is too big to keep to themselves.

Standing there in the Children's Section of the Laurel Ridge Library, surrounded by the community that had carried her through loss and healing, Megan felt something she hadn't in seven long years:

the certainty that her story was still being written—and that the best chapters were yet to come.

EPILOGUE

The soft glow of candlelight transformed the Laurel Ridge Community Church into something ethereal on Christmas Eve. Dozens of white candles flickered from the windowsills and along the altar, their warm light dancing across deep red poinsettias and evergreen garlands, filling the sanctuary with the scent of winter and celebration. The familiar pews were filled with faces Megan had known for years—neighbors who had brought casseroles during her darkest months, volunteers who had worked tirelessly at fundraisers and through the Hands of Grace Ministry, friends who had watched Lauren grow from an infant into a bright seven-year-old who now bounced with excitement in her red velvet dress.

Megan stood in the small room that served as the bride's preparation area, smoothing the skirt of her ivory silk dress with hands that trembled only slightly. The dress was simple but elegant, with long sleeves and a modest neckline that felt appropriate for a Christmas Eve ceremony in the church where she'd first learned to pray through grief. Pearl earrings that had belonged to her grandmother caught the light from the small window, and her hair was arranged in a soft updo that Lauren had declared "perfect for a princess."

"You look beautiful," Heather said softly from beside her, adjusting the small spray of winter white roses and evergreen that served as Megan's bouquet. "Absolutely radiant."

Through the closed door, Megan could hear the gentle murmur of conversation as friends and family settled into their seats. The church organist was playing quiet Christmas carols—"Silent Night" and "O Come, O Come Emmanuel"—melodies that spoke of hope arriving in unexpected ways, of light breaking through darkness, of promises fulfilled in God's perfect timing.

"I keep thinking about how everything in my life has fallen into place the past few months," Megan said quietly, her voice filled with wonder. "About Matt coming home, and loving Lauren and me unconditionally. About how natural it feels to have him in our lives. I never imagined I could feel this complete again."

Heather squeezed her hand. "It's a blessing. You've all found exactly what you needed in each other."

A gentle knock interrupted, and Graham peered in with a grin that so clearly echoed his older brother's that Megan's heart caught. "Ready, ladies? They're waiting for you."

Megan drew in a steadying breath, and nodded. "More than ready."

Graham stepped inside and offered his arm with a touch of old-fashioned gallantry. She slipped her hand into the crook, and Heather placed the bouquet securely in her other hand. With a reassuring smile, Graham guided her toward the sanctuary doors.

The sanctuary fell silent as the organist transitioned into the processional music. Through the gap in the door, she could see Matt standing at the altar beside Pastor Andrew, his hands clasped behind his back and his face bright with anticipation. He wore his Marine dress blues, pressed and immaculate, though it was the warmth in his eyes—not the polished brass buttons or the crimson stripe down his trousers—that held her gaze and made her heart flutter.

Earl and Sylvia Smith sat in the front pew on the right, Sylvia dabbing at her eyes with a handkerchief while Earl beamed with paternal pride. Across the aisle, Henry and Ruthanne Miller sat with Megan's parents, Bill and Helen Houser, and her sister Shanna, who had come home to celebrate the holiday season with them.

"This is it, my friend," Heather whispered as she stepped in front of Megan to take her place as matron of honor. "Let's go get your happily ever after."

With a quick kiss to Megan's cheek, Graham turned to Heather and offered his arm, ready to lead her down the aisle.

The sanctuary doors opened, and Lauren appeared in the doorway—a vision in red velvet, a basket of white rose petals clutched carefully in both hands. She glanced back at Megan, her eyes sparkling with excitement, and gave a quick little wave before beginning her walk down the aisle.

Lauren had taken her role as flower girl very seriously, practicing her steps for weeks and insisting her basket must hold "enough flowers to make the whole church beautiful." Now she moved forward with deliberate grace, scattering petals with the focused concentration of someone entrusted with a sacred duty. Halfway to the altar, she caught sight of Matt, and her face broke into a grin so radiant it sent a ripple of soft chuckles through the congregation.

When Lauren reached the front of the church, she took her place beside Ruthanne, who wrapped an arm around the little girl's shoulders and whispered something that made Lauren nod solemnly.

Graham guided Heather up the aisle, to her place on Megan's side, while he crossed to stand beside his brother as best man. They settled into position, a living frame for the moment everyone had been waiting for.

Then the music swelled, and every person in the church pews stood and turned toward the back of the church.

Megan stepped into the doorway alone, having chosen to walk herself down the aisle as a symbol of the journey she'd made through grief and healing, through fear and into courage. The sight that greeted her took her breath away. The church was full.

But it was Matt's face that held her attention as she began her walk. His expression transformed from anticipation to wonder as he saw her, his eyes reflecting the candlelight and something deeper—the kind of love that had grown slowly and surely from friendship to romance to commitment. This was the man who had fixed her sink on a summer evening, who had read bedtime stories to her daughter, who had wrestled with guilt and fear because he loved them so much he was afraid of dishonoring the past. Now he stood waiting for her, with peace on his face and promise in his eyes.

Each step down the aisle felt deliberate and meaningful, carrying her from the life she'd built as a widow to the life she was choosing as a wife. The congregation's faces were warm with affection. This wasn't just a wedding; it was a community celebration of love's power to heal and transform.

When Megan reached the front of the church, Matt stepped forward and offered his arm. She placed her hand in the crook of his elbow and felt the solid warmth of him beside her as they turned to face Pastor Andrew together.

"Dearly beloved," Pastor Andrew began, "we are gathered here on this most holy of nights to witness the union of Matthew Earl Smith and Megan Grace Miller in marriage. It seems fitting that we celebrate their love on Christmas Eve—a night that reminds us that

God's greatest gifts often come in unexpected ways, in His perfect timing, wrapped in grace we don't deserve but are invited to receive with grateful hearts."

"Marriage is more than the joining of two lives," Pastor Andrew continued. "It is the creation of a new family—the weaving together of histories, dreams, and daily acts of love into something stronger than the sum of its parts. Matt and Megan, you come to this altar not as strangers learning to love, but as friends who have chosen to deepen that love into commitment, as two people who have discovered that honoring the past can open doors to the future."

He paused, looking out at the congregation with the gentle smile that had comforted so many in seasons of trial. "Before we hear your vows, Henry and Ruthanne would like to speak."

Henry Miller rose from his seat, his face composed yet deeply emotional as he looked first at Matt, then at Megan, and finally at Lauren, who watched with rapt attention.

"Matt," he said, his voice carrying clearly through the hushed sanctuary, "when we lost our son David, we feared we might lose Megan and Lauren too—not to death, but to isolation, to the kind of grief that makes people pull away from community and love. Instead, we've watched Megan build a beautiful life for herself and for our granddaughter, and we've watched you step into that life with respect, patience, and genuine love."

Ruthanne stood beside her husband, tears streaming down her cheeks as she added, "David would be proud of the man you've become, Matt, and grateful beyond words that his family has found love and security with someone who honors his memory while building something new. We give you our blessing—not because you are replacing our son, but because you are loving his family the way he would have wanted them to be loved."

Pastor Andrew nodded, his own eyes bright with emotion. "Matt and Megan, you have prepared your own vows. Matt, would you like to begin?"

Matt turned fully toward Megan, taking both her hands in his as his voice steadied with conviction. "Megan, when I came back to Laurel Ridge, I thought I was just coming home to run a business and find my place in civilian life. I had no idea God was bringing me back to discover what love really means. You've taught me that love isn't about replacing what was lost—it's about honoring what was beautiful while having the courage to build something new."

His gaze moved to Lauren. "Lauren, I promise to love your mom with everything I have, and to love you not as a substitute for the father you never knew, but as the man who gets to help raise you into the amazing woman, you're already becoming. I promise to tell you stories about your daddy, to make sure you always know how much he loved you, and to help you understand that having two fathers is a double blessing."

Turning back to Megan, his voice softened but remained sure. "I promise to be your partner in all things—in joy and in sorrow, in serving others and building our family, in the daily work of love that makes a house into a home and a collection of people into a family. I promise to choose us—every day, in every season, for the rest of my life."

Megan's vision blurred with tears, but her voice was steady as she began her vows. "Matt, you came into my life carrying your own grief and questions, and instead of that driving us apart, it drew us closer. You showed me that vulnerability isn't weakness—it's courage. The courage to let someone see your heart and trust them with it."

She turned to Lauren. "I want you to remember this—love doesn't get smaller when it's shared, it only grows bigger. And I promise to love you with everything I have, and to make sure you always know how deeply you are cherished."

Her eyes returned to Matt's, finding there the reflection of her own joy and commitment. "I promise to be your wife, your partner, your friend through whatever life brings. I promise to help you build the future you dreamed about during all those years of service, to make our home a place where love grows, where laughter is welcome, and where everyone who enters feels cherished. I promise to choose us—to choose this family—every day, for the rest of my life."

Pastor Andrew smiled as the vows came to their close. "The rings, please."

Graham stepped forward with the simple gold bands they'd chosen, and Matt and Megan exchanged them with words that echoed through the candlelit sanctuary.

"With this ring, I thee wed," Matt said, sliding the band onto Megan's finger.

"With this ring, I thee wed," Megan repeated, her voice clear and strong despite the tears that shimmered in her eyes.

"By the power vested in me by God and the state of West Virginia, and in the presence of this community who promises to support and encourage your union, I now pronounce you husband and wife. Matt, you may kiss your bride."

Matt's hands framed Megan's face with the same gentle reverence he'd shown that night in the library when he'd kissed her for the first time in front of the community. But this kiss was different—not tentative or wondering, but confident and claiming, the kiss of a man claiming his wife and his future with equal certainty.

When they broke apart, the church erupted in applause and tears and joyful laughter. Lauren bounced on her toes, clapping her hands together.

"Ladies and gentlemen," Pastor Andrew announced over the celebration, "it is my joy to present to you Mr. and Mrs. Matthew Smith, and their daughter Lauren."

The organist launched into Mendelssohn's "Wedding March," but before Matt and Megan could begin their recessional, Lauren darted forward and grabbed both their hands.

"Can I walk with you?" she asked, looking up at them with eyes that reflected all the joy of a child whose deepest wish had just been granted.

"Always," Matt said, scooping her up into his arms before offering his other arm to Megan. "We walk together now."

The three of them moved down the aisle together, Lauren giggling from her perch in Matt's arms while Megan held his elbow and felt the love of their community following them. The faces that lined their path were bright with happiness.

They reached the back of the church just as the bells in the steeple began to ring, their bronze voices carrying across Laurel Ridge in celebration. Pastor Andrew had arranged for the Christmas Eve bells to ring for their wedding also, connecting their personal joy to the community's celebration of hope and new life.

The church doors opened, and they stepped out into the December night to find snow beginning to fall—soft, fat flakes that caught the light from the church windows and the streetlamps. The world looked transformed, made magical by the gentle blanket of white that was settling over the town like a blessing.

"Snow on your wedding day," Sylvia said as she emerged from the church behind them, her face bright with joy. "That's the best kind of luck."

"Everything about today feels like luck," Megan said, but then she corrected herself with a smile. "No, not luck. Grace. All grace."

The church bells continued to peal as friends and family spilled out into the snowy night, forming a circle of warmth and celebration around the new family. Children from Lauren's school dashed about, catching flakes on their tongues, while adults lingered to offer congratulations and share in the joy that seemed only to grow the more it was passed around.

"Mrs. Smith," Matt said softly, testing the name as he drew Megan close with an arm around her waist. "How does that sound?"

"Perfect," she replied, leaning into his warmth.

Henry and Ruthanne approached, their faces radiant with peace. "Thank you," Henry said simply, shaking Matt's hand before pulling him into a brief but heartfelt embrace. "For loving them. For honoring David. For becoming the man our granddaughter needed."

"Thank you for welcoming me into your family," Matt answered, his voice steady with gratitude.

As evening deepened and snowflakes drifted steadily from the darkening sky, the celebration gradually shifted from the churchyard into the glow of the recreation hall, where laughter and music mingled with the scent of evergreen. The Christmas Eve candlelight service would begin at nine, and many who had attended Matt and Megan's wedding planned to return to the church to watch the youth perform their Christmas play and hear Pastor Andrew's short sermon.

After a while, though, Megan slipped away from the crowd, needing a moment to absorb the magnitude of what had just taken place. She stepped onto the porch outside the recreation hall, her gaze lifting to the church steeple rising toward the star-filled sky.

Seven years ago, she had stood in this very spot after David's funeral, convinced her story had ended before she'd truly had a chance to live it. Tonight, she stood here as a wife again—part of a family that honored the past while embracing the future—as a woman who had learned that sometimes the most beautiful chapters come after the ones that break your heart.

Snow fell more steadily now, dusting the churchyard in quiet magic.

"Come inside before you freeze," Matt's voice called gently from behind her. She turned to see him approaching with Lauren's small hand tucked in his.

"I was just thinking," Megan said softly. "About how different this Christmas Eve is from the last one. About how much can change when you have the courage to let it."

Matt pulled her close, Lauren snuggling easily between them as though she had always belonged there. "And what were you thinking about specifically?"

"About stories," Megan said, her gaze lifting to the church. "About how every ending is really just a new beginning in disguise—and how the best love stories are the ones where people choose each other, again and again, in every season, through every change."

Lauren tilted her face toward the falling snow. "I think Daddy would be happy about our story. Don't you?"

Tears filled Megan's eyes, but they were tears of gratitude, not grief. She kissed her daughter's cheek. "Yes, sweetheart. I think he would be very happy."

"And I think," Matt added quietly, drawing them both tighter into his embrace, "he would be proud of the strong, beautiful women you've become—and grateful that his love was only the beginning of a story that still has so many chapters left to be written."

Leave A Review

If you enjoyed this book, please consider leaving an honest review on Amazon

Visit Our Website:

www.tarabaisden.com

Visit Our Amazon Author Page HERE

Find Us On Social Media:

Facebook

Facebook Author Page

Instagram

About The Author

Tara Baisden is a Contemporary Christian Inspirational Romance author who proudly calls the beautiful state of West Virginia her home. Nestled on a sprawling mountainous property, she is surrounded by the peace and serenity of nature. Her days are happily spent in the quiet of country life, writing heartwarming stories of love, faith, and second chances. Tara also enjoys quilting, working in her garden, tending to her beloved pets, and soaking in the beauty of her surroundings.

With deep roots in West Virginia, family is everything to Tara. One of her favorite pastimes is gathering on the front porch with loved ones, sharing stories, laughter, and enjoying the simple, meaningful moments that life offers. When she's not crafting her novels, Tara can often be found exploring the rich history of her home state, visiting local historical sites, and, of course, stopping by every bookstore she passes! Her passion for reading and discovery always fuels her next adventure.

Tara is the author of the Laurel Ridges series of novels, as well as the Riverbend Valley series of novels, of which have been beloved by fans of inspirational romance. Her novels reflect her love for faith, family, and the timeless beauty of the world we live in.

Known for her sweet and clean romances, she creates characters that feel like family and settings that make readers want to visit again and again.

You can find out more about Tara and her latest releases at www.tarabaisden.com or follow her on social media for updates and behind-the-scenes glimpses of her writing process. Stay connected—you won't want to miss the heartfelt stories of love and family she has in store!

About Laurel Ridge

Welcome to the fictional town of Laurel Ridge, West Virginia!

Nestled deep in the heart of the Appalachian Mountains, Laurel Ridge is a place where time slows down, allowing visitors and residents alike to enjoy life's simple pleasures. With its quaint, brick-paved streets, historic storefronts, and the ever-present backdrop of rolling hills and dense forests, Laurel Ridge is a hidden gem that attracts tourists looking for both serenity and adventure.

A Rich History

The town was founded in the early 1800s by pioneering settlers who were drawn to the fertile land and abundant natural resources of the region. Laurel Ridge began as a small logging community, relying on the towering forests that covered the surrounding mountains. The New River, one of the oldest rivers in the world, provided an essential transportation route for lumber, as well as a lifeline for the early settlers.

As the years passed, the town evolved from a logging outpost into a thriving hub for craftspeople and artisans. By the late 19th century, it had developed a reputation for its hand-crafted furniture, textiles, and pottery, all made by skilled locals. The town's proximity to the New River also made it a destination for adventurous souls seeking to kayak, fish, or hike along the riverbanks.

A Place of Renewal

Though the logging industry faded by the early 20th century, Laurel Ridge adapted to the changing times. Its natural beauty and deep connection to West Virginia's mountain heritage drew travelers from near and far, transforming it into a beloved tourist destination. Local shops, run by generations of the same families, line the town square, offering handmade goods, locally sourced foods, and, most of all, warm hospitality.

The town's signature event, the Harvest Festival, began in the 1930s, celebrating the craftsmanship, music, and traditions passed down through the generations. Each year, visitors flock to enjoy live Appalachian music, taste locally grown produce, and witness demonstrations of old-world techniques like blacksmithing and weaving.

A Town of Faith and Community

At the heart of the town stands Laurel Ridge Community Church, a small, white clapboard building with a steeple that reaches toward the sky. Built in 1876, the church has been a pillar of faith and strength for the community for over a century. Its bell, crafted by the town's original blacksmith, has been ringing on Sunday mornings ever since, calling townsfolk to worship and reminding everyone of the enduring values of faith, hope, and love.

The church's history is intertwined with the town's, serving as a refuge in difficult times and a gathering place in moments of joy. Over the years, the church has grown to include an outreach center that supports local families and tourists in need, providing everything from free meals to spiritual counseling. The church's welcoming atmosphere reflects the town's deep sense of unity and service.

A Growing Tourist Haven

Today, Laurel Ridge has grown to a population of around five thousand people, yet it has managed to retain its small-town charm.